Unjust Deserts

Unjust Deserts

Stuart Russell

The Pentland Press
Edinburgh–Cambridge–Durham

To the several friends who
encouraged me to persevere

First published in 1994
by The Pentland Press Ltd
1 Hutton Close
South Church
Bishop Auckland
Durham

ISBN 1-85821-191-3

Typeset by Carnegie Publishing Ltd., 18 Maynard St., Preston
Printed and bound by Antony Rowe Ltd., Chippenham

To Andrew, Kate and Nick

and

Lizzie,

whose faith made it possible

'Importunate life.
It should have something better to do
Than to hang about at a chronic street corner
In dirty weather and worse company.

> (Christopher Fry, *The Lady's not for Burning*)

McKendrick:	'Why did they search you?'
Anderson:	'They thought I might have something.'
McKendrick:	'Did you have anything?'
Anderson:	'I did in a way.'
McKendrick:	'What was it?'
Anderson:	'A thesis. Apparently rather slanderous from the State's point of view.'
McKendrick	'Where did you hide it?'
Anderson:	'In your briefcase.'

> (Tom Stoppard, *Professional Foul*)

FOREWORD

The ex-British colony of Tujan probably lies somewhere in Africa. It is a huge land, large tracts of which are wasteland. Through it, from east to west, runs the river Elin, originating near the Western capital of Muja and flowing along several hundred miles of desert, through the capital Omeldoum and on to the Tujanian coast.

At the time of our story, Tujan has, for many years, been wracked by famine and civil war, its population ravaged and demoralised, particularly in the West. Thousands of Westerners have seen their homes burnt and their families and friends obliterated, finding hope in neither the actions of the government nor the attitude of the international community. The hostility that exists between the two parts of the country is reinforced by the great divide of religion, the West being Christian, the East Muslim.

On this deep seam of human misery, a layer of expatriates has been imposed, men and women, predominantly British, recruited by various aid agencies to bring peace, friendship and enlightenment to this troubled land. Unsparing in their work, unswerving in their self-denial, they strive to provide the few crumbs of comfort the citizens of Tujan manage to glean. It is to this noble band that this novel is dedicated. Or would be if they and the place were not figments of the author's imagination!

PROLOGUE

I

The tortuous progress of the overcrowded lorry along roads that were increasingly non-existent was interrupted by an insistent knocking coming from the vicinity of the left front wheel. The vehicle groaned to a halt and the passengers got out. All were Tujanian apart from a tall Englishman in jeans and tee shirt who looked at the tyre and made a few desultory comments to the driver. No doubt the puncture would be 'repaired' by stuffing the tyre with vegetation.

The Englishman turned and surveyed the wasteland. The river had subsided in the last month or so. Mud flats were exposed and colonies of wading birds searched languidly near its shores, the water glistening in the late afternoon sun. It was their second day out from the Western capital of Muja and a long journey stretched ahead; four days of heat and dust, of iron rations and security checks. He was relieved that he now had nothing to hide.

Behind him lay the West, its population ravaged by war and starvation, the road thick with corpses. The fittest survived the longest, thinning out like the vegetation until there were no bodies and few trees. Only the desert lay ahead.

The man went down to the river and paddled in the shallows, splashing water over his face and into his beard before returning to the truck. The other passengers were sitting by the roadside: skeletal bodies, barely clad, all their worldly goods tied up in bundles of frayed cloth, talking with the driver in high pitched urgent voices, mothers nursing babies on dried up breasts. A few of them were changing the wheel and the Englishman went over to help them.

A gust of wind scoured the landscape. Sand swirled into the passengers and they covered their faces. Then the wind died, night fell, and a deep melancholy settled over the wasteland.

II

The major in the Tujanian army showed his pass and was escorted into the office of the Minister for Internal Affairs. Hands were shaken, pleasantries exchanged, cups of tea ordered. Then the minister seated himself behind his desk and spread his hands expansively. Behind him, the picture of the President hung rather crookedly on the wall.

'So, what did you discover?'

'That a submission is being planned.'

'What kind of submission?'

'It is supposed to contain reports of atrocities committed by Government troops.'

'Are the reports true?'

The major hesitated. 'Our forces have occasionally been a little . . . tactless in the methods used.' He shrugged. 'Usually they have no choice.'

The Minister was thoughtful. 'That won't matter to the rest of the world. You know what it will say – no smoke without fire. What are they planning to do with this submission?'

'No one knows. But it suddenly became a matter of urgency to get it done. And the aim is obviously to give it as much publicity as possible. Putting two and two together, that can mean only one thing.'

'You mean . . .?'

The major nodded. 'They want it to be ready for the visit of the British Foreign Secretary.'

The Minister stood up and began pacing the room. 'How many signatories do they have?'

'More than ten thousand if the rumours are true.'

The Minister wheeled round. 'More than ten thousand!'

'The numbers may be exaggerated.'

The other shook his head. 'It's a risk we can't afford to take.' He resumed his seat. 'Did you find out anything else about this document?'

'Such as?'

'How they propose to get it here. How they propose to present it.'

The major shook his head. 'Not really. Our chaps got the impression that it would be presented by an expatriate. There are several Western sympathisers in Omeldoum among the expatriate community. One in particular.'

The Minister's eyes narrowed. 'Do we know who this person is?'

'We have our suspicions. But it could be one of a hundred people.'

The Minister fixed the major with his reptilian eyes and the latter felt uncomfortable. He remembered the Minister's reputation for ruthlessness. 'I shall make you responsible for finding out, Major. What about transporting the document? How are they getting it to Omeldoum?'

'We think it's being carried by an expatriate, returning by road. They think a white man is less likely to be suspected.'

The Minister smiled and his attitude softened. 'You have done well, Bakheet. But your job is less than half done. That document must never be allowed to reach its destination. That is the rest of the job and it is your responsibility. I trust I have made myself clear.'

III

'Tujan!'

The man at the desk in the Foreign Office looked up at the strange figure in front of him with the hooked nose and mandarin moustache and nodded. 'We need to send someone to organise a top-level visit. The Foreign Secretary's due there in a few weeks' time.'

'But why can't the Embassy in Omeldoum deal with it?'

'Well, they would, normally. But the Aid Secretary's due in UK for talks just before the Visit and they want someone to make sure everything goes smoothly. It also gives the thing a bit more prestige – you know the score.'

'But why me?' A jet of spray came from the tall figure's mouth as he spoke and the man at the desk swayed his head slightly.

'Because you're the only one available of sufficient seniority who knows the language.'

'What language?'

'Tujanian.'

'But . . .'

'But what, Anderson?'

Anderson Frank said nothing. He had learnt Tujanian only because he had needed another language for promotion to his present grade in the Foreign Office. Also, he had a six months' assignment in Fiji lined up in a few weeks time. That would now be out of the question.

The man at the desk was sympathetic. 'I know it's not what you wanted but it's an important job and shouldn't do your career any harm. And Tujan's not so bad.'

Frank looked up sharply. 'You've been there, have you?'

'Well, no, I can't say I've actually been there but . . . Oh for God's sake, it's only for three weeks . . . I'll arrange for you to have the necessary jabs and get your visa organised. You'll be leaving in about sixteen days.'

Anderson Frank nodded glumly and left the office. It was bad enough missing Fiji and having to go to Tujan without being made to feel like a pin-cushion before he went.

After he had gone, the man's secretary came in.

'Did Mr Frank agree?'

'Agree to what?'

'To go to Tujan?'

'Really, Deirdre, how did you find out about that?'

The secretary persisted. 'Did he?'

'Well, yes, if you must know, he did.'

Deirdre said something that sounded like 'shit'.

'Why, what concern is it of yours?'

'We just hoped he'd get the job in Fiji, that's all.'

'I had no idea you were so interested in Mr Frank's welfare.'

Deirdre shook her head. 'It's not that. It's just that the job in Tujan is only for a few weeks, isn't it? We hoped he might be away longer.'

'We?'

'The girls in the office. We can't relax while he's here. He's always . . . you know, touching us up.'

The man winced. 'That's a most unfortunate expression.'

'Unfortunate or not, it's still true. Mr Frank's a bit of a menace where women are concerned.'

As Deirdre went out, the man pondered. He'd heard the same complaint from his wife and his wife's friends. The unfortunate Anderson Frank with his drooping frame, his hooked nose and his protruding teeth had laboured for thirty years under the delusion that women found him irresistible.

IV

Stephen Talbot watched the urn lowered into the earth and heard the vicar pronounce the valediction with a feeling of unreality. A picturesque church-yard in Devon seemed an unlikely place for the ashes of Joe King to be laid to rest. The old sod whose life had encompassed the sordid and the deprived and who had spent years in the fleshpots of Jamaica and the squalor of Tujan, had arrived at his last billet. The old hulk had reached its lea shore. A few family and friends had gathered: his daughter and grandson; one or two colleagues from grammar school days.

Stephen didn't know quite what he felt. Incredulity perhaps. He couldn't believe that the experiences, the intellect, the aging face with its innocent blue eyes, the many physical handicaps, the sense of humour, had been reduced to this.

A handful of dust.

It shouldn't have been a surprise. Old Joe had lived closer to death than anyone he had ever known, yet, perhaps because of this, he had, in a strange way, defined life and pointed towards a kind of immortality.

Jack, the vicar and Joe's oldest friend, was giving a lunch to commemorate Joe's departure. The small party retired to the vicarage where Stephen munched on tender sirloin and rather soggy Yorkshire pudding.

'Yes. Died at the airport. Lucky in a way. Could have suffered a lot more.'

Joe's daughter came up to him. 'You're going to Omeldoum, aren't you?'

'Yes. Next week.'

'You couldn't do me a favour, could you? Sort out his luggage?' She grimaced. 'I can't face it.'

'I sorted most of it during my last visit.'

'I know. Just give the books to the university and throw the rest away. I've got the house to deal with. God, the rubbish. You've no idea the kind of things he thought were worth keeping. So if you could . . .' She looked appealingly at him.

'Of course.' She smiled her thanks. Apart from her youth and sex, she could have been Joe's twin. They hadn't got on together until near the end.

Jack came over and topped up Stephen's wine. 'Good of you to come. Joe would have appreciated it.'

'I wanted to. It was the least . . .'

Jack rested his hand on Stephen's arm. 'I know. Joe thought a lot of you.'

'We were closer than I realised.' And Stephen said something he couldn't have predicted before Joe's death. 'I shall miss him.'

Jack nodded. 'We all will. Did I hear you say you were going to Tujan?'

'Next week. I should have gone a month or so ago but there's been a bit of trouble there.'

'The war's still going on, isn't it?'

'I wasn't talking about the war. The project I'm involved with. The chap who's taken it over has made a lot of mistakes.'

'How often do you go?'

'Twice a year. I write courses in UK and go to Omeldoum to try them out. Financed by the British Council.'

'Who's the Council rep ?'

'Chap called Andrew Late. I met him on my last visit. Looks a bit like Fidel Castro. Seems he's made a few mistakes as well.'

'Who – Castro or the rep?'

Stephen smiled. 'Both, probably.'

Jack nodded thoughtfully. 'Well, I'm sure you can sort it out. Joe seemed to think you could sort anything out.' He produced a bundle of tickets from his pocket. 'What about buying some raffle tickets? Help our roof restoration fund?'

'Of course.' Stephen smiled again as he handed over two pounds. Old Joe had had many qualities; the ability to assess the capabilities of his friends hadn't been one of them. He looked at a reproduction of a Van Gogh self-portrait on the lounge wall. For a second, the gaunt face and sunken blue eyes transformed themselves and it was Old Joe who hung there, a look of absolute mischief lighting up his features. Stephen should have known then that the omens for his visit were not propitious.

CHAPTER I

I

'So what do you think of the way Fairfax is organising things? Made a pretty impressive start, don't you think?'

Stephen looked into the face of the man opposite, Andrew Late, British Council representative in Omeldoum. It could have been the face of a Cypriot terrorist except for the eyes which were bright blue with something in them that looked like an appeal.

Stephen shrugged, thinking of the nasty little man he had encountered the previous September in UK and then briefly in Omeldoum in November. He thought of all the correspondence that had passed between Tujan and UK on 'the way Fairfax was organising things'. He thought of the Polytechnic English Language project that had received so much time and effort during the previous twelve years.

'I'm not yet in a position to judge.'

'Oh, come on.' Late's impatience simmered. 'Fairfax's methods have met with opposition among the local staff, and even among some of his expatriate colleagues.' He looked closely at Stephen. 'You must have heard rumours?'

'Not really. I did begin to wonder about my visit though. I should have been here six weeks ago.'

Late fingered his beard. 'To be frank, er . . . didn't want you to come earlier. Wanted things to settle down a bit, let the staff get used to Fairfax's methods. I think he's an administrative genius. We can all learn a lot from him.' There was a slight but unmistakable emphasis on the 'all'.

'So why did you want me to come now?'

Late closed his eyes and clasped his hands together. 'Erm . . . London's idea.' He paused, weighing something up. 'In a few weeks time, we have a VIP visiting us. What you might even call a VVIP . . . Can't tell you who it is . . . sworn to secrecy. Fewer people who know the better.'

'I know who it is.'

Late looked up in surprise. 'You know?'

'They told me in London.'

'Bastards. Told me they wouldn't tell anybody.'

'I think they felt they had to tell me so that I would know why you'd finally decided to invite me. I'd almost given up on a visit this year.'

'I know.' Late shook his head. 'Didn't think it would be much good you coming before. Thought if we delayed it a bit . . . London think you're the right man for this particular job.' He leapt to his feet and patted Stephen on the shoulder. 'I do too, Stephen. Good to have you here again.'

'The right man for which particular job? I thought I was here to try out teaching materials as usual.'

'That's right. It's just that . . . things being as they are and with this VIP chappie just around the corner, as it were . . .' Late tailed off in confusion, the appeal in his eyes more pronounced. He drummed his fingers on the desk before continuing.

'Can't afford to have the boat rocked at this stage. Thought you might have enough sense to provide a bit of ballast. There. You've got the image. I'll say no more.'

Stephen certainly had got both the image and the message. He'd spent long enough in Omeldoum to have the respect of the local staff and the Council wanted him to steady the ship, suppress the unrest, use his influence to ensure that 'the visit' was a success. 'After all,' he could hear them saying, 'a lot may hang on it. Increased aid to the starving masses, more money for education, diplomatic intervention to end the war in Western Province.' Not to mention the careers of Andrew Late and Fairfax Gomes-Little.

Late changed the subject. 'Good flight?'

'Not bad.'

In fact, it had been bloody awful. The previous flight had been cancelled owing to a strike at air traffic control and two flights had been merged into one. The result had been predictable – delays, a sardine-like crush, poor service and a low irritability threshold. The two men on his left had talked interminably as he had alternately tried vainly to sleep and to read. He had drunk too much and the timbre of the main talker had hit a raw nerve in his brain, streams of low sound sequences firing him up like an unanaesthetised dental assault, putting his teeth on edge and affecting his sinuses and his glands. He had tried to bury his throbbing head in one of the pigmy cushions that on airlines pass as pillows. The announcement of the descent into Omeldoum had come as a great relief.

'Yes, I must say British Airways is first class these days. Absolutely A1. Fairfax meet you at the airport?'

'He was there, but I came into town with Alena.'

Late's face clouded. 'We booked you a room . . . at the Hilton.'

'I know. I'm honoured. But I think I'd rather stay with Alena.'

'I'd rather you stayed at the Hilton. At least until after the visit. Alena's been . . . a bit of a problem recently.'

'Then perhaps I should see as much of her as possible, help sort her out a bit. Besides, she's offered me her car. If I stayed at the Hilton I'd have no transport.'

'Thought of that. Told Gabriel to get the spare Land Rover ready for you.'

A room at the Hilton *and* a Council Land Rover! They were certainly pulling out all the stops.

'Thanks, Andrew, but I think I'll be more relaxed at Alena's. We've always worked pretty well together.'

Late was now looking thoroughly unhappy, signs of weakness showing clearly through the confident exterior. Stephen noticed that his lips were cracked and his beard had dandruff.

'You know Alena's husband is here.'

Stephen nodded.

'Strange man. Writes articles on birds for the local press. Some people think they're subversive.'

Stephen stood up. 'Some people thought Jesus Christ was subversive.' He was gradually finding the confidence to deal with this man. He realised with surprise how short Late was. His bushy hair was thinning on top and he suddenly looked very distressed.

'I suppose so. Gabriel will give you the keys on the way out. Er . . . drinks at my place tomorrow. Seven o'clock. Hope you can make it.'

'I'll try.'

'Do. And Stephen,' Late put his hand on Stephen's arm as Stephen was on the point of leaving. 'I do want this visit to be a success.'

The words were said calmly, without apparent threat; Stephen fully understood the implications. He took the Land Rover keys from a smiling Gabriel and paid a visit to the toilet where urine splashed on to his dusty brown shoes and he painstakingly read the Tujanian graffiti scrawled on the whitewash.

'Better never than Late!'

As he followed Gabriel to the Land Rover, Stephen was glad to be back. The morning was warm although the oppressiveness of summer couldn't be far away. Birds were twittering in the neem trees, and the sun shone through their dancing leaves making latticed patterns on the wall above the dusty pavement. It was difficult to believe that within the city confines were the street kids, the refugee camps and, a few hundred miles away, the highways littered with corpses – the television pictures flashed into his mind – insect-like creatures with huge stomachs and matchstick limbs, crushed between their 'liberators' and their 'protectors'.

Stephen thrust the images aside. He wasn't here to tackle all the problems of this troubled land. His brief was to deal with one, a man called Fairfax Gomes-Little.

II

Stephen held up his hand in protest. 'No more, Alena, I couldn't eat another thing.' His stomach was already ballooning uncomfortably against his waist-band.

The mountain of food on the table testified to the generosity of his hostess. Alena's plump face registered hurt resignation. 'Well, if you don't like my cooking . . .'

'It's terrible, isn't it Stephen?' Alena's husband Bert piled his plate for the third time.

'Look at him.' Alena pulled a face. 'Eats as much as he likes and never puts on an ounce. Come on.' She stood up. 'Let's leave him to stew in his own disgusting appetite. You and I have things to discuss.'

Alena and Bert lived in a spacious first floor flat in the centre of the city. Stephen looked out of the window as Alena poured two glasses of wine, the burglar bars a harsh reminder of Tujan's rising crime rate. He shielded his eyes from the glare of the sun.

'I hear Bert's been writing subversive articles,' he said as they sat down in the lounge.

Alena suppressed a giggle. 'David Old asked him to, to liven the thing up a bit. The trouble is the paper's so bloody political they think Bert's articles are satire. "Bird Migration" means the demise of the present government, or something like that. And there've been all kinds of letters asking about the European sand martin, and the little green bee eater. Somebody even wanted to know who the little green bees were!'

'He wants to be careful,' Stephen warned. He had seen people deported for less in some of the countries he had worked in.

'Oh rot. Look, if we have to start worrying about Bert's articles as well as everything else, we may as well pack up.' She looked at Stephen imploringly, her big blue eyes set above plump cheeks showing a touching innocence beneath the formidable façade. 'Why didn't you come earlier? You knew how much we needed you.'

'Don't think I didn't try. I'm only here now because London used their weight. I have a bit more influence there than I do here. So, what's the situation?'

'Same as ever. The gnome behaves like God and expects us to take him at his own valuation. When we don't, he threatens us with the high jump.'

'And the local staff?'

'Hate his guts, to a man – and woman.'

'And the union?'

'Still to make a decision.'

'Any idea what it'll be?'

'Well, the staff think it'll be in their favour. If that'd been the case, I think they'd have said so by now. I think they'll drop it.'

'Why, for God's sake? They've got the evidence. All the complaints are in writing, aren't they?'

Alena nodded. 'Perhaps they think the evidence isn't enough.'

'Bullshit. Perhaps they think they'll lose their scholarships. That's nearer the truth.'

'I don't think the chaps worry much about scholarships when their pride's at stake. Our chaps didn't anyway.'

'So there's nothing we can do?'

'I was hoping you'd come up with something.'

'How much does Gomes-Little know about my involvement?'

'He *knows* nothing. But I'm sure he suspects *everything*. Why else would he block your trip?'

'We don't know for certain that he did. But I agree, it's likely. Late was very nervous when I saw him this morning.'

'They're all shit-scared about the Visit, Stephen.'

'I know. He was wittering on about me providing ballast.'

'So what *are* you going to do?'

Stephen shook his head. 'I don't know. Talk to the staff, wait for the Union decision, see if things can be patched up, I suppose.'

'They can't.' Alena was emphatic as she topped up his wine. The home brew was more than acceptable.

'Have you talked to anyone else about this?'

'Only Maurice. He's away at the moment. And Derek.'

'Derek?'

'Derek Lomas. The Head of the Distance Education Scheme for Displaced Westerners.'

Stephen knew Derek well. He had worked for the Council in Muja and before that they had been contemporaries in Zambia. 'What does Derek think?'

'He thinks the Union is our last chance. And he thinks it's a slim one.

This country has so many problems, Stephen. We shouldn't be wasting all this time trying to sort out imported ones.'

'What does Bert make of it all?'

Alena smiled. 'Bert's a lovely lovely man and I couldn't wish for a nicer husband. God knows how I'd have managed without him these last few months.'

'But . . .'

'Well, whatever people say about his articles, he's not in any way political. This isn't his scene. He's much happier birdwatching than trying to sort out the shits we have to deal with at the Poly.'

'Are there any specific problems with the gnome at the moment?'

'No more than usual. They all hate his guts, that's the perennial specific problem.'

'Why are you speaking in the third person?'

She smiled grimly. 'I'm not allowed to hate his guts. Council managerial arrangements forbid it.'

'So he's just like I thought.'

Alena struggled to her feet and replenished his drink. 'Worse. We have absolutely nothing in common – oh, apart from our briefcases.'

'What?'

'Our briefcases are identical.' She giggled. 'He took mine one day by mistake.'

Stephen was alarmed. 'There weren't . . .'

'Relax.' She put her hand on his arm. 'I was worried shitless for a time until I realised there was nothing incriminating in there. I wouldn't take your letters to the Poly, anyway.'

'But there are no new problems at the moment?'

'No. . .o. Oh, only with Valentine Luko.'

'Do I know him?'

'No, he was recruited just after your last trip. Nice bloke – they all are.'

'So what's the problem with Luko?'

'He's from Western Province. You've heard what it's like out there. Valentine heard that his family was in trouble and asked the gnome if he could take two weeks leave. The little sod refused, said it was term time – he would have to wait for the mid-year break. Valentine asked him if he could arrange to have the war stopped until the mid-year break. The gnome sent him a memo accusing him of insubordination.'

'So what happened?'

'Valentine's gone. Taken French leave. But I wouldn't like to be in his shoes when he comes back.'

'But isn't this something the Union should deal with?'

Alena looked scornful. 'This is an East-West issue, Stephen. The Union will never take the side of a Westerner. The gnome's treading a bit warily with the rest of us at the moment, keeping the peace until "the Visit" is over. The problem is that the Poly management likes the way he does things, not to mention Late. Basically, they're *all* bloody tyrants.'

'So there's no chance of getting rid of him?'

'Not if the Union lets us down. Unless you can come up with something. Anyway, don't look so gloomy. Enjoy your visit, show the staff there are still a few decent expatriates left, and look forward to your next project. That's what I'm doing. Cheers.'

Stephen raised his glass. But he couldn't be infected by Alena's mood. And he knew that underneath she wasn't as carefree as she seemed. If things didn't change, it seemed likely that most of the local staff would resign and ten years' work would go up in smoke.

III

Charles Digley sat by the pool at the Omeldoum Club and sipped a Pepsi. His appearance drew a few frowns from some of the bathers but that didn't bother him. Bloody colonialists!

Not that he could blame them for objecting to his appearance. He hadn't trimmed his beard for six weeks, hadn't changed his clothes for almost three and the mixture of dirt and dried sweat must have left him more than just visually unsavoury.

Not that he cared very much. Even at his best he had never worried about his appearance and the six months he had spent as a VSO on an aid project ten miles from the Western capital of Muja had rarely seen him at his best.

The Club, a short distance from Alena's flat, was the Mecca of the city's expatriates, the pool, the squash courts and the stylish colonial buildings fringed by well-tended lawns and well-stocked gardens enabling them to forget for a while the awful reality of what lay outside.

Charles looked at the sparkling waters with privileged bodies radiating health, and as he closed his eyes the nightmare of those other bodies came back to him, wraithlike, moving inexorably towards death on the hot, dusty roads, humourless grins on doomed faces. He opened his eyes and was aware of one face in particular, a woman's face, not like the rest.

The face was bending close to him, pretty, with a wide mouth, deepset eyes and a brow furrowed with concern. And below the face, a slim, tanned body in a white bikini.

'Are you all right?'

He looked at her, not understanding.

'Are you all right? You looked a little . . . off.'

'Did I?'

She nodded. 'You sort of . . . cried out.'

He wanted to say, 'You'd have cried out, you overprivileged bitch, if you'd been where I've been these last few months instead of . . .'

The woman was joined by a squat, balding man in bathing trunks.

'Is he all right?' The tone was unsympathetic.

'He seems to be.'

The man gave Charles an appraising look and led his companion away.

'Probably nothing that a bloody good wash wouldn't put right.' Charles heard the remark, as he was meant to, but the look the woman gave him as she walked away was ample compensation.

A couple of minutes later, Derek arrived, as fat as ever, his large intelligent face a mixture of cheerfulness and concern. The two men greeted each other, and Derek ordered two Pepsis as they sat down.

Charles smiled at him. 'You need a diet.'

Derek smiled back. 'And you need a bath!'

'So I've been told.' He indicated the couple now lounging with a few companions by the poolside.

'Mr and Mrs Basil Earl. He's Aid Secretary at the Embassy.'

'You sound as if you don't like them.'

'She's all right. He's a prick of the first order.'

'So I gathered.'

'Anyway, I didn't come here to talk about the Embassy crowd. Have you got it?'

'Not here. It was too risky with all the road blocks.'

Derek looked worried. 'Where is it, then?'

'I gave it to a chap coming back by plane. I thought he'd have a better chance of getting it through. And I was right. I've never known so many checks. And they virtually stripped me at each one.'

'Who is this chap?'

'His name is Luko. Works in the English Language Department at the Poly. Poor sod had just heard his family had been wiped out.'

Derek grimaced. 'Family wiped out *and* works at the Poly. Hardly one of the chosen few. I hope you've done the right thing. A man with so many problems might not be the best . . .'

'He was totally committed, almost snatched the thing out of my hand. I'm sure he'll look after it. He's got more reason than us for wanting it here.'

'I hope so. It's those poor buggers' only chance of making anything of a case.'

They were silent for a moment and then Derek said, 'How is it in Muja, anyway? As bad as it sounds?'

Charles nodded. 'Probably worse. It's genocide, Derek. These bastards are trying to wipe the whole bloody lot out.'

IV

Maggie Earl waited by the pool as her husband went off to change. He had lost his squash match and as ever he had excuses, as ever he had looked unfit and middle-aged at the end of it. She found it hard to admit it but she was beginning to find him repulsive.

She looked again at the man sitting in the shade at the other end of the pool, the plebs' end, as Basil called it. He had been joined by another man, someone she recognised as the organiser of a refugees' training scheme. She had seen something in that man's eyes that she had forgotten existed. It wasn't there in the Embassy socialites. Their eyes were empty of all but parties and public schools, flights home and perhaps, for the very bored, a 'bit on the side'. It wasn't there in the commercial people she occasionally met. Their eyes were even emptier – except when it came to hard currency and good deals. It wasn't even in Basil's eyes, although as Aid Secretary it should have been. Sometimes she thought his eyes were the emptiest of all. She had seen pain in that man's eyes, an awareness that he was in a country where people were suffering.

But there had been other things there as well, a contempt for all that she represented, for a start. And honesty, a basic sincerity, at once appraising and accusing, leaving her confused and defenceless. She found it surprising that one brief contact should have made such a deep impression.

V

Fairfax Gomes-Little sat in the first floor flat he had inherited from his predecessor and contemplated his first five months at post. True, there had been problems as he had introduced his own brand of efficiency into the Department. There had been murmurings from the local staff and the bitch

Alena Collingwood had made life difficult for him by leaking complaints to the Council.

Or thought she had made life difficult for him. His lips spread slightly in the thinnest of smiles. What none of them understood was that he thrived on confrontation, regarded it as something to be fostered rather than avoided. He had the Council's ear (Andrew had been marvellously supportive) and also the Polytechnic hierarchy was convinced that the department was woefully inefficient and needed more than a few kicks up the backside to sort it out.

His smile broadened as he remembered how he had identified the two prime troublemakers and branded them communists. And Alena (never everyone's cup of tea) was now nicely discredited with the Council. It was only a matter of time before she was dismissed and he would see to it that she never landed another job funded by the British taxpayer.

He softened a little as he remembered how easily he had won over the Polytechnic authorities. A good command of Tujanian had helped. He wasn't sure of the Principal who was a wet in the worst liberal tradition but the rest were splendid, particularly the Academic Secretary, Bakheet. Beautifully decisive, wonderfully reactionary, he should have been a European; such qualities deserved better than being entombed in a dark skin.

Not that he was entirely taken in by their declarations of support. They were worried sick that aid would be cut off and their annual excursions to the fleshpots and bars of the United Kingdom curtailed. He would use this fear to get the kind of department he wanted, staffed with his kind of people, run in his way. Yes, on the whole, he decided, the first five months had gone well.

He stood up and walked thoughtfully around the room. He was a small man, so much so that his height and frame scarcely suggested a man at all, more a nervous adolescent watching anxiously as puberty caused startling growth in his peers and wondering when his own body would be given the same genetic promptings. The impression of adolescence was belied by his face which looked older than its forty-five years, hair receding in a widow's peak, eyes ghoulishly enlarged by the huge lenses of his spectacles, skin sallow and lifeless. He had no family. Through the years he had gained his kicks from fast cars and small planes and his sex drive, once considerable, had atrophied through lack of opportunity. His movements were short and sharp, as though someone were pulling strings.

But nobody pulled the strings of Fairfax Gomes-Little. On the contrary, he saw himself as the puppet-master, controlling those around him, bending all to his will.

There were, however, two factors in his life that he didn't control. The first was the Polytechnic Teachers' Union. Frustrated in their attempts to find support from any other quarter, the staff had taken their complaints to the Union and Gomes-Little cursed himself for not doing his homework. He had only recently discovered who the key members of the Union were and the opportunity to talk to them might well have passed. Their decision was expected any day now and it would have the weight of a command. Their conclusion was unpredictable and Gomes-Little hated unpredictability. He hated it almost as much as he hated unions which if he had his way would all be banned. But they weren't and there wasn't much he could do about it except hope that, if the decision went against him, the Polytechnic authorities would maintain their resolve not to be dictated to by a bunch of agitators.

The second factor was Stephen Talbot, the project's London-based consultant who had arrived that morning. At Andrew's suggestion, he had arranged to meet Talbot at the airport, had even got up at two in the morning to do so. But the bitch Collingwood had been there and Talbot had given him little more than a curt greeting before leaving in her car. He wasn't used to being cold-shouldered by subordinates, particularly at two thirty in the morning! Not only that but there had been a self-assurance about Talbot which he found disturbing. Talbot was reputedly thought highly of by the men in London.

He lit another cigarette from the stub of the one he had just finished and looked out of the picture window, his composure returning. The afternoon was settling down into early evening over the untidy landscape that spread before him. The scene at the airport had offended his pride and he was annoyed with himself for confusing anger with insecurity. Talbot was an irritant, no more. He would make sure this was the last visit.

But the Union was a different matter and he didn't know what else he could do on that score. He had sown his seeds among the people he thought mattered, scattering doubts about aid and scholarships. All he could do was hope he had sown them in the right places.

He relaxed a little as he thought it through. The one thing all were certain of was the importance of 'the Visit'. And the Union held no brief to stop him dealing with the bitch. Or Talbot, come to that. Not to mention that damn Westerner, Valentine Luko.

CHAPTER 2

I

The music was grotesquely inappropriate – the soundtrack from *Chariots of Fire*. Several guests sat round tables in the garden of Andrew Late's house in a leafy suburb of Omeldoum on a pleasantly cool evening. There was nothing but the insatiable mosquitoes to disturb their equanimity yet there was an uncertainty in the air, like the uncertainty in a theatre when the time for curtain up has passed and the play hasn't begun. Late, in spite of his attempts to present a suave demeanour and his home with all the accoutrements of culture, was an unpredictable and neurotic host, never having resolved the social equation that his position in the Council had set him. He didn't really know how to entertain. It didn't help that on such occasions he seemed determined to live up to his name.

The music reached a crescendo as Stephen Talbot was shown in by the gateman and Late, resplendent in white *tobe*, emerged from the house. All eyes turned towards him and he gave a slight bow.

He noticed Stephen and ignored him. He walked round tables calling waiters to dispense drinks and chatting to people with a robust bonhomie that he hoped would hide the acute uncertainty that had overtaken him. His mouthwash had run out the previous day and the knowledge that his breath was almost certainly rancid made him lose confidence in his attempts at social intimacy. He had a standing order for mouthwash with the local import/export agency but the last consignment had arrived without it. These import/export agencies were about as useful as the Pope's penis, he thought viciously. Without his mouthwash, he felt a bit like a batsman facing a demon fast bowler without his box: hesitant, vulnerable, his first inclination being to back away.

The guests were the usual offering – Embassy and Council with several from other expatriate communities, and a few underlings and Tujanians to sustain the Council's liberal reputation. Basil and Maggie Earl sat primly as Late ebbed and flowed around them. Flanking them were Gomes-Little, looking dapper in stiffly pleated safari suit, and Derek Lomas, all beer blubber and fat. Gomes-Little smoked continuously and his huge lenses peered around, belying the ease suggested by his posture. A far table rang with laughter as Late, moving swiftly round, successfully attempted some witticism to a gathering of teachers. Among a group of Tujanians, sitting apart and drinking Pepsi, Stephen recognised the Principal and the Academic Secretary and felt more relaxed.

Late belatedly acknowledged Stephen's arrival and swept across the lawn. His *tobe* was almost incandescent and there was something quite awesome about him. Then Stephen remembered the cracked lips, the thinning hair, the specks of dandruff in the beard.

'Stephen.' Late took him by the arm. 'Glad you could make it. Thought you might be too tired.'

'I've rested all day.'

'So you haven't . . . er . . . seen Fairfax yet?'

Stephen looked across to where Gomes-Little's lenses were now turned towards him. 'Not since the airport.' He raised his hand in a greeting which Gomes-Little acknowledged with a slight smile.

'Ah yes, the airport.' Late's mask slipped for a moment. The unease he had shown the previous day returned. Stephen suddenly registered a strange aroma, the source of which he identified as Late's mouth. Late saw his screwed-up nose and immediately moved back two paces.

'Is Alena coming?' Stephen knew the answer to this, having spent the day with Alena and Bert.

'Er . . . no.' Late paused, unhappily, and Stephen waited. 'Thought it best, as it . . . er . . . were . . . not to invite her.' Stephen still waited. 'Her husband, you know . . . those articles.' On the point of floundering, Late summoned a waiter. 'Come on, we're getting too serious. Have a glass of wine.' Stephen took the glass and sipped approvingly. 'French. Occasionally pays to have diplomatic contacts even though most of them bore the arse off me.'

The crudity of Late's remark jarred. Looking as he did like a rather stout archangel with 'Jerusalem' blaring out in quadraphonic splendour, somehow words like 'arse' should have had no place in his conversation. He ushered Stephen across to the table where the Principal and the Academic Secretary were sitting. They stood on his arrival and Late hovered nervously, like a fiancé introducing his betrothed to appraising parents. 'You know Stephen, of course.'

The Principal extended his hand. 'Of course.' And with a glance at the Academic Secretary. 'We thought you had deserted us.'

Stephen shook his head. 'I would have been here a lot earlier but . . .' He tailed off, uncertain how to continue.

'But the good life of the UK proved too accommodating.' The Principal laughed. 'Don't worry. We understand.'

'It wasn't that . . .' Stephen began but Late interrupted him.

'Anyway, he's here now . . . should prove absolutely invaluable in these few weeks up to . . .'

The two administrators nodded and Late repeated under his breath, 'Absolutely invaluable.'

Stephen polished off his wine and helped himself to another. He was beginning to enjoy himself. He turned to the Principal.

'So, how are things?'

The Principal smiled, his sad face heavily touched with humanity. He looked older than his forty-odd years.

'What things, Stephen? The English Language Department? The Polytechnic? Tujan?'

Stephen smiled back. They both knew he meant, 'How are you coping with this new and pernicious influence in the English Language Department?'

'Perhaps we should talk about Tujan.'

The Principal turned to the Academic Secretary. 'So, how is Tujan, Bakheet?'

His colleague shook his head, anger taking over his ravaged features. 'I think Stephen knows how Tujan is. What was it you once wrote, Stephen, the fastest decaying country in the world?'

Stephen smiled, embarrassed that one of his few sorties into journalism should be so accurately remembered. 'It wasn't a very serious article. I'd only been here a few weeks.'

Bakheet put a cold hand on Stephen's arm. 'It was very . . . perceptive of you. You said that our banknotes, held together by Sellotape, were a metaphor for the country; the sewage seeping up through every crack the image of our future. You see, I remember it perfectly.' He tightened his grip on Stephen's arm. 'Do not be embarrassed, Stephen. There was only one thing wrong with your article. It was an understatement. And since then it has become more of an understatement. Mustafa will tell you. The country has decayed like a bad tooth. It is full of rebels and traitors, people who want to destroy the very little we have left.'

Stephen used the excuse of another glass of wine to extricate himself from Bakheet's grip. There was no doubting the Academic Secretary's anger.

'We see some terrible pictures from the West.'

'Ah, the West.' The anger in Bakheet's eyes deepened and the hand holding his drink began to shake. 'We all know about the West.' He turned to Mustafa who nodded uncertainly. 'One day, Stephen, when we are not guests in another man's house, I will tell you about the West. And what we are going to do about it. But the problem is not only the West. There are traitors much nearer home. In the East. Here in Omeldoum. You may have heard rumours.'

'Rumours?' Stephen recalled the similar conversation with Late the previous day.

'Yes. About your English Language Department.'

Stephen glanced at Mustafa who was looking uncertain and unhappy. 'I heard there were a few problems.'

'I will be frank, Stephen. My country is not rich. When a country like Britain gives us something, it is the duty of our staff to accept it.'

Mustafa looked even more unhappy and Stephen felt it incumbent on him to say something. 'Even if they think what they've been given is bad for the country? Surely they should be allowed to form their own judgements.'

'Form their own judgements!' Bakheet was derisive, his hand shaking so much that his Pepsi slurped out from the top of the glass. He put it on the table. 'They cannot form their own judgements. All their judgements are based on prejudice, all their interests are their own. They have no concept of what is for the good of the country.' He gestured in the direction of Gomes-Little. 'Some of them have tried to make life difficult for your new boss.'

Stephen feigned surprise. His acting would have convinced no one except a man certain that his audience shared his preconceptions.

'Trivial complaints about him – nothing that means very much. It is amazing, Stephen, how small-minded we Tujanians can be.'

'You say tried. So they haven't succeeded?'

Bakheet shook his head. 'They will *never* succeed. Fairfax is certain that what he is doing is right for the Department, right for Tujan. He has some very good ideas and his administrative control is excellent. He has our full support.'

Bakheet looked at Mustafa as he said this and Mustafa lowered his eyes. Stephen wondered how Mustafa had possibly become Bakheet's superior. He surpassed him only morally, in being infinitely the nicer man, and the Third World wasn't noted for rewarding such qualities. Stephen thought of Gomes-Little's failure to reply to any of the four letters he had written during the previous two months and wondered how anyone with such a slight grasp of communication needs could be said to have excellent administrative control. In retrospect, he was surprised at the length and intensity of this interchange. Feelings had obviously been running high. As Stephen excused himself and moved towards the next table, Mustafa's eyes turned towards him and gave a reassuring flicker. It said more clearly than any words: 'I understand, don't worry', and Stephen went to have the expected chat with Gomes-Little with his confidence greatly increased.

Late, having retired briefly to his balcony to survey the scene, saw Stephen in conversation with Mustafa and Bakheet, and smiled. Bakheet was a godsend. Then Stephen moved to Gomes-Little's table and Late saw him being introduced to Basil and Maggie, and exchanging greetings with Derek Lomas. Late wasn't at all sure that Derek with his well-publicised Western sympathies was a suitable person to be attending a Council soirée but he had to be responsive to all shades of opinion. The Council must always appear even-handed in the dispensation of its favours and Late smiled again at his own deviousness, recognising with relish the Machiavellian promptings in the motives of all men called to high office.

Before returning to his guests, Late checked the kitchen to see that the snacks were on the way and finally made a visit to the bathroom to clean his teeth. There he cupped his hands round his mouth and breathed slowly into them, taking the breath back up his nose and smelling the slight rancidity. He looked with distress at the empty mouthwash bottle.

II

At the time Andrew Late was sampling his own breath, Charles Digley was showering at the Omeldoum Club. Derek had suggested that it would be a good thing if he washed, that his gesture of solidarity with the oppressed peoples might not go down too well with the distinctly unoppressed members of the club. He had first had a game of squash and as his frayed jeans and Save-the-Children tee shirt had become soaked with sweat, he had begun to relish the thought of a shower.

While he was towelling he felt an acute pain in his back and for the second time that day he cried out. He slumped on to one of the low benches that ran round the changing room and a few seconds later rose gingerly, relieved to find no major problem. He felt a slight discomfort as he bent down to put on his sandals but walked slowly out of the changing room and round the pool, gradually increasing his pace. The discomfort had gone and he concluded that the distress had been only temporary.

He glanced into the dining room but didn't really feel like eating at the Club. There was some rule about no collarless shirts after seven o'clock and a ridiculous old woman who ensured the rule was obeyed. Even if he'd managed to bring a few starving Westerners with him, he was sure food would have been withheld until they'd been kitted out with collars and ties!

He walked a hundred yards or so to a small café that sold take-away beefburgers. To the left was a rubbish dump around which were the inevitable street kids, little grey monkeys foraging for scraps among newspapers and plastic bags and mango pips. A few came towards him, hands outstretched, insistent, demanding. He went into the beefburger place, leaving them gesturing outside until the doorman dispersed them with a few waves of his truncheon.

He ate two beefburgers, relieving the dryness of the bread with a glass of mango juice. Outside, the children had returned; small black noses flattened against the window. He ordered six more beefburgers and handed them to the creatures in the street. Immediately he was besieged and as a few bigger boys fought for the initial offerings, the rest clamoured round him, begging, beseeching, threatening. He tried to move away, fighting them off as best he could, helped by a couple of night watchmen who emerged from the alleys and began flailing with their sticks. The street kids scattered and Charles ran to the sanctuary of the Club, aware of the irony of a man of his principles taking refuge in a haven of privilege. As he sat down with a Pepsi, he noticed that the pain in his back had returned.

III

Chariots of Fire had given way to Tchaikovsky's Violin Concerto by the time the food arrived. Stephen had left Mustafa and Bakheet and had been received coolly by Gomes-Little. The little man had introduced him to the other people at the table: Derek Lomas, smiling satirically, and Basil and Maggie Earl who maintained the Gomes-Little coolness, the one frostily, the other more engagingly.

'At the risk of sounding clichéd, what do you do here, Mr Talbot?'

Stephen looked approvingly at the elegant woman on his left. She was one of only two females present, the other being a large woman dressed in a kind of ethnic bell-tent seated at the far table with the teachers. Maggie Earl, by contrast, was slim and suntanned with a face that was almost beautiful.

Gomes-Little answered for him. 'Stephen's one of our course writers. He's here for his spring holiday.' The little man laughed, but there was no humour in his eyes. Stephen gave him a token glance and turned towards Maggie. 'As Fairfax said, I write courses for the Poly.'

'And the holiday bit?'

'If Fairfax works me as hard as he should, I shall need a holiday when I leave. What about you?'

'Basil's the Aid Secretary at the Embassy. I'm part of his accompanied baggage.'

'And that's all?'

'Before I met him, I trained as an osteopath.' She said with deliberate enunciation, 'I manipulate bones.'

'I see.'

'I know what you're thinking, Mr Talbot. Not particularly relevant to the needs of Tujan. But then, what is? Materials writing?'

Stephen was a little taken aback. 'I suppose if you're a student needing a course or a man who's put his back out, we're both pretty relevant.'

'Do you think what you're doing is important?'

'It's difficult to say, just like that.'

'Oh come on, Mr Talbot.'

'The name's Stephen. And it is difficult without defining what we mean by important.'

'At least I relieve pain, when people come to me, that is.'

'And when they can afford it?' Stephen murmured.

'My charges are based on the ability to pay.' She looked directly at him. 'Are yours?'

Stephen smiled and used Andrew Late's gambit. 'I think we're getting too serious.' He was coming off worst with this elegant woman who showed every sign of being able to put him firmly in his place. What added to his irritation was that the conversation was taking place within earshot of Gomes-Little who was reacting approvingly to Maggie Earl's attack.

But Stephen didn't know that beneath the sophisticated façade, Maggie Earl felt woefully inadequate. Yes, she did manipulate the bodies of people who came to her in pain, but in the main they were privileged people nursing injuries sustained pursuing privileged activities. She longed to get involved in the real problems of this puzzling land, which was why she held people like her husband and Stephen Talbot in some contempt. They *were* involved in development, in solving problems; they could have tried to straighten the spine, the tortured frame of the country, could have alleviated a little of the pain. But they didn't. They were only paring the fingernails. A phrase from Graham Greene came back to her '. . . providing sewing machines for starving seamstresses . . .' or something like that. Wasn't that just what Basil and the whole aid industry were doing? The look in Stephen Talbot's eyes wasn't so different from the look in the eyes of her husband and she thought again of the man by the pool.

IV

At the time two small children were fighting in the dust for the last scrap of the food dispensed by Charles Digley, Stephen was popping his fourth prawn vol-au-vent into his mouth. Late had certainly spared nothing on the catering. Even on a hefty expense account, snacks and waiters from the Hilton must have set him back a bit. He saw Derek looking at him and raised his glass in a gesture of cheers before going over and sitting in the seat Gomes-Little had vacated.

'Nice to see a friendly face.'

'Even if it is only mine.'

'Same old Derek. Always putting yourself down.'

'With my figure it's the only way I can survive.'

Stephen patted Derek's gut playfully. 'It's expanded a bit.'

Derek looked worried. 'It's terrible, being so overweight. Most people think I just eat too much. I try to explain that it's hormonal.'

'Rather than habitual?'

Derek broke into his compelling laugh. 'Well, I suppose I do like my beer. When I can get it, that is.' He became serious. 'Have you seen Alena?'

'I'm staying with her.'

'Then you know about the mess at the Poly?'

Stephen nodded and looked round. There was a general mingling and Late's incandescence was flitting from group to group. He now had the large bell-tented woman by the arm and was stepping theatrically around. He caught Stephen's eye and swept his companion over. They made a strange couple, like a miscast sun and a large stormcloud in some morality play. 'Stephen, meet Dolores. Dolores, Stephen. Treading the boards together next week, aren't we, my sweet? Victorian melodrama. You must all come to see it. Great fun.'

Late whisked his stormcloud away and Stephen watched him making expansive gestures. Obviously an impromptu rehearsal was going on. Before he turned back to Derek, he noticed Gomes-Little talking earnestly with Bakheet.

'So the rep's still going strong?'

'I think that's overstating it. Would they have Late in it if they were "going strong"?'

'Good point. What's he playing?'

'The villain.'

'Typecasting?'

'Desperation, I think. I've seen a bit of it. It promises to be absolutely bloody awful.'

'Nice to know some things don't change. Anyway, what about this other business?'

Derek lowered his voice. 'Alena's over-reacted. Now, don't misunderstand me. I don't like our two friends here one bit. The gnome has put a lot of backs up, and Late seems constitutionally incapable of handling anything properly. It's just that Alena herself has handled it pretty badly. She's been desperate for you to get here.'

'I know.'

'Pity you couldn't have come sooner. Still, it's not my problem. This country has enough problems. The gnome is pretty small beer.'

'Not in my book.'

Derek bent towards him. 'In two years he'll be gone, finished.'

'The English Language Department might be gone with him.'

'It might, but I doubt it. But the war won't be gone, the famine won't be gone, all the injustices won't be gone!' Derek's eyes glinted with indignation. 'I once showed a film to some students in the West. It was a war film, one of those red badge of courage things the Americans love to make and our students love to watch. Anyway, one scene in this film showed the aftermath of a battle with the medicos treating the wounded. And they had to cut the leg off one bloke's trousers so that they could dress a wound. The students were appalled.'

'So?'

'The point is that it wasn't the battle or the wounded leg that appalled them. It was seeing a perfectly good pair of trousers destroyed! Can you imagine? We're talking about a place where trousers have a greater value than legs! Compared to this, is your English Language Department so important?'

'Paring the fingernails of a dying man.' Both men jumped and found Maggie Earl standing behind them. She smiled. 'Don't look so worried, Mr Talbot. Sorry to eavesdrop, but I'm afraid I must agree with Derek.'

'You'd be a fool not to,' Stephen said as Derek moved off in search of a drink. When they were alone, an elfin impulse came over Maggie.

'I didn't realise. How much you dislike Fairfax Gomes-Little, I mean.' And as Stephen began to protest she moved closer. 'So you've really come here to get rid of him?'

Stephen looked at her. 'Don't jump to too many conclusions.'

She put her hand lightly on his arm. 'I'm just interested, that's all. When

all you do is manipulate bones, you like to watch people manipulate . . .
other things.'

'Such as?'

'Oh, power, emotions, you know. Don't worry, I won't tell anyone. Your
secret is quite safe with me.'

That night, Stephen lay on his bed in Alena's spare room and contemplated the evening. He had made a bad start. Maggie Earl knew of his
campaign before it had even begun and he felt uneasy. Frustrated wives of
Embassy officials didn't make the best confidantes.

She was right of course. As was Derek. Gomes-Little was insignificant
when set against the other problems of the country. Paring the fingernails of
a dying man. He examined his own nails. The following day he would be
at the Poly and somehow he had to get down to the business. He had little
heart for the task and few ideas. He thought of the massacres in the West,
finding it difficult to believe they were taking place in the same country as
the prawn vol-au-vents, the French wine, the *Chariots of Fire* music. The
empty grandeur of the evening appeared in stark contrast to the unimaginable
despair cast over so much of the country and its people. He suddenly realised
he had no real stomach for the task of paring the dying man's fingernails and
hoped the Union would do it for him.

CHAPTER 3

I

Talking to Gomes-Little was a bit like playing chess – long silences broken by short exchanges, including, of course, the atmosphere of conflict, of a possible winner and loser. Stephen worked hard during the initial skirmishes though he felt after half an hour or so that Gomes-Little was ahead, perhaps on position, perhaps even a pawn or so.

'There have been a few problems,' Gomes-Little confided, completing the opening phase. 'Nothing that I couldn't handle, of course.'

'I suppose they found you a bit different from Malcolm.'

Gomes-Little nodded. 'That was the main trouble.' He was working hard to create the image of a reasonable man. Stephen felt the tension in the situation, the potential for conflict along all the verticals and diagonals.

'If there's anything I can do to help.'

The other smiled. 'As I said, everything's under control.'

Stephen didn't tell him that he knew about the Union and the threat hanging over him. For a second, he almost felt sorry for the little man. Then he remembered the problems, the bitterness, the opposition of all the staff, and his attitude hardened.

'I'd like to see the staff fairly soon. Not many of them in evidence today.'

Gomes-Little waved a hand. 'Most of them work at home – when they're not teaching. There's so little space here, I told them there was no need for them to be here all the time.'

This was patently untrue. Gomes-Little had forgotten that six months previously, Stephen had briefed him on the new office space, the furniture and equipment that had been installed to create a viable, integrated department. He went on the attack.

'Why didn't you answer my letters?'

The other assumed an attitude of patient boredom. It was the attitude Stephen remembered most clearly from their previous meetings.

'Because I had nothing I particularly wanted to talk to you about.'

'I asked questions about the department, the work, my future role. I've received no answers.'

'Because I haven't thought them out. These things take time. Running a project like this isn't the piece of cake outsiders think it is.'

Stephen had to take his hat off to the man. In one statement he had been characterised as an outsider and put firmly in his place as a man with no real administrative experience. Gomes-Little moved quickly to reinforce his position. 'Also, I assumed you'd be getting your information from another source.'

'Meaning?'

'You've got friends in the Department. I thought one of them might have kept you informed. Abdallah, say. Or . . . Alena.'

'Did you ask them?'

'I often find it hard to track them down. And I've had a lot of things on my mind. But surely Alena must have written to you. After all, you're working on the same materials.'

Another clever ploy. Now to deny contact between himself and Alena would be tantamount to admitting professional negligence. He wondered why he had been chosen for this game of diplomatic chess. He wasn't very good at it and was seemingly up against a grandmaster.

'Of course Alena and I wrote to each other a couple of times. As you say, we had to.'

Gomes-Little smiled. He looked like a man who knew he could contain anything his opponent might throw at him.

'About work?'

'To start with.'

'But not later?'

Stephen hesitated. He had lost track of the strategy and wasn't sure of his next move. But inspiration came.

'Well, naturally, when I was getting no reply from you, I asked her if everything was all right and to check if you'd received my letters.'

'And what did she say?' Gomes-Little still behaved like a man in control but some of his certainty had gone.

'She said there had been a few problems. She didn't go into details herself, just sent me a list of the staff's complaints.'

'So she *did* leak them. Thank you Stephen. That's what I've been trying to find out.'

'"Leak" is putting it a bit strongly. She sent them as a possible explanation as to why you hadn't answered my letters.'

'She never asked me about your letters. I wonder why.'

Now it was Stephen's turn to smile. He had a better idea where the ploy was leading even though the admission about the 'leak' appeared damaging.

'Perhaps she had as much of a problem finding you as you had of finding her. And she passed no opinion on the complaints except to say she thought they were exaggerated.'

This was palpably untrue and under most circumstances Stephen would have felt guilty. But he had created an element of uncertainty in his opponent's mind. His last statement had taken Gomes-Little by surprise; his next one underlined this. 'Anyway, Alena's not so important. She's always been a bit difficult. The important thing is for you and me to work together, don't you think?'

He was gratified to see that this threw Gomes-Little into total confusion. The last thing he had expected was any show of disloyalty towards Alena, and Stephen didn't know exactly why he was doing it except that he felt instinctively that the way to beat the little shit was not by confrontational techniques at which he was obviously a master. He had to be taken by surprise, weakened from the inside. The Union decision was the key. If it went against them, they would need a whole new strategy and Stephen felt it would be easier to develop one if he gained Gomes-Little's confidence.

He left it at that. The position was interesting but, to mix his sporting metaphors, he felt he had shaded the first round.

II

Valentine Luko joined the crowd at Muja airport. There was an urgency about them that bordered on panic. Rumour had it that this was the last scheduled flight to Omeldoum and he had taken a calculated risk. He knew the place would be crowded and that the despair of people fearing abandonment in a living hell could well be lethal. He also knew that the vast majority of the crowd would not have tickets and that there was a danger he might not make the flight.

He could have left much earlier in fact. His younger brother, the last of his family, had died two weeks previously, and if he had left then, he would have been assured of a flight. But he would also have been subjected to a rigorous security check and this was what he wanted to avoid.

Valentine had become a man with a mission, haunted by the vision of his home, burnt and looted, his parents dead and disfigured. Only a photograph remained, the family on his graduation day, clutched in his mother's hand as she reached out towards her husband. His ten-year-old brother died in Valentine's arms two days later, a victim of disease and appalling medical supplies. There had been little time to grieve. The emptiness he had feared never came, being held in check by things worse: by roads littered with corpses; by the eastward trek of a people threatened with extinction; by the cheapness of human life; by paper-thin babies suckling the breasts of dying mothers.

He had met a volunteer who had taken him to what had previously been the Refugees' Training Centre. Now it was a kind of soup kitchen, dishing out watery liquid from huge earthenware pots, and a greyish substance that passed as bread. It was here that he told his companion of his bereavement. And then, as the nothingness was beginning to take hold, he heard of the submission.

As he jostled through the crowds at the airport, he felt the papers, stitched into the lining of his jacket. It was stiflingly hot and at any other time wearing a jacket might have aroused suspicions. But security was preoccupied trying to identify the legitimate passengers and he wasn't even frisked. He managed to get one foot on the steps leading to the plane and hauled himself up into the overcrowded aircraft. Troops with machine guns stood menacingly while others laid about them with truncheons, separating the ticket holders from the rest. Valentine's last view of his home was of a thousand screaming people held in check by a cordon of soldiers.

He sat in a window seat, hot and uncomfortable. The engines started fitfully and the plane struggled into the skies. Now the view of his home changed. The blue river meandered through green bushland and the roads gradually faded, the detail blurring as the plane gained height and wheeled eastwards in a long arc towards Omeldoum.

It was then that the full import of the situation hit him. So many emotions were churning inside him that when he started sobbing it was not for any single reason. It was everything: his family, his home, his mission. They were sobs of loss and sobs of relief. If only he could have shared his family's pain, been able to warn them or protect them. But he hadn't been there. The delay over his leave had meant . . .

His sobs subsided. He thought back to the days in Omeldoum when he had filled in so many forms, waited so many hours for people who never came. And he realised that there was one person he hated more than the people who had killed his parents and destroyed their home.

III

Stephen's first morning at the Polytechnic was going better than he had expected and a strategy, to worm his way into Gomes-Little's confidence, was developing. He didn't know whether Gomes-Little would fall for such a ploy or how long he could sustain it. But he knew instinctively that it would be easier to outwit Gomes-Little as a friend than outfight him as an enemy.

He suddenly remembered his promise to Joe King's daughter and decided to deal with Joe's luggage as soon as possible. The following day was the weekly rest day. Joe's personal effects were stored at the Embassy and he decided to ask Maggie Earl to arrange for them to be sent to the Club.

A messenger brought a note requiring Gomes-Little's attention and Stephen took the opportunity to phone the Embassy. He could hear Gomes-Little addressing the messenger in Tujanian. Although he understood little of the content, the tone was clear – abrasive, accusing, threatening – the age-old assertiveness of the little man coupled with a kind of vestigial racism, the superiority many Englishmen still felt in the presence of a darker skin.

The Embassy gave him the Earls' number and Maggie answered his call.

'Mr Talbot, what a surprise! Haven't put your back out, have you?'

Stephen made his request.

'I think it's my husband you should be contacting. He's the one who works at the Embassy. I just live here.'

'I know. I just had an idea that you might be more sympathetic to deal with.'

'Even after last night?'

Stephen suddenly felt extremely irritated at the offhand treatment he was receiving from this woman.

'Will you do it? Just a straight yes or no.'

'All right. It's no big deal, anyway. I'll get Basil to get the cases sent to the Club. You'd better make sure the Club's expecting them.'

Stephen rang off, still irritated. Gomes-Little had disappeared so he wandered across to the admin. block to have a chat with Mustafa. He was tempted by breakfast at the staff club but he wasn't really hungry, having eaten a large bowl of Alena's bean stew about two hours previously.

The Poly compound hadn't changed. A vague attempt at landscaping had produced unkempt lawns with bougainvillaea bushes providing welcome splashes of colour. Between these, dotted randomly, were the piles of rubbish and the containers that had once brought machinery purchased by British Aid. The college bus remained where it had broken down years before, one front wheel skewing wildly in a right-angled turn like a dislocated elbow. On the wall of the engineering workshop, the clock stood at twenty to three as it had ten years previously. Groups of students stood languidly about, their demeanour suggesting the opposite of academic fervour. From the Students' Union tent came the broadcast rantings of the Muslim extremists, spreading their militancy to the four corners of the campus. He thought of the war and a nation in the last stages of collapse but the abiding impression, over-riding the urgency of the broadcast, was of a benevolent indolence, a complete absence of purpose. A stiff breeze suddenly blew across the campus, scattering dust, disturbing the calm. It subsided as quickly as it had arisen.

He climbed the steps to Mustafa's office and knocked on the door. Mustafa was in the middle of a meeting but Stephen had no doubt that his arrival would lead to the meeting being abandoned and he wasn't disappointed. The Principal's face wreathed in smiles as he entered. The two men with Mustafa gathered up their papers and left after a few perfunctory handshakes. Mustafa went with them as far as the outer office to order tea.

'Good to see you again, Stephen. I assume you want tea.'

Stephen nodded. 'What would Omeldoum be without tea?'

The other laughed. Stephen noticed how much older he looked. A youthful face worn by the cares of office in a troubled land. A forty-year-old body whose shoulders had drooped alarmingly. Stephen felt a wave of sympathy for his old friend and a rising anger for the British Council for compounding his problems.

Suddenly it wasn't only his anger that was rising. Disquieting rumblings started inside him and his bowels began moving like a well-oiled machine. Alena's bean stew having jogged round the first few laps of the intestinal track was now sprinting for the tape. Stephen hastily excused himself and dashed from the office. Too late now to follow the well-worn path to the Hilton, to read the local paper in air-conditioned splendour while bowels and bladder smoothly discharged. With a stiff-legged sprint he reached the Poly toilets, visited only in direst emergencies. This promised to be an emergency of epic proportions. Holding his nose, he squatted awkwardly as his bowels exploded and brown liquid covered the three turds already in the pan, beached like logs on the dried-up rapids of a river. Insects swarmed upwards and he swatted wildly, almost losing his balance, buttocks exposed to the bloodlust of mosquitoes.

His innards subsided and he realised the worst was over. Like a mother discharging the afterbirth, his bowels continued with a few sterile contractions while he looked for something to wipe himself. Eventually, in a deep corner of his pocket, he found the raffle tickets he had bought at Old Joe's funeral. A minute or so later he emerged into the sunshine, taking great gulps of comparatively fresh air, and went to Bakheet's office.

Bakheet's secretary smiled when she saw Stephen. She had been his student several years before.

'Mr Stephen!' The greeting was enthusiastic. 'Bakheet is not far, but please, go in and wait. He would wish it.'

There was an opulence and coolness about Bakheet's office that contrasted sharply with the squalor and heat of the rest of the Polytechnic. The inevitable picture of the President hung behind the desk next to a picture of a younger Bakheet in mortar board and gown. Stephen glanced at the papers strewn on the outsize desk and one caught his eye. It was written on English Language Department notepaper and, after a quick look behind him, he picked it up. It was clear and to the point.

Dear Bakheet,

I refer to the future of Alena Collingwood in the English Language Department. She will soon be applying for contract extension or renewal. In view of the problems we have had in the Department this year and her liaison with disaffected and rebellious members of staff, I feel that the Department can only suffer from her continued presence and consequently I shall be recommending to the British Council that when her present contract expires, her tenure in the Polytechnic should be terminated forthwith.

I am sure this recommendation will meet with your full approval.

Yours sincerely

Fairfax Gomes-Little
Head, English Language Department

Noises in the outer office caused him to replace the memo on the desk and retire to one of the armchairs. He stood a moment later as Bakheet and another man entered the room.

'Stephen!' Bakheet advanced towards him, hand outstretched. 'Nice to see you.' He indicated his companion. 'My nephew, Major Bakheet.' The white *tobe* wouldn't immediately have signified an army officer.

The two men exchanged greetings.

'He's enjoying some well-earned leave. Just back from Western Province.'

Stephen joined the other two as they took seats by the desk. A messenger came in with tea.

'Stephen's here to sort out our English Language Department. To make some of our stupid bastards see sense.'

Stephen addressed himself to the impressive figure at Bakheet's side, aware of a growing discomfort between his buttocks. The raffle tickets had done a pretty superficial job.

'So how is the West? We hear some pretty dreadful rumours.'

Major Bakheet shook his head. 'The rumours are not as terrible as the facts. What the local tribes are doing – it is dreadful.'

'We hear that the fault lies mainly with the Government troops,' Stephen said, feeling a desperate urge to scratch.

The other smiled but his eyes were steely. 'Then you hear wrong, Mr Talbot. Without the troops things would be much much worse.'

Stephen thought back to the TV pictures. Much much worse? Was it possible? He adjusted his position on the chair, trying to relieve what was fast becoming a major irritation.

The elder Bakheet obviously didn't like the way the conversation was going. 'Stephen, you are here to sort out the English Language Department. Leave the West to us.'

Stephen smiled wanly. 'It just seems a bigger problem than the English Language Department.' Suddenly the West, Gomes-Little, everything, seemed vastly unimportant compared to this over-riding need to scratch.

Now it was the major's turn to smile. 'Just a little bigger, yes. But, as my uncle said, we shall deal with it.'

'But how?' Stephen persisted, carrying on a conversation he was no longer interested in. The messenger brought another tea and he drank it mechanically, the cloying sweetness sticking in his throat. 'We hear all kinds of things – mass starvation, food convoys being attacked . . .'

'Yes, that is true, Stephen. But by the rebels, not by us. By the Westerners themselves. Those people have a lot to answer for.'

But surely, Stephen thought, the irritation between his buttocks almost driving him mad, the corpses, the skeletons, the children with swollen bellies and matchstick limbs, they *are* Westerners. They *are* the local people.

'Is the government thinking of withdrawing?'

The major laughed and the eyes of the older Bakheet flashed angrily.

'Never!' His body was tense with indignation. 'Last night I said that one day I would tell you what we are planning for the West. Now you ask me if the Government will withdraw. I will tell you, Stephen. We shall withdraw only when the last Westerner is dead.'

The major nodded slowly. Stephen excused himself, found a quiet place and relieved his agony. Only then did he realise the horror of Bakheet's last words.

IV

Andrew Late put down his dictaphone as Stephen and Gomes-Little entered his office to discuss Stephen's programme. He stood up, the smile on his face twitching slightly, a long way from the incandescent figure of the previous evening. The collar on his grey woollen shirt was frayed and his charcoal trousers were baggy. His eyes were bloodshot and something suspiciously like egg yolk was caked in his beard.

Late looked at his two visitors as a parent might look at two offspring suspected of delinquency. But Stephen played up to his new ploy of befriending Gomes-Little and the latter was charm itself. So, as the discussion went on, Late became increasingly relaxed until at the end he was smiling broadly. As they got up to leave, he turned to Gomes-Little.

'Need to see you soon about arrangements for the visit.' He turned hastily to Stephen. 'Can't discuss it now. You understand, Stephen. These things . . . pretty well top secret. Fewer people who know, the better, that sort of thing. Not that I think you'd . . . er . . .' He broke off uncertainly. Stephen reassured him.

'I completely understand.'

'Good man, good man.' Late came within an ace of patting him on the head. He turned back to Gomes-Little. 'Monday? Ten o'clock?'

'An evening would be better.'

Late shook his head. 'Can't make an evening. This melodrama the rep's putting on. Taking a hell of a lot of time. So, is Monday all right?'

Gomes-Little nodded. The two men were leaving the office when Late called Stephen back, his smile exuding gratitude. Stephen noticed an incipient boil on the side of his neck.

'Really do appreciate your attitude about all this.'

Stephen drove the Land Rover to Alena's, feeling suddenly optimistic. His act had been good enough to convince Late. But he had no doubt that sterner tests lay ahead and he still had not the vaguest idea what to do if the Union failed them.

V

There were five people in Alena's flat: Stephen and the hostess, and three Tujanians, colleagues from the English Language Department. Bert had disappeared on one of his bird-watching expeditions and Alena was dispensing refreshments, clearly loving the spotlight. But in spite of the initial laughter, the business was serious.

'I tell you, Stephen, the man is evil.' It was Said Mohamed talking, a poet and a devout Muslim. 'He says I am a communist. I am not a communist. I am a very happy Muslim. This man is mocking my faith, abusing me, undervaluing me.'

'Come on, Said.' Amani Osman was more practical. 'Stephen wants to hear things that have happened to us, not things we feel.'

They looked at him appealingly and Stephen felt touched and not a little inadequate. He was glad no one knew about his ablutionary antics the previous day. After the Union, he was their last throw and he had an uncomfortable feeling that he might let them down.

'I might need something more tangible to take back to London.'

'Tangible!' Said was indignant. 'We gave all the tangible things in our complaints to the British Council. And what happened? Nothing! We are unhappy, Stephen. Can you not see it in our faces? What can be more tangible than that?'

'Well . . .'

'It's true.' The third person present, Omar Hassan, spoke. 'Every word Said says is true. We do not want this foreigner in our country. Give us good people like you and Alena and Malcolm. Tell the British Council that Mr Gomes-Little must go.'

'And if he doesn't?'

The other three shrugged and the two men were adamant. 'Then we shall resign. And most of the others will resign too.'

'Have you made this clear to Mustafa?'

There was open derision. 'Mustafa! Stephen, compared to Mustafa, a jellyfish is strong!'

'But he supports you?'

'He would support us, perhaps, if he could support anybody. The real power is Bakheet. And Bakheet hates us. He would like us out to get more of his cronies in.'

They fell silent, looking hopefully at him, and Stephen was at a loss. Their assessment of the Poly management was astute and realistic. Their only illusion was about how much he himself could achieve. After they had left, Alena waited for his reaction.

'The Union decision. When's it expected?'

'Some time next week.'

'And if it goes against us?'

'Then they'll resign. You heard them. The Department's a shambles, Stephen. You must have noticed. Nobody's there, nobody does any work. All they think about is keeping out of his way.'

'And you?'

She laughed. 'I've told you, don't worry about me. I'm a survivor. In fact, in a perverse sort of way I've almost begun to enjoy it.'

'So how long can you continue to enjoy it?'

'As long as I have to. I've applied for an extension to my contract, by the way. So that we can finish the work we've started.'

'Until when?'

'Next January. Though there won't be much point in finishing the work if that lot resign.'

Stephen remembered the note on Bakheet's desk. He looked at the large trusting figure of Alena and felt again the hopelessness he had felt with the Tujanian staff. He declined her offer of bean stew and suggested the slightly less risky option of lunch at the club.

CHAPTER 4

I

Stephen found Joe King's luggage on a first floor balcony in the residential section of the Club. He recognised the boxes – nine in all – he had packed during his previous visit. Since then Joe had died and his luggage had remained in a kind of diplomatic limbo. The Embassy had never before housed anything like Joe's personal possessions, he was certain of that. Apart from the books, the rest could probably be consigned to the nearest skip.

He arrived at the Club early, hoping to spend as little time as possible on what threatened to be a rather harrowing task. He missed Joe. The city wasn't the same without him. The death of Joe had happened a few weeks before the arrival of Gomes-Little and it had been an unhappy exchange. The presence of Joe, frail and uncertain as he was, had given a kind of stability to the place. With Joe there, the problem of Gomes-Little might never have arisen. A curt 'Who's this little fucker?' would have cut him down in an instant.

By common assent, Omeldoum wasn't the most hospitable city in the world. But that Friday morning, Stephen's little part of the city was a cocoon of warmth, tea and gentle good humour. The *agids* were cheerfully going about their work and the view of the city from the first floor balcony was one of foliage, trees, birds flitting about, and the tops of buildings neat and congruous.

He opened the ragbag of boxes, cases, plastic bags and holdalls and scanned the contents. Used air tickets, a random collection of yellowed newspapers, old coins carefully wrapped in bits of cellophane, a passport-size photograph from a machine, a postcard from Joe's wife in happier days. There was a new-looking biscuit tin with a snarling tiger on its front and and an even more lethal-looking collection of medicaments inside. An old spectacles' case, dirty shorts, an odd sandal down-at-heel and buckled with string, objects that had somehow escaped the first filtering.

The *agids* showed interest, standing on the edge of the miscellany like a couple of old hens. Stephen said they could have what he threw away and tossed them a dirty plastic bag. They began pecking methodically at it, strewing its contents on the floor. A broken alarm clock came to light and Mohamed, the senior *agid*, cocked his head querulously, then squawked greedily away, planting it with his growing hoard on top of the refrigerator. A bunch of keys was examined quizzically and Mohamed's face was a picture as he discarded them one by one.

Then on to the books, the real treasure trove. Books had been Old Joe's life. He had a feeling for books that he reserved for little else and it soon became clear that his feelings for other people's books had been even stronger than for his own. It turned out that the beneficiary of Joe's legacy already owned most of it – about three-quarters of the books were from the University library. Two or three dozen were from the Club. A set of Tom Stoppard plays was from Stephen's own collection, having 'gone missing' from his bookcase during his full-time residence in Omeldoum: *Dirty Linen*; *Jumpers*; *Every Good Boy Deserves Favour*.

And *Professional Foul*.

Before lunchtime, the business was complete. The *agids* had gleaned their treasures and helped Stephen pack the books in various boxes consigned to sundry places. A huge amount was dumped on the skip. Only one cloud remained on the horizon of Joe's luggage, a trunk that had been left in Joe's old room at the Green Grange.

Stephen stood on the balcony and looked out over the Club premises, the pool blue and sparkling in the centre. He saw Maggie and her husband arrive and watched them walk towards the changing rooms, his attraction to this elegant woman muted by her brittle and offhand manner. An afternoon by the pool tempted him, particularly when Maggie emerged in her bikini a few minutes later, but he decided to spend the day finishing off Joe's luggage. A spot of lunch, and then an afternoon in the old guest house by the river.

Lunch was a barbecue. Stephen joined the crowd in the shade around the hissing charcoal burners and helped himself to a chicken leg and a piece of burnt steak complemented by a variety of salads. For sweet there was chocolate trifle tasting of washing powder. All the club sweets tasted of washing powder. He waved to Maggie Earl, who briefly acknowledged him, and sat with an old acquaintance and colleague of Old Joe's, a portly middle-aged man of some scholastic distinction. He had stayed too long in Omeldoum and was now marooned there, beached like the turds in the Poly loo. As they ate their lunch he leaned across to Stephen.

'We hear dreadful things about the Polytechnic these days.'

Stephen chewed a mouthful of what looked like potato salad.

'What kind of things?' In Omeldoum, rumours, like sewage, seeped through every available crack.

'Internecine strife! Duels to the death between Alena and the new man!'

Stephen removed a piece of polythene from his coleslaw. 'The rumours are exaggerated.'

The other tried to swallow a piece of steak. 'So there is no trouble?'

Stephen hesitated. 'Well, you know what they say, no smoke without fire.'

'Especially in Omeldoum.'

'Yes. But it's not really concerned with Alena although the Council is making out it is. The real problem is between the local staff and Gomes-Little.' Stephen picked up his chicken leg and bit into it. It was stringy and, beneath the charred skin, the flesh was pink.

'Is it serious? – I wouldn't eat that if I were you.'

Stephen agreed. He had no wish to repeat his experience in the squatters' loo and put the offending limb back on his plate.

'Well, they're all thinking of resigning.'

The other looked surprised. 'That *is* serious. So you're here to sort it out.'

'I'm here as usual to assist with the teaching programme. It's up to Late to sort the other thing out.'

They began picking at the trifle. Stephen's companion grimaced and pushed his plate away. 'Same as ever. They may as well not bother.'

Stephen followed suit. 'They don't rinse the dishes properly.'

The other wiped his mouth and poured himself a glass of water. 'So whose fault is it?'

Stephen knew he wasn't talking about the dishes. 'I've no idea. Obviously it's not as clear cut as the local staff would have us believe. I haven't seen that much of Gomes-Little but he seems a decent sort of bloke. Do you know him?'

'Not very well. I've been to a couple of films at the Council with him. And I see him here from time to time. As you say, he seems pleasant enough.'

Stephen looked at his watch. It was after three, time to make a move if he was to deal with the last bit of Joe's luggage. He excused himself, paid his bill, took a surreptitious look at Maggie Earl in her white bikini and left for the Green Grange.

II

The Green Grange was situated by the river about two miles west of the city centre. The Council Land Rover had predictably proved less than reliable and Stephen took a taxi. The driver, a swarthy man in a dirty *djelabia*, did several clever things with wires and a bent screwdriver and the engine spluttered into life. Stephen took his seat in the back, carefully negotiating a lethal-looking spring that had burst from its covering. In Tujan, it wasn't only the currency that was held together with Sellotape.

The taxi trundled along, skewing this way and that to avoid the pot-holes that had eroded large areas of the road's surface. Dogs lazed in the dust and the afternoon sun, looking incapable of the snarling aggression that surfaced at sundown. The wide tracts of the river came into view with the two great bridges leading, in effect, nowhere. The heat shimmered on the water.

At the Green Grange, there was the inevitable argument about the fare. The amount requested was so ludicrous that Stephen forgot about the spring and scratched his leg badly as he got out. This did nothing to improve his temper. He stood there shouting at the surly man behind the wheel. The driver shouted back, neither understanding more than a smattering of what the other was saying. A couple of labourers in the adjoining fields watched in amusement.

Stephen made his way into the grounds of the Green Grange and the taxi drove off, the driver still cursing. Stephen wondered what particular aspect of the endlessly versatile wrath of Allah was currently being brought down on his head. But from a practical point of view, the altercation did present problems. He had intended asking the driver to pick him up in an hour or so and he now had no means of getting back to town.

The Green Grange was something of a legend in Omeldoum. Stephen had heard of this strange academic residence long before he found out where it was. For years he had travelled round the city looking for a palatial building with fairy turrets hewn out of emerald marble. When it was finally pointed out to him, he understood his mistake. The Green Grange was more like a Victorian mausoleum than a palace. It had reputedly been built as a residence for an Arab prince, but by this time anything less resembling an imperial residence would have been hard to imagine. As he went in, he felt as he had on his only previous visit, depressed and apprehensive. It was seedy and dark, smelling of decay and rats' urine, its walls a lurid turquoise discoloured by years of sandstorms and grime. Rotten linoleum, crumbled plaster and rat droppings covered the floor and two fans hung from the ceiling like the twin propellers of an obselete plane. He looked briefly outside, at the sink with its one brass tap, discoloured like the fingers of an albino chain smoker. A corroded battery sat irrelevantly underneath.

Next to the Green Grange, beyond the rubbish tip, separated by a high fence topped with barbed wire, was the Mogasi power station supplying electricity to two thirds of Omeldoum. By the fence was a lone palm tree, brown and moulting, like an old bird of prey whose pride had wilted with its plumage.

Joe had lived in the Green Grange for only a few months and then under the most severe protest. His room lay off the central dining area to the right and Stephen was surprised to find the door open. He tapped lightly and put his head in. Three or four holdalls were lying on the floor and there were clothes on the chair. Sprawled on the bed, naked except for a pair of boxer shorts, was presumably the owner of these objects. He was sure this was Old Joe's room. The old tin trunk with J. KING painted on it in black letters confirmed he was right.

The man on the bed opened his eyes and saw Stephen's face peering round the door. He struggled to sit up, propping his elbow on the two pillows underneath his head. He was lean and brown with an unkempt beard and intense eyes. The air was oppressive; beads of sweat stood out on his skin; the fan above the bed circled tortuously.

'Sorry,' Stephen said, 'I thought . . .'

'No. Please don't . . .' The other cried out in pain as he tried to sit up. 'They told me this room was empty . . .'

'It is. A friend of mine used to stay here.'

Charles Digley eased himself on to his side. 'Will he be coming back?'

'No. I've come to sort out his trunk.'

Charles looked at the tin trunk in the corner. 'Oh, that's his. I wondered . . .' He groaned again as he shifted his position.

'You seem in some pain.'

'It's my back. I don't know what happened. I thought if I rested it . . .'

'How long have you been like this?'

'Two days. It doesn't seem to be working.' Charles thought of all the things he had to do. The visit was approaching and here he was, laid up and useless.

Stephen lugged the trunk across the room. 'I'll take this outside, then I won't disturb you.'

'Sorry I can't help you. I can hardly move.'

'It's not heavy.'

He heaved the trunk through the doorway and turned back. 'If there's anything you want, I'll be here about half an hour.'

'Thanks. I've got a drink. Don't feel much like eating.'

Stephen closed the door behind him and opened the trunk. More hallmarks of Old Joe confronted him: more plastic bags, more scraps of paper covered with notes, more newspapers from the fifties and sixties; more books in brown paper covers; more jars of ointment and pills. Stephen took a deep breath and dived in. At least sorting out Joe's luggage was one of the less demanding aspects of his trip. Virtually everything could be classified as rubbish and treated accordingly. Pity he couldn't deal with Gomes-Little in the same way.

As he shovelled out the piles of papers, his mind wandered over the events of the previous few days. And as always, when the body was engaged in a mechanical act and the mind was given free range, the thoughts it came up with were not pleasant. He was certain some of the vilest crimes had been planned on the flimsiest of pretexts while the protagonist was doing nothing more sinister than painting a wall. War, rape, murder, atrocities of the most horrific kind – nothing, he felt, was beyond him during these periods when the mind was free to pursue its own track of grotesque distortion. And it wasn't Late or Gomes-Little that preoccupied him as he sifted through the bits and pieces that made up the residue of Joe's life. It was Maggie Earl, that bitch from the Embassy who had treated him with such amused disdain since the evening at Late's. He hated her, and as his eyes looked unseeingly at headlines proclaiming Britain's entry into the Common Market and the resignation of John Profumo, he was certain that he'd never hated anybody more in his life. 'How would she cope in this morguelike shit-hole?' he wondered. A colleague of Old Joe had lived here for twenty-five years which was among the most amazing statistics Stephen had ever come across. Twenty-five years! A silver jubilee among the rat shit. He'd like to see Maggie Earl last twenty-five minutes. How would she manage if she suddenly found herself in Old Joe's room with only a broken fan to relieve the heat?

A thought struck him, a thought which in his present state of mind he could only classify as brilliant. He straightened up from his task and poked his head round the door.

'I've been thinking about your back. I know an osteopath who might be able to help.'

Charles looked doubtful. 'I don't think I can afford an osteopath.'

'Don't worry. Her charges are based on the ability to pay. She may not charge you at all.'

'But where would she see me? I can't move very far at the moment.'

'I'll bring her here!' Stephen's delight was increasing by the second. 'Tomorrow afternoon, if she's free. She said she wanted a chance to help the world's oppressed.'

'You can hardly call me oppressed.'

'Everyone in pain's oppressed. So, tomorrow afternoon. You never know, she might get you back on your feet.'

Stephen resumed his task, a look of absolute delight on his face. Now he would see Maggie Earl's elegance crumble as she worked on a body caked with sweat in a room where a hundred malodorous smells came together in one huge stink, in a place where the stench of failure was like the dust in the air, visible, tangible. Now she would have to put her self-righteous principles where her mouth was. Not only that, it would give him a chance to be alone with her. He found it difficult to contain his glee as he went to work on the last layer of Old Joe's trunk.

III

In the bottom of the trunk, he found a long, thin parcel. It was wrapped in newspaper and stuffed into the inevitable plastic bag. Stephen was about to throw it into the box of rubbish when curiosity got the better of him. He pulled the bundle out of its covering and unwrapped it.

Whatever guesses he might have hazarded as to the contents, he would have been woefully wide of the mark. A huge rubber phallus revealed itself to his astonished eyes. Ten inches long, with the thickness of a baseball bat, swollen red glans and protruding veins, There were straps too and a small tube of cream called 'Eros Jel'. What that was for was anybody's guess. In fact, what was any of it for? No wonder Old Joe had always been so careful that no one should pry into his personal possessions! But what had he used it for? And who, if anybody, had he used it on? Stephen held the thing at arm's length and gazed at it in awe, aware that his experience in many fields was sorely limited.

Voices in the adjoining corridor caused him to look up in alarm. In a country where sexual pleasure was a sin, where girls were circumcised at puberty, where lechers were whipped and adulterers stoned, what unimaginable wrath would fall on anyone caught in possession of the joystick he was holding. He quickly wrapped the thing in a sheet of newspaper, thrust it into the plastic bag, threw the bag into the rubbish box and dumped the box on the tip. He went back to the trunk to complete his task, feeling that when the shock had died down, he would spend many a fertile hour speculating about Old Joe and the 'thing'.

He jettisoned the last of Joe's possessions and headed again for the tip. As he turned the corner, what horrors met his gaze! How could he have forgotten the local capacity for scavenging? There, ankle deep in the debris from the trunk, were the two workers from the adjoining fields. They had unearthed a few objects which were placed in piles, like archaeological relics. Stephen saw that the 'thing' had not yet been found, then noticed the taller of the two eyeing the plastic bag he had thrown away a few minutes earlier. He sprinted the twenty yards or so to the tip and as the man picked up the bag, tried to snatch it from his hand.

But the man wasn't letting go of it so easily and for a few seconds the two of them performed a ludicrous tug-of-war, pulling so violently that Stephen felt sure the bag would break and its monstrous contents be exposed. He appealed to his antagonist's friend. 'This is mine,' he heard himself say in a voice he hardly recognised. 'I threw it away by mistake.' He was suddenly struck by the absurdity of the situation, an impoverished labourer and a British Government consultant wrestling on a rubbish tip for possession of a rubber penis, the one petulantly, the other with the urgency of a Methodist minister sprinting away from a clip joint.

The man's friend nodded and spoke to his colleague who resentfully released his hold. Stephen muttered his thanks, and went back towards the building, sweat pouring from him. As an afterthought, he turned and beckoned the two men, explaining that he was giving them the trunk. They looked at it and touched it. Both were smiling now, white teeth in dark faces, eyes shining at this unexpected treasure, and Stephen nodded to them encouragingly. He went to say goodbye to Charles and confirm the possibility of a visit from Maggie Earl the next day. But Charles was asleep and Stephen left quietly.

The heat of the day had melted into a pleasant evening. The sun was dropping in the sky and the trees by the river were dark against the orange glow of the water. But Stephen had no time for the beauties of nature. He was too concerned with finding transport back to town and getting rid of the 'thing'. His first instinct was to hurl it unseen into the nearest bush but this was easier said than done, for the terrain, deserted an hour or so earlier, was now a hive of activity. Groups of men were talking in loud voices, youths had organised an impromptu game of football, the ubiquitous dogs were stirring from their languor and yapping threateningly. The place was a maggot heap of life.

Stephen scanned the area for a place to deposit his parcel but could see none. He looked with loathing at the dogs. Even if he found a place, he was sure those canine scavengers would retrieve it. Torn apart by savage street dogs, with curious onlookers trying to identify their bone of contention! What a sad end for an object of such proud pretensions. Tucked under his arm was the improbable substitute for Old Joe's manhood. He wrapped a hand round it. The girth was astonishing. He reached the road and proceeded warily, skirting the snarling packs and beginning to think he might have to walk all the way.

Suddenly a cloud of dust heralded a Land Rover, driven at speed and banging from pothole to pothole. Stephen stepped off the road to allow the vehicle to pass but, to his horror, it screeched to a halt and Late popped his head out of the driver's window.

'Stephen!'

Late's voice portrayed the bonhomie he had exuded since his doubts about Stephen's loyalties had been dispelled. Sitting next to him was the large girl from the drinks evening and a couple Stephen didn't recognise were in the back. Late leaned across and opened the passenger door.

'Jump in.'

'What?'

'Jump in. We'll give you a lift.'

'Er, no, it's all right. I'm enjoying the walk.' He slipped the plastic bag behind his back.

Late persisted. 'Jump in. Can't have you wandering around with all these dogs about. Not only that,' he continued in mock reproof, 'you're improperly dressed. Don't want you falling foul of the Fundamentalists. You know what they think of white men in shorts! Move over a bit, Dolores.'

Stephen had no option but to obey. The woman in the passenger seat smiled at him and he felt events slipping beyond his control as he climbed in beside her. Late let out the clutch and immediately drove into a Grand Canyon of a pothole that shook every suspension bolt to its foundations and caused the plastic bag to leap from Stephen's hand. Dolores picked it up and handed it to him. He thanked her mechanically, panic welling as he felt it was only a matter of time before his grotesque package was revealed.

The vehicle lurched on and he was thrown against Dolores, his thigh pressing hard against the flabbiness of hers. She smiled at him again. 'Intimate little cab, this.' He removed his thigh, pressing both legs together against the door to avoid further contact. He wondered how advanced her sense of touch was and whether she had been able to feel the veins through the thin plastic as Late unerringly homed in on another huge crater.

'Bloody roads! No wonder we can't keep any vehicle going more than a week at a time. Shopping?'

It was a while before Stephen realised the last remark had been addressed to him.

'Mmm?'

'The bag. That thing you're clinging on to for dear life. Have you been shopping?'

'What? Oh, well, just a little er . . .' He tailed off, now in total disarray.

'What can you buy down here? Didn't know there were any shops.'

'Well, no, there aren't. I didn't actually get it down here. I just haven't been back to er . . .'

'Just been to rehearsal, haven't we, gang? Bloody good it was, too. You can have your Shakespeare but for the average run-of-the-mill rep, can't beat a good melodrama.'

'I thought it was being put on at the Club.' Stephen hoped his relief at the change of subject wasn't too obvious.

'It is, it is. Just been out to Clifford's place.'

'Clifford?'

'The producer.' Late's tone suggested that Stephen should have known who Clifford was all along. 'A dress rehearsal and a line rehearsal, wasn't it, team? And I must say we were pretty nearly word perfect.'

The lady in the back snorted. 'All except you and me, Andrew.'

'Yes, well, not as young as I used to be.' Late was still oozing good nature. 'What's your excuse? Oh, you don't know each other, do you? Stephen Talbot, Queenie and Louis Pratt. Stephen's visiting from UK. Giving advice on ELT at the Poly. Doing a first rate job as well.'

There was another screech of brakes and the passengers pitched forward in their seats. Stephen realised with alarm that they had stopped outside Late's house and Late was bellowing for his watchman to open the gate.

'Just a short stop, Stephen. Come in and have a drink. Then drop you all . . . still at Alena's, are you? Got to do a quick change. Reception at the Marlborough. You know how these things are?'

'I don't think I will, Andrew.'

'Nonsense. Won't be more than ten minutes, then I can see you all home. Won't have you wandering around after dark. It's not safe, so there's an end of the matter. Let's get these costumes into the house, shall we? Louis, can you bring the stuff off the back seat?'

Stephen got out of the Land Rover with all the enthusiasm of a bather entering shark-infested waters. He offered Dolores his hand. She looked him straight in the eyes before glancing down at his bundle, a glance that made him certain she'd guessed its contents. Bugger Joe, Stephen thought. Why did the dirty old sod have to lumber him with such a monstrosity?

'Perhaps we can all help Louis with those,' Late said as the rather puny Louis tried to carry a pile of assorted costumes. The others each took an item from the top of the pile, all except Late who led the way, looking like the head of a Christian crusade bringing clothes to the Indians.

'Hang them up there.' Late pointed to the hooks in his entrance hall. 'I'll get Josiah to organise some drinks while I go and change. Beer all right for everyone?'

The others went into Late's lounge and Stephen heard Late bellowing again for five beers, cold and quick. He hoped it wasn't home-brew. He imagined Late's incompetence would comfortably extend into the field of beermaking. He excused himself and went into the toilet. There he took out the thing and gazed at it in morbid fascination. What a specimen! For a second the pattern of veins on the side took on the semblance of Old Joe grinning malevolently.

Stephen shuddered and put the thing back in the bag. He dared not take it into the lounge. He could imagine Dolores organising a game of twenty questions, 'just to find out what Stephen's got in his precious bag'. 'Vegetable with strong animal connections, my dear. No, you can't eat it, well; I wouldn't wear it myself . . .'

He opened the door and peeked out. He could see Josiah in the lounge dispensing drinks, hear Late above in the shower, thundering out some Gilbert and Sullivan number. Quickly, he took the thing from the bag and shoved it into the inside pocket of a black cloak hanging on the coat hooks. Then he slipped back into the toilet and replaced it with a cylinder of Harpic. Feeling much more relaxed, he joined the rest in the lounge.

'Your beer.' Dolores pointed to a glass of dark liquid on one of the side tables. Stephen picked it up and sipped it. His worst suspicions were confirmed. 'I think I'll give it a miss.' He rubbed his midriff. 'Touch of the squits.' He had no wish for a repeat of his experience at the Polytechnic.

Louis Pratt nodded sympathetically. 'Don't blame you,' he said confidentially. 'How these two can drink it beats me!'

The singing from the first floor had stopped. There was a period of heavy gargling, then a door banged and footsteps scurried down the stairs. The next minute Late appeared, resplendent in evening dress, hair sleeked down, shoes highly polished.

Dolores gave a wolf whistle. 'My, aren't we the smart one!'

Late beamed. The boil on his neck had grown. 'We do our best.' He looked at the full glasses. 'Drink up! Must be on our way.'

Louis coughed. 'Do you mind awfully if we don't, Andrew?'

'Don't. Not a bit of it.' Late picked up a glass and examined it closely, his confidence wavering. 'Not one of my better brews, I must admit. Don't know what went wrong. Must come again when I've got a really good one on tap. Come on, then. Oh, Stephen, you've forgotten your shopping. What *have* you got in that bag, by the way?'

'Alena wanted something to clean her loo.' He showed them the Harpic.

'Didn't know you could buy that locally.'

'Well, only if you know where to go,' Stephen replied and thought guiltily of the phallus nestling in the cloak on Late's hallstand.

CHAPTER 5

I

'No, I'm not pulling your leg . . . Yes, severe pain. You'd be doing him a big favour . . . I'll meet you at the Club then . . . Three o'clock? . . . Fine.'

Stephen put the phone down and did a little jig. He'd told Maggie Earl the bare essentials and couldn't wait to see her face when she saw the man she had to treat and the place she had to work in!

He'd spent a couple of hours that morning with Gomes-Little, going over plans for the Department. He'd heard very little about the Foreign Secretary's visit although he knew the Poly featured large on the agenda. Gomes-Little's fears about his intentions seemed to have been dispelled as completely as Late's but he remained vigilant. If the little shit was as devious as the note on Bakheet's desk suggested, nothing he said could be taken at face value.

'I'm preparing a brochure for the visit.'

'Oh.' Stephen tried to invest the monosyllable with as much interest as possible.

'Yes. On the work of the department, past, present and future. There'll be a few articles in it, a copy of the department magazine, some of the better materials – some of your stuff, of course. I'd like your opinion on it before it goes to press.'

Stephen alerted all his senses. 'Like your opinion' had tripped off Gomes-Little's tongue as though it was a phrase he used all the time.

'When will it be ready?'

'I hope to have the draft prepared in the next day or so. The final thing will take a week to ten days to print and collate. It'll be finished well in time for the visit.'

'Do we know the plans for the visit?'

The other smiled. 'We're not allowed to tell you, Stephen. You heard Andrew. The instruction is to tell as few people as possible.'

Stephen nodded. Why did he get the impression that Gomes-Little was enjoying this?

'There's something else I want to talk to you about.' Gomes-Little's cough indicated he was approaching a sensitive subject.

'What's that?'

'Alena. I hope all the problems we were having earlier haven't made her feel unwanted. We never see her now unless she's teaching and this is such a shame.'

'What do you want me to do?'

'I don't really know. Tell her how much we value her, perhaps. You see, the way things are, I suspect she won't renew her contract and this would be . . . well . . . a great loss to the Department.'

Stephen remembered the note on Bakheet's desk. He needed no further proof of Gomes-Little's deviousness. But he also felt a strange kind of superiority. If the little shit was going to play his vindictive games, he should make sure his Tujanian allies were as careful as he was.

II

Maggie Earl was waiting when Stephen arrived at the Club. She looked cool and relaxed in a plain cotton dress, hair swept back from her forehead, her fine face needing no make-up. The Land Rover was still out of action so they decided to use her car. Her dress rode up slightly as she drove off. She noticed Stephen looking at her brown thighs and pointedly pulled her hemline lower.

'I'm glad you've found me some work.'

'I don't think it'll pay very well. The man you're treating isn't very well off.'

She shrugged. 'Is he a local?'

'No, he's an expatriate, but I don't think he has much money.'

They drove along the road to the Green Grange, Maggie avoiding all the pot-holes that Late had found with such consistency the previous evening. Stephen thought of the phallus and wondered if it was still in the black cloak. He also wondered how close a check Late kept on his domestic supplies, realising that even a brain as unpredictable as Late's might associate the disappearance of a can of Harpic from his toilet with the appearance of an object of similar size and shape in the inside pocket of a cloak in his entrance hall. He wondered what the prim female at his side would make of the penis. Perhaps she needed a quick flash of something like that to shake her from her infuriating air of superiority and self-control.

He pointed out the entrance to the Green Grange and looked for some reaction, some surprise at the nature of the place in which she was expected to work. But the air of superiority remained, her lips slightly parted, suggesting a smile indefinitely postponed.

They parked the car and got out. As they entered the hall, she spoke for the first time since the early part of the journey.

'What an interesting place! What is it?'

'It's a residence for university lecturers and other down-and-outs.'

'Surely it wasn't built as that?'

'No, it was originally the local residence of some Arabian prince. Come down a bit since those days.'

'Oh I don't know. I think it's fascinating.' She looked round again. 'Such atmosphere!'

They walked on towards Charles's room, Stephen feeling a little non-plussed at Maggie's reaction. He quickly decided it was the paternalism of the pseudo-liberal, finding compensation in squalor, nobility in the striving of the oppressed classes, architectural value in an outside shithouse. Why wouldn't she recognise this place for what it was: morbid, filthy, depressing, an insult to all who had to stay here?

He knocked quietly on the door of Charles's room and poked his head in, gratified that the smell of sweat was still prominent. Charles gave a weak gesture.

'Hi.' Stephen pushed the door open. 'I've brought the osteopath I mentioned.'

Maggie came into the room and Stephen was again surprised as he saw the look of recognition on her face.

'Hello.' Now the smile actually happened.

Charles made an attempt to struggle up. Maggie stopped him. 'Don't. Leave it a while.'

'You know each other?' Stephen's little plot was showing signs of misfiring.

'We met briefly at the Club.' There was an edge of pain in Charles's voice. 'I didn't know you were an osteopath.'

'I'm glad it doesn't show!' Maggie took a handkerchief from the pocket of her dress and mopped her brow. 'It's hot in here.'

'It's good of you to come.' Charles made a more successful effort to prop himself up. 'You can't be used to working in places like this.'

She went to the window and opened one of the shutters. 'I was a volunteer before I met Basil.'

The two men were astonished. It was the last thing they had expected. The cool, poised wife of the Aid Secretary a volunteer! 'Three years in West Africa. I'm used to working in places a lot worse than this.' She looked at Charles. 'You're a volunteer too, aren't you?'

'Yes. Just back from the West.' Maggie looked at him, and remembered the impression he had made on her at the pool. Now there was a different pain in the intense blue eyes.

'How did you get yourself in this state?'

'I don't know. I'd just finished a game of squash and I felt it go. It seemed all right until I woke the next morning and could hardly move.'

'It happens. Now I'm not going to ask you to stand. Do you think you can sit up on the edge of the bed if I give you a hand?'

Charles struggled up on to his elbow. She went across and put one arm round his waist, pulling him up with the other hand while Stephen looked on helplessly. Maggie Earl showed no sign of being repulsed by the unkempt nature of her patient. Well, she wouldn't, would she? As a volunteer in West Africa, she must have seen and handled far worse. He felt a sudden self-disgust at his own puny motives, a feeling that intensified as he thought of the people depending on him, the trust of the Polytechnic staff. Guilt nagged at him like a bad tooth as he watched Maggie running her hands down Charles's spine.

'You won't need me for a while.'

Maggie half-turned her head. 'No. But the manipulation won't take long. Don't wander too far.'

She spoke to him as to a child.

'Thanks,' Charles shouted after him. 'For being the Good Samaritan yesterday. Sorry there's nowhere you can get a cold drink in this place.'

'That's all right. I'll just have a walk round.'

He went out into the hall where the previous day he had found the phallus. A few scraps of newspapers remained. He went down the steps into the compound near the rubbish tip. The heat was only just bearable. He rested his hand for a moment on the low wall at the bottom of the steps; it was hot enough to fry an egg.

The rubbish had been burnt and was now smouldering. Breezes had scattered the charred papers. He picked up one sheet, its edges blackened. It was in Old Joe's handwriting.

Things fall apart, the centre . . .

Mere anarchy is . . .

And on another scrap:

A terrible beauty is . . .

A feeling of dissatisfaction came over him, of wastefulness and loss, of grossly inflated self-importance, of hugely erect conceits hiding the small limp penis of his humanity. He saw himself as in a play wrestling for possession of a strange aberration while another part of his mind planned the humiliation of Maggie Earl. Meanwhile, Gomes-Little was still securely in place.

And thousands were dying.

He went back to the room. Charles was lying on the bed and Maggie was talking to him. There was sweat on her forehead and her dress was streaked with perspiration and dirt.

'So you should be all right, providing you rest completely today. You'll need another manipulation to get it completely back in place. In three or four days you should be . . .'

'Three or four days! I can't wait that long.' Charles thought about the submission and the Westerner he had to contact. And he had to see Derek. Why hadn't Derek contacted him?

He looked at Stephen. 'Do you know a chap called Derek Lomas?'

Stephen glanced at Maggie. 'We both do. Why?'

'Could you ask him to come and see me? It's pretty urgent.'

Stephen nodded, glad to feel useful again.

Charles turned to Maggie. 'What about tomorrow?'

'Tomorrow what?'

'For the next treatment.'

'That's much too soon. Your body needs a good rest after a session like that.'

'Oh, come on. I'm young and reasonably fit. And you've got me walking after one session. It's amazing.'

Maggie compromised. 'I'll come and see how you're getting on. No more. And although you feel you can walk now, don't. Rest it. At least until tomorrow.' She turned to Stephen. 'I shan't need you tomorrow. I can find my own way here now.'

It was the final brush off.

III

The following morning, Stephen had arranged to go into the Polytechnic with Alena. He had spent a large part of the previous evening in gloomy self-appraisal. Alena and Bert had been out and he had listened to Brahms and got quietly pissed on home-brew. He woke with a hangover and, far from feeling like the day when he would get to grips with the real business of his visit, it felt like another day when he would get to grips with nothing at all.

Raised voices coming from Gomes-Little's office greeted their arrival at the English Language Department. Alena arched her eyebrows and peeped in. A minute or so later, after more shouting, a man stormed out, slamming the door behind him.

'Valentine.' Alena grabbed the man's arm as he went towards the stairs. He angrily shook himself free.

'Valentine. What is it?'

He gestured towards Gomes-Little's office.

'That man! That compatriot of yours!'

'Come and have a coffee and tell us about it.' She pointed to Stephen. 'This is Stephen Talbot, a colleague of ours, and a very good friend.'

Valentine managed a curt greeting, still seething. But the line between anger and despair was very thin; there were tears of helplessness in his eyes.

They went down the stairs to Alena's car. A few minutes later they were sitting in the Hilton, quiet music playing, the air cool, and three cups of fresh coffee in front of them.

'Now, Valentine, tell us what happened.'

He looked at them and shook his head, not knowing where to begin. 'Take your time,' Alena reassured him. Stephen was impressed with her handling of the situation.

'You see . . .'

'It's Stephen,' Alena prompted.

'You see, Stephen, I come from Western Province. My people are dying.' His eyes clouded over. 'All of them. The government wants to kill them.' He buried his face in his hands. Alena gave Stephen a 'Can't you *do* something?' look and Stephen tried to ward off a familiar feeling of inadequacy. He cleared his throat.

'What about your family, Valentine?'

'I wanted to see them. Alena knows how much I wanted to see them. But Mr Gomes-Little would not let me go. He said I must wait till half term. I told him half term would be too late.'

'So you went?'

Valentine nodded, calmer now. 'I *had* to go. What would you do if your family was threatened with death?'

'So, did you see them? Are they all right?'

A look of grief as intense as anything Stephen had ever seen came over the man's face. 'When I got there they were . . . dead. House burnt, all their things stolen, gone . . . everything.'

'Oh, Valentine, I'm so, so sorry. You must be so sad.'

He shook his head. 'Not so sad now, Alena. But angry.'

'What was Mr Gomes-Little saying to you?'

'He said I was suspended from duty.'

Stephen was shocked. 'Did you tell him about your family?'

The other nodded. 'He was very sympathetic, he said, but rules were rules. He had to let the procedure take its course. I had been absent without leave. He very much regretted it but I would probably lose my job.'

Stephen took a deep breath. Alena was looking at him intently. 'But this isn't the army.'

'He thinks it is.'

'Would you mind losing your job? You could get another.'

'I am a Westerner, Mr Stephen. It is not easy for Westerners to get jobs. I was happy to have my job at the Polytechnic. Alena was very good to work with, and Mr Gomes-Little had promised me a scholarship.'

'You're talking of it in the past.'

'I know.' He gave a gesture of hopelessness. 'My home burnt, my family dead. And now my job gone because I tried to see them.'

He began sobbing and as Alena comforted him, she looked accusingly at Stephen.

'Now do you see the kind of man we're dealing with?'

IV

The same evening Major Bakheet signalled to his driver to stop outside the Refugees' Training Centre. Half a dozen of his company waited in the Land Rover while his sergeant accompanied him to the door.

The watchman responded aggressively to the strident knock, the aggression fading as he opened the door.

'I would like to see Derek Lomas.' The major addressed the man first in Tujanian, then in impeccable English. The man was probably a refugee, perhaps even a Westerner. His heart beat faster. This place promised to be a real nest of vermin.

The man turned and led the two soldiers into the inner office where Derek was sitting at his desk poring over some papers and didn't immediately look up. When he did, his plump face paled under its tan.

'Mr Lomas?' The major spoke politely, lips smiling thinly under cold eyes. He remembered his instructions, the threat implicit in the Minister's words: 'I hold you responsible for finding this expatriate who sympathises with the West.'

'Yes.' Derek struggled to his feet.

'I am Major Bakheet. And this is Sergeant Mohamed. We would like to ask you one or two questions.'

'About what?' Derek resumed his seat and indicated two chairs; the major pulled one to the desk, the sergeant remained standing.

'About what you do here to start with.'

'Surely you know?'

'If I knew I wouldn't ask, Mr Lomas.'

'This is an education centre for refugees. A distance education centre.'

'Distance education?'

'Yes. We write materials and send them out to refugees in distant places. What used to be called correspondence courses.'

'And your position?'

'I am the Director.'

'I see. And you have only refugees here?'

'What do you mean?'

'You have no . . . Westerners.'

'Yes, we have Westerners. I worked hard to get them admitted. It seemed to me unfair that nationals of other countries could get help while Tujanian nationals, equally in need, couldn't.'

'So you think Westerners are Tujanian nationals?'

'What other country are they nationals of?'

The major pursued a different tack.

'You spent a lot of time in Western Province, did you not?'

Derek nodded. 'Five years.'

'During that time, did you . . . form an attachment to the people out there?'

'I got to know them and like them, if that's what you mean.'

'And do you still . . . know them and . . . like them?'

'Of course. These things don't change overnight.'

'Would you say you know and like them so much that in the present conflict your sympathies are with them rather than with the elected government?'

Derek took a deep breath.

'I try to see things objectively. If this means seeing justice in the Westerners' cause then . . .' He shrugged.

The major looked sternly at him. 'That is a very serious admission, Mr Lomas.'

'Many people feel like that. Not all of us can support what you are doing.' He paused, then continued. 'It's not a crime to sympathise with a cause. This is supposed to be a democratic country.'

'Perhaps you've forgotten that there is a state of emergency in operation. Such sentiments as you have just expressed could easily be classified as treason.' Bakheet stood up and the sergeant advanced to his side. 'I must ask you to come with us.'

Derek was aghast. 'You're arresting me?'

'Let us say, we are taking you into custody for your own protection. Views such as yours are not popular with Eastern people. The British Ambassador will, of course, be informed.'

The sergeant summoned two of the soldiers and a stunned Derek was led away while Bakheet watched and smiled. Now he could tell the Minister that he had apprehended the man whom he suspected of being the chief Western sympathiser. And perhaps a thorough search of the premises would reveal the submission.

V

Stephen looked out of his bedroom window at a bright red sky. Dawn had broken but the sun hadn't yet risen. The air cooler was trundling away ineffectively but for once his head was clear.

The offices of the Educational Centre for Refugees were a short walk from Alena's flat. Stephen made his way there after declining a breakfast of bean stew and settling for a cup of instant coffee and a piece of toast.

As he approached Derek's office, he was aware something was wrong. There was a soldier on duty outside and the door was hanging open. The soldier stood up as he approached.

'Derek Lomas?'

The man looked at him uncomprehendingly before barking something in Tujanian. Stephen felt his lack of the local language as keenly as ever.

He pointed to the inside of the building. 'I want to see Derek Lomas.'

The soldier was now confused and Stephen went towards the open door. 'No, no, no!' The soldier came towards him waving his index finger. Stephen tried to pull him towards the door but the soldier wouldn't budge.

The voices brought Derek's assistant to the door and Stephen went towards him, gesturing to the soldier to stay calm. The soldier relaxed a little but kept his rifle at the ready.

'You're Derek's assistant.'

The man nodded. 'And you are Mr Stephen from UK.'

'That's right.' He indicated the soldier. 'What's going on?'

The man spoke to the soldier in Tujanian and the soldier lowered his rifle. 'He is not a bad man. Only doing his job.'

'Where's Derek?'

The other looked distressed. 'Late last night, Special Branch took him away.'

'You mean he's . . . arrested?' The man nodded.

'Why?'

'They believe he is helping the West. They thought he was hiding something.'

'What makes you think that?'

The man moved towards the open door. 'I'll show you.' He said something to the soldier who smiled good-naturedly. Then he led Stephen into the building, pushed open the office door and pointed dramatically.

The office had been ransacked. Not a drawer had been left untouched, not a paper uninspected. Everything had been taken apart.

'And this is not all.' He led Stephen to Derek's private apartment at the back of the building. The same story. Everything turned upside down.

'When did this happen?'

'Just after Mr Derek was arrested. Soldiers, perhaps ten, twelve, came and . . .'

'Did they find what they were looking for?'

The man shook his head. 'I don't think so.'

'Does anyone else know of this?'

'Major Bakheet said he would phone the Embassy. But in case he forgot, I phoned them myself.'

'Major Bakheet?' Stephen frowned. He wondered how many Major Bakheets there could be in the Tujanian army. So he would have to tell Charles there would be no visit from Derek. They went back into the street, the soldier looking relieved when he saw them emerge. A taxi drew up on the other side of the road and Stephen watched in surprise as the familiar figure of Valentine got out and crossed the road to the Refugee Centre. The soldier's smile froze and he brandished his rifle menacingly.

Valentine had slept badly. A power cut had deprived his room of its fan and air cooler and the heat had been oppressive. He had slept in the garden to the obvious delight of the mosquitoes. His thoughts as he lay there had been turbulent, full of loathing for the little man in charge of the English Language Department but also concerned that his personal problems might interfere with his mission. When Charles had handed the Westerners' submission to him in the soup kitchen in Muja, they had made arrangements to meet in Omeldoum. Charles had told him to contact the Director of the

Refugees' Educational Centre, so the following morning he set off in a taxi, the submission still stitched into the lining of his jacket.

Valentine greeted the two men with the ritual handshake. The soldier, at a sign from Stephen, had subsided like a dog brought to heel. But his tail wasn't wagging. He was looking at Valentine and keeping up a warning growl. Valentine himself looked dreadful. His crinkled hair was matted, his eyes were bloodshot and his face was drawn and grey.

'I am looking for Derek Lomas.'

Derek's colleague, though friendly, was wary. 'Why?'

'A man I met in Western Province told me to see him.'

'You have been to the West?'

'Valentine's just back.' Stephen said. He added gently. 'His family was killed in the war.'

The other's attitude softened. 'I'm sorry.'

'No, Mr Stephen, they were not killed in the war. Soldiers are killed in war. My family was murdered. They were not fighters, they were no threat. They were murdered in cold blood.'

There was an uneasy silence. Finally Stephen asked, 'Why did you want to see Derek?'

Valentine looked around. Something in the attitude of the two men and the presence of the soldier finally got through to him. 'What has happened here?' He looked at the open door.

Stephen said quietly, 'Last night Derek was arrested.'

Valentine put his head in his hands. 'Now I don't know what to do.'

A thought struck Stephen. 'Valentine, the soldiers turned Derek's office and home upside down. Have you any idea what they were looking for?'

Valentine hesitated, then shook his head. 'I must go. I need time to think.' He set off down the road. Stephen saw him hail a taxi and watched as he got in and the car disappeared. He then said his final commiserations to Derek's colleague and walked back to Alena's. He hadn't noticed the soldier who, as Valentine left, had gone to his radio and contacted headquarters.

VI

Charles Digley could hardly believe it when the elegant woman he had seen at the Club followed Stephen Talbot into his room at the Green Grange. When Stephen had said he knew an osteopath, Charles had visualised the kind of stout, frumpy creature that habitually lurked on the fringes of the medical profession. Maggie had been a pleasant surprise.

He had thought about her a lot since their meeting by the pool. Her position and privileges had provoked his usual anger but other thoughts had intruded, inspired by the look she had given him as she walked away.

He hadn't been mistaken about that look. It was there again when she came into his room and recognised him. Her eyes had held his a second longer than necessary and during the treatment her hands had been as much caressive as manipulative. Perhaps that was the way of all osteopaths, but he doubted it.

After she had left, he walked quietly round the confines of the Green Grange, even venturing outside and taking a look at the river. It seemed a long time since his journey from Muja, impossible that the river he was staring at now was the same river he had stared at two weeks previously four hundred miles west.

His back felt stiff – she had said it would – but the agonising pain had gone. He knew he should be thinking about contacting Derek and getting in touch with Valentine Luko. He had no idea how the submission was to be presented or even if it had arrived safely in Omeldoum. And the VIP visit was now only two weeks away. But he found it difficult to think beyond the elegant woman with the lovely smile and the eyes that refused to leave him alone.

VII

Maggie was looking forward to the afternoon with a schoolgirl eagerness. The previous night she had lain awake long after Basil had performed his ritual – she could never have called it 'making love' – frustrated, staring at the ceiling, wondering what it was all about. She found herself thinking of the man in the Green Grange, his brown skin, the muscular body that had felt so good as she massaged it. She was pleased that she had helped him, although another session the next day would be very unwise. Still, at least they could have a 'consultation'. And this time that idiot Stephen Talbot wouldn't be lurking around.

CHAPTER 6

I

'Ah, good to see you, good to see you.'

It was Andrew Late's finest hour, the opening night of the little known Victorian melodrama, *Night of the Stallions*. The plot was predictable, the local interpretation of it less so. It featured Late as a power-crazed villain anxious to get his hands on the money (and other things) of Queenie Pratt, while Dolores played Queenie's faithful maid and Louis her long-lost love.

Late was at the Club gates, greeting all who came in. There had been concern that the attendance would be low, particularly in view of the last two cultural events organised by Late at the British Council. But the impoverishment of the Omeldoum entertainment circuit ensured that people would come along if only for something to do. It was the accepted duty of all expatriates to patronise these events and to try and dress the part. Strings of pearls, diamond necklaces, even old moth-eaten fox furs were dug out and dusted off. Then the wearers took their seats in the temporary theatre in the Club grounds, happy in the knowledge that at least one aspect of European subculture occasionally poked its head above the growing tide of barbarism that was the third world.

'Good to see you! Good to see you!' Late was bouncing up and down with enthusiasm. 'To be frank, we never expected so many people. Ah, Stephen.' Late shook Stephen warmly by the hand. His greeting to Alena and Bert was markedly cooler.

'Why *Night of the Stallions*, Andrew?' asked Alena. 'Are we going to see horses charging across the stage?'

'You'd be surprised,' said Late mysteriously. 'No, I won't give anything away. Just let your imagination work on it.'

'It's got to be an improvement on his last two efforts,' Alena said, as they sat down in the open air theatre.

The first act proceeded predictably with much audience participation, regular hissing and booing, lines left out, clangers dropped. The play's title referred to the heroine's likely demise, a variation on the railway line theme, when the hapless Kate (played with tremulous uncertainty by Queenie Pratt) would be tied to a woodland path along which, once a year, a hundred black stallions came rushing. It soon became clear that whatever qualities had elevated Late to his exalted position in the British Council, acting ability wasn't one of them and Stephen found himself fidgeting with embarrassment. He exchanged knowing looks with Alena while Bert sat with a faraway expression on his face, no doubt dreaming of that rare, unidentified wader.

The interval came and went and Stephen found himself looking increasingly at his watch, when a waiter peered into the audience and beckoned him. He rose quietly and followed the waiter to the Club entrance, relieved to have a reason for skipping part of the proceedings.

Valentine Luko was there, pacing up and down.

'Stephen!' They shook hands. 'I had to see you. Can we talk?'

'Of course.' He signed Valentine in. 'Let's have a Pepsi.'

They were sitting with their drinks when Stephen said, 'How did you know where to find me?'

'The staff at the Poly. Alena said you'd be coming here tonight. I had to find you. You told me Derek Lomas's office had been searched?'

Stephen nodded. 'It was a pretty thorough job. They were desperate to find something.'

'I know what they were looking for.'

'You?' Stephen was surprised. 'How?'

'Because I have it.'

Stephen raised his eyebrows. 'Well, what is it? It might get Derek out of jail.'

Valentine shook his head. 'Nothing can get Derek out of jail. Not for a while. But I will tell you what it is.' And Valentine told Stephen the story of the submission, how he had smuggled it from the West, the last throw of a people threatened with extinction.

Stephen listened. To start with, he was intrigued. Valentine's story was vastly more interesting than the antics on stage. By the finish, he was not a little saddened by the hopelessness of it all.

'But why are you telling me all this?' Stephen said at length. 'What have I got to do with it?'

Valentine hesitated. 'I would like you to take it.'

'Take what?'

'The submission.'

Stephen was appalled. He felt he was being tipped the modern equivalent of the black spot.

Valentine clutched his arm. 'No one will suspect you. I am sure Special Branch are on to me, and they will be suspicious of the man who gave it to me. They will suspect anyone who has recently been to Western Province. You are a respected person here. You have not been to the West. You have not even been in Tujan very long.'

'Valentine, I don't really think I could . . .'

The grip on his arm became tighter. 'Stephen, you are my last chance. If I keep it I know they will get it.'

Stephen was still noncommittal. 'What are you planning to do with this submission?'

'You know there is a visit from the British Foreign Secretary?'

Stephen nodded.

'We hoped we could present it then.'

Stephen shook his head.

'Impossible. The schedule for the visit is top secret. No one knows what it is apart from one or two people.'

Valentine was silent for a while. 'Then perhaps you can contact Charles Digley. Ask him what to do.'

'I know Charles.' An image of the Green Grange and Maggie came into Stephen's mind.

'Then take it to him. Talk to him about it. Decide between you what to do. Or take it back to UK when you go. Show it to someone there. Just make sure someone important sees it.'

Stephen looked hard at Valentine. 'You realise what you are asking me to do. Betray the trust of my employers, carry out an act of subversion against the Government here. At the very least it could cost me my job.'

Valentine spoke quietly. 'Mr Stephen, I know that. And I do not ask lightly. But we are not talking about jobs here. Remember yesterday in the Hilton. We talked about my job. And I was upset. But I went away and thought about it and realised it did not matter.' He shook his head. 'We are not talking about jobs. We are talking about thousands and thousands of people dying and being killed.'

Stephen was suddenly deeply impressed by Valentine's commitment and his desperation in trying to hand over such an important document to a virtual stranger. The trust that was being placed in him was staggering and, as ever, he felt supremely unworthy. Joe King's judgement of him as a kind of poor man's superman had extended to people who hardly knew him.

'All right,' he said and wondered how many times he would regret that statement.

Valentine sighed. Then he smiled, his face relaxed, and he looked ten years younger.

'Mr Stephen . . .' he began but Stephen cut him short.

'Just give it to me before I change my mind. Where is it?'

Valentine patted his jacket. 'I will go to the toilet. You follow me. When I come out I will leave the submission there.'

'What if someone beats me to it?'

'I won't come out until you arrive. Whistle a tune to show me it is you.' He downed his Pepsi and stood up. 'Where is the toilet?'

Stephen explained and Valentine disappeared. Stephen waited a minute or so before following him, whistling the same Gilbert and Sullivan nonsense that Late had rendered so enthusiastically a few nights before while Stephen had been lurking in another loo. There were two other men waiting, no doubt fellow refugees from the melodrama. They gave him the half smile that establishes the camaraderie between people waiting to move their bowels or empty their bladders. He smiled back, inwardly cursing the men, both of whom had prior claim to occupancy of the toilet that Valentine was on the verge of vacating. He whistled more loudly in an effort to warn Valentine to stay put. The flushing sound indicated that he had failed.

Fortunately, years of making spontaneous responses to unlikely situations had left his imagination perfectly honed to coping with them. He suddenly began hopping around clutching his stomach. The others looked at him.

'You all right, old man?'

'Yes . . . er . . . I mean no, not really, touch of the trots. Do you mind if I . . . ?' Without waiting for an answer he slipped into the loo as Valentine vacated it.

'Bean stew!' he enunciated, not without feeling, as he closed the door. The two men nodded sympathetically.

Stephen locked the door and looked around. In the corner was a blue and white plastic bag, similar to the one that had held the phallus. This one contained a thick wad of papers. The writing was in English and most of the pages were covered with signatures, thousands of them. He put the papers back in the bag and went to open the door, pausing as he thought of the men outside. He had been there barely a minute, hardly time to relieve an attack of diarrhoea. Not only that but the eruption that invariably signalled the relief of gut rot hadn't occurred. He waited a minute or so before pulling the chain, wisely suppressing the urge to attempt an oral simulation of an anal explosion. Then he went out, nodding his thanks, another plastic bag tucked behind his back.

II

Stephen resumed his seat, just as the play was building up to its climax. Alena looked at him.

'Any problem?'

'No, just a guy I said I'd see.' He hadn't yet worked out the implications of having a submission from the West in his possession but he knew it was a monumental undertaking and the fewer people who knew about it the better. He cursed himself for his humane qualities, for being a soft touch. Bloody milk of human kindness by the gallon, he thought bitterly. The submission had all the symptoms of a major personal disaster. It was a recipe for hot water, a navigational aid leading inexorably to the human sewage farm, a question only of time, he felt, before it landed him well and truly in the shit.

On stage, a tragedy of sorts was unfolding. Dolores and Queenie were bemoaning their likely fate just as Late appeared with a bellow of 'Ah-ah!'

The two girls cowered before the onslaught of the wicked Late. To an accompaniment of boos and hisses, he grabbed Queenie by the arm and wheeled her round the stage.

'I have a note from your lover, my pretty one.'

'What? But that's impossible. He only writes me notes on Sunday.'

'You forget, my pretty. Today *is* Sunday. And I have intercepted his silly note. I have it here.'

With an attempt at a flourish, Late put his hand in his inside pocket. A lack of slickness had characterised his entire performance but even allowing for this, he was still taking an inordinately long time to produce the dreaded note. Perhaps it was a production gimmick intended to make a virtue out of Late's cackhandedness, Stephen thought, realising immediately that it wasn't. He suddenly knew, beyond any shadow of doubt, the cause of Late's difficulty. For the cloak Late was wearing bore a marked similarity to the one . . .

Late looked at the girls as they tried to suppress their giggles.

'You'll be sorry you laughed at me,' he brayed, ad-libbing admirably. 'What I have in store for you is a fate worse than . . .!' And to the astonishment of all present, he pulled from his pocket something that looked like a giant penis. He pulled it out, looked at it, then thrust it back again.

A deathly silence followed. And only Stephen, hiding his face in his hands, knew the truth.

Minutes later the play ended. A subdued cast took their bows, a subdued audience applauded and left, still amazed at what they thought they'd seen.

Alena glanced coyly at her two companions and started to giggle.

'Now we know why it was called *Night of the Stallions*.'

Bert chuckled. 'The only trouble was it was spelt wrong. "Stallions" should have had an apostrophe before the s!'

Stephen clutched the bag holding the submission and laughed, more in hysteria than amusement. He caught sight of the President's picture in the Club office. Once again the baleful face assumed the features of Old Joe. And Old Joe was laughing till the tears rolled down his cheeks.

Backstage Late was weeping tears of frustration.

'I tell you I did *not* plan it. One of you lot played a trick on me.'

Dolores looked at him scornfully. 'Don't be silly, Andrew. Do you think I'd waste a magnificent object like that on some cheap theatrical effect! Come on, let's have another look at it.'

But Late had gone, his big night reduced to farce, his world crumbling around him. The cast had been invited to drinks at the Ambassador's. He didn't want to go. His face burned in shame and humiliation and he even forgot to remove his make up.

But an invitation from the Ambassador couldn't be spurned. He decided to brazen it out but first he drove down to the river. There he took the odious thing out of his pocket, eyed it with a hatred he had rarely felt before and, with a grunt like a serving tennis player, hurled it far into the murky water.

III

There were a dozen or so people at the Ambassador's and as Late entered, all eyes turned to him. He blushed, fingered the boil on his neck and gave what he hoped was a cheery 'Hello'. He suddenly understood a lot of things, such as how Custer must have felt. Late felt very much that this could be *his* last stand – although he shied away from the word 'stand' – much too reminiscent of . . .

The Ambassador came over to him.

'Would you like a drink?'

Late nodded absently. He couldn't stop thinking about the moment when his hand, feeling for a small billet-doux had come into contact with a pliant, knobbly thing. Why hadn't he left it where it was? What demon in his brain had sent those infernal signals instructing his muscles to propel it into the spotlight? And how the hell had it got there in the first place?

The Ambassador looked hard at him. 'I'll get you a brandy. I should think you need one.'

Late muttered his thanks. He glanced up, aware of people looking at him and looking quickly away.

'Here.' The Ambassador pressed a large brandy into his hand. 'Mind you, some of us were convinced you must have been drinking already.' He

lowered his voice. 'What on earth got into you? We could hardly believe
our eyes. You've shocked an awful lot of people, Andrew. The only
consolation is that many of them actually *can't* believe their eyes. They're
convinced they were the victims of a mass illusion.'

Late realised with astonishment that the Ambassador thought he'd done
it on purpose.

He tried to say something. Only a strangled gurgling came out. The
Ambassador eyed him sternly and Late gave up. Sexual mania or gross
incompetence. A tendency to wander in the darker areas of life looking for
sexual aids of unlikely proportions, or an inability to prevent someone
planting such objects in his inside pocket. Either way, he couldn't win.

The Ambassador sighed. 'The most we can hope is that nothing comes of
it.'

Late looked at him, aghast. 'What do you mean?'

'Well, in case you haven't noticed, this *is* a Muslim country, Andrew.
And, being a Muslim country, its opinions on some matters are pretty
puritanical. What I mean by hoping nothing comes of it – for your sake, not
mine – is that I hope there were no Muslim Fundamentalists in the audience,
for example. That's one of the things I mean by it. And I hope there were
no foreign diplomats in the audience, that's another thing I mean by it.
They'd have an absolute bloody field day! Not that I could blame them. I
don't think I've ever seen a crasser example of bad taste in my life. And as
that includes service in at least a dozen countries, you can imagine what I
think of your behaviour.'

Late tinkered with his brandy and wanted the earth to swallow him up.
At the back of his mind was a vague feeling that somebody had it in for him.
Strangely, he felt no malice towards his malefactor, only a sorrow and a
curiosity as to who it could be.

For the Ambassador, it was the last straw. He had enough on his plate
with the Visit now only two weeks away. As if that wasn't enough, that fool
Derek Lomas had got himself arrested. And now this! He looked at Late,
half-cowering in the corner, and felt a deep contempt for the man. Where
did the British Council dig them up from?

CHAPTER 7

I

Just before Late's monumental blunder, Valentine Luko had left the Club feeling more relaxed than at any time since his return to Omeldoum. The submission had become a burden. He wasn't worried about his personal safety; in fact, since the death of his family, he had felt that his own death couldn't be far away and he was curiously indifferent to it. He would willingly have sacrificed himself to ensure that the submission reached its target and in recent days he had begun to feel vulnerable. He had a strong suspicion that Special Branch was on to him and unless he got rid of the submission soon, he was sure it would be discovered. Now he could forget about it and concentrate on his other obsession. There was a look of grim determination on his face as he went down the main street of town and took the turning towards the residential area of Juddah where Fairfax Gomes-Little lived.

The streets were deserted apart from the occasional group of street kids and a couple of taxis parked by the roadside. There were the dogs too, responding to the manic barking of their most aggressive member and posing a snarling, collective threat. Valentine picked up a stone and pretended to throw it. The dogs scattered, still snarling but now unsure. A gust of wind scattered rubbish along the gutterways and a couple of sheep, disturbed from their slumbers, shot to their feet and staggered across the road, a mixture of reproof and alarm on their idiot faces. Valentine walked on towards Juddah; behind him the dogs were barking again.

Juddah was a residential area for wealthy Tujanians and expatriates on rent-free contracts. Each residence was protected by a night-watchman whose main concern was to ensure that no disturbance, however alarming, should interfere with the body's need for a good night's sleep. Consequently, when Valentine opened the gate to Gomes-Little's residence, the only evidence of the watchman was a gentle snoring coming from the garden. He closed the gate and listened for a while. Apart from the snoring, all was quiet. The Land Rover in the drive indicated that Gomes-Little was in; the darkness suggested he might well be asleep. Keeping his ears cocked, Valentine rang the bell.

Had Valentine's instinct for self-preservation been sharper, he would have realised as he was walking along the main street that the barking behind him indicated another presence; and a presence in the deserted night might well have sinister implications.

II

Since his visit to the Refugee Centre the previous day, Valentine had been a marked man. The soldier on duty had reported that a Westerner had been along to see Derek Lomas, and had given a full description. Even before this, he had been under surveillance as a man who had recently visited the West. So when news of his visit to the Refugee Centre reached Special Branch, Major Bakheet suspected that Valentine might be pretty hot property. But he had resisted the urge to have him picked up immediately. Since the abortive ransacking of Lomas's place, the major had felt the need to act more circumspectly. There was still ample time to find the submission before the Visit. He determined not to make the same mistake with Valentine as he had with Lomas. He would put a tail on him, give him a bit of rope, find out who his contacts were.

Lance Corporal Mohamed Abbas had been assigned the job of tailing him and to start with it had been easy. Valentine had gone nowhere, seen no one. Abbas had waited so long for Valentine to emerge from his house that he had become careless.

Lance Corporal Abbas was a handsome young man and, like many handsome young men, he was frequently subjected to temptation. It wasn't long before several women, Westerners in the main, had become aware of this stranger in the vicinity of their homes. And Abbas, with his easy smile and sharp conversation, had responded quickly to their offers. He liked Western girls. Sex for them wasn't taboo as it was for Muslims. They were available; not only that, they enjoyed it. He wasn't in uniform or the girls might have felt differently. All Westerners were suspicious of men in uniform. It was on the third invitation that he entered the house.

He emerged, drained and guilty, a couple of hours later and Valentine had gone. He made enquiries of a watchman propped up against a tree and was told that Valentine had left by taxi an hour or so before. The man thought the taxi driver had been given directions to the centre of town.

Cursing his lack of self-control, Abbas himself took a taxi to the main street. He gave instructions for the driver to stop and waited for a few minutes by the kerb, uncertain what to do next. He had made a bad mistake and if his superiors found out . . .

These morose thoughts were passing through his mind when he saw a man coming down the main street. As the man walked past his taxi, Abbas couldn't believe his luck. It was Valentine. He offered a heartfelt prayer to Allah, vowed future celibacy and wondered what to do next. He had been saved by the skin of a mosquito's teeth. He didn't know where Valentine had been and thought it unwise to guess or pretend. The last hour would have to be struck from the record. He just had an uneasy feeling that it might have been important.

He paid the taxi driver and set off. His eyes were accustomed to the darkness and he had no difficulty keeping Valentine in his sights, cursing the dogs for announcing his presence. He was a good tail or Sergeant Mohamed wouldn't have chosen him. He watched Valentine go into Gomes-Little's residence and took up a position by the gate.

Valentine had rung the bell several times before lights were switched on in the house and Gomes-Little opened the door cautiously. He was dressed in brown fluffy pyjamas that looked like a pantomime costume. His irritability threshold, never particularly high, was at its lowest at night. He realised too late that it was Valentine and that Valentine was not paying him a social call.

Gomes-Little tried to close the door but Valentine thrust out a foot and forced his way in. Seconds later, Gomes-Little was overpowered and frog-marched up the stairs into his lounge for a renewal of the hostility that had characterised their relationship in recent weeks. Only now the hostility was on Valentine's terms; looking at Valentine's face, Gomes-Little realised that for him it might well be terminal.

Corporal Abbas went into the garden and waited. He knew nothing of his job except that something had been smuggled out of the West and that it had to be found. A man paying a visit so late at night could mean only one thing: his quarry and the occupant of the house were up to no good.

He had noticed a group of soldiers from the nearby barracks laughing and joking down one of the side streets. Making sure the occupants of the house were firmly ensconced, he doubled back. Four of the soldiers were still there. He flashed his Special Branch card and explained to them that there were two men, perhaps more, that he wanted to apprehend in a house just along the way. The soldiers followed him to Gomes-Little's residence. The same gentle snoring was coming from the garden. They padded up the stairs, and flung open the lounge door. Inside, Valentine had Gomes-Little in a death-lock and was choking the life out of him.

Abbas pointed. 'Those are the men.'

Valentine looked at the soldiers and cursed. His hands left Gomes-Little's throat and the latter slumped to the floor like a rag doll. The Westerner looked around for some means of escape but, seeing none, held up his hands and sat down in an armchair. Choking noises were coming from the little man on the ground as the blood returned to his brain. He struggled to his feet and addressed the soldiers in Tujanian.

'I can't tell you how happy I am to see you. This man was going to kill me.'

Abbas was curt. 'Save it.'

'What?'

'Save it. We know what you're up to.'

For one of the few occasions in his life, Gomes-Little failed to cotton on to the prevailing train of thought.

'I'm sorry, officer, I don't quite catch your meaning.'

'You have a telephone?'

'Of course.' Gomes-Little, still rubbing his throat, pointed to the other side of the room. Abbas dialled and the conversation that followed left Gomes-Little's jaw hanging lower and lower. When Abbas rang off, Gomes-Little stormed over to him, bristling like a turkey cock.

'Explain yourself.'

Abbas scarcely looked at him. 'What?'

'Explain yourself. What do you mean by saying you had found the Westerner's expatriate contact and that when you arrived an unconvincing act of assault was going on. Dammit man, that was no act. The man was trying to kill me. Look! Look at the bruises!'

Abbas ignored him and went across to the soldiers. Gomes-Little followed, his short steps and teddy-bear pyjamas giving him the air of a petulant schoolboy beside the tall soldier. In despair he turned to Valentine. 'You tell them,' and as Valentine remained silent. '*Tell them!*'

Valentine looked at Gomes-Little in derision. He was calm now. His initial attempt at satisfaction had failed. He had no doubt that he would be arrested and he saw the chance of taking Gomes-Little with him.

'Well?' Abbas addressed himself to Valentine. Valentine looked at him and told the truth.

'This man is no friend of mine. I came here to kill him.'

Abbas turned away, smiling. He had his evidence. These Westerners! All they ever did was lie!

III

Half an hour later, Major Bakheet arrived at the house of Gomes-Little. Valentine had said nothing in the meantime and Gomes-Little, after some initial ranting, had also kept quiet. He had justice on his side and, while he was no believer in the fair balance of the scales, he couldn't believe that on this occasion justice wouldn't prevail.

Bakheet had met Gomes-Little on two or three occasions at the Polytechnic and knew that his uncle thought highly of him. But his mission forced him to over-rule personal feelings. He explained to Gomes-Little that Valentine would be taken out and searched. Then his quarters would be searched. If they found what they wanted, all well and good, otherwise they would have to search Gomes-Little's place as well.

The little man spread his hands in an expression of incomprehension. 'But why? What are you looking for? This man tried to kill me. He's a member of my staff who has a grudge against me.'

Bakheet smiled reassuringly. He went out with a passive Valentine and left two soldiers with Gomes-Little. The latter heard him explaining that they were not to let the 'little gentleman' out of their sight until he got back. So Gomes-Little sat with the eyes of the two men on him for almost three hours. He even had to put up with the indignity of being chaperoned to the toilet. At length, just as he was reaching breaking point, Bakheet returned.

'You haven't heard the last of this, Major.'

Bakheet smiled. 'Relax, Mr Gomes-Little. I'm afraid we found nothing on your friend or in his rooms.'

'How many times do I have to tell you he is *not* my friend?'

Bakheet nodded unconvincingly and Gomes-Little fumed some more. Why could you never get through to these people?

'So we must now search you.'

And Gomes-Little watched while half a dozen soldiers pillaged through his personal belongings. Files, papers, books, neatly stored away, were scattered around the house. Carefully folded shirts and trousers were tossed aside. His mattress was overturned, cushions were unzipped and their innards spilled. And finally, Gomes-Little, still in his pyjamas, had to suffer the experience of a body search. Strange, dirty hands everywhere! He cringed in revulsion.

Throughout all this, Major Bakheet had been looking increasingly unhappy. The smile on his face was wavering and he was beginning to think that he might have made a colossal blunder. At the end, he turned to a seething Gomes-Little to offer his apologies.

'For what?'

'For disturbing you in this way.' He barked instructions to his soldiers to clean up the place. As they began shoving clothes back into drawers,

Gomes-Little yelled at them to stop. They hesitated and Bakheet indicated they should do as Gomes-Little said.

'Once again, Mr Gomes-Little, I am sorry.'

'Why? I told you, your men saved my life. Now will you please *get out!*'

After the soldiers had left, Gomes-Little looked around at the wreckage of his house and began sobbing in anger. Someone would pay for this. In the morning, he would lodge an official complaint with Bakheet. And then he would get straight on to Andrew.

IV

'What?'

'Late last night. Six soldiers came into my home and turned it upside down.'

Andrew Late, his hand shaking as he held the receiver, managed a somewhat noncommittal 'Oh.'

'Yes. Just burst in. No warrant, no permit or anything. Actually it was lucky they did in a way. That bloody Westerner, Valentine Luko, had burst in a few minutes earlier and was trying to strangle me. I tell you, these people are crazy.'

'I see.' Late realised a semblance of interest was called for but in his present state of mental numbness, he couldn't find the right vocal inflection. 'Have you told the Polytechnic authorities?'

'Not yet. I thought I'd tell you first.'

'Well, these things happen here. We have to expect it. Report it to the Polytechnic authorities. Let them deal with it.' And Late put the phone down.

Gomes-Little was open-mouthed. Whatever reaction he had expected from Late, being cut off in mid-call hadn't been one of them. He had expected Late to support him. He always had before. He had expected expressions of outrage with a fair measure of indignation thrown in. He certainly hadn't expected, 'These things happen here'! And what on earth was he talking about? Surely he wasn't implying that being half-strangled by a mad Westerner and having your house ransacked by military thugs was normal, that such things should be expected?

But Gomes-Little hadn't been to the first night of the melodrama. If he had, he would have found Late's attitude more understandable.

V

The previous night Late had left the Ambassador's early, deciding to go home, have another brandy and try and get things in proportion. All he'd actually done was pull a rubber penis out of his pocket. A huge rubber penis! In full view of a theatre audience! In a country noted for its puritanism! He groaned. The more he tried to think it down, the worse it became. He closed his eyes quickly, opening them again as a ten-inch phallus appeared in his mind's eye. Try as he might, he couldn't get rid of the image. Every time he closed his eyes, there it was, growing bigger, like Jack's beanstalk. Hours later, as dawn was breaking, the thing disappeared and Late sank down in temporary relief.

Inevitably he had overslept. He drove to the office, unwashed and unkempt, dark glasses hiding bloodshot eyes, looking more like a fugitive from a howling mob than the head of a respected British institution. He gave a furtive greeting to his secretary.

'Oh, Mr Late?'

Late half-turned, looking like an Armenian bandit challenged while walking through town and knowing that the game is up. She lowered her eyes. It was obvious that *she* had heard.

'Mr Gomes-Little has been trying to phone you. He says it's urgent. He sounded a bit upset.'

Late nodded and wandered into his office, having given instructions that he wasn't to be disturbed. He had no wish for phone calls, however urgent, so that when Gomes-Little phoned again a short time later, he couldn't summon up what he knew in his heart was the required level of sympathy. But Gomes-Little had had trouble with his staff from the beginning; it seemed a logical continuum that one of them should try to kill him. Perhaps he had backed the wrong horse.

The thought of horse brought him back to stallions and was a direct line to . . . He groaned and groaned. From the far wall, the Queen and the Duke of Edinburgh eyed him severely. Here he was, their representative, responsible for the spreading and perpetuating of British cultural values in the wider world and for showing its citizens the full value of British life. And what had he actually shown them?

A giant penis!

The phone rang and he shook as he answered it. But it was only one of his underlings with a transport problem and he left the phone off the hook.

He remembered a major in *Catch 22* who, in a few square yards of enemy territory, had managed to make himself invisible. Perhaps he could give his secretary instructions: 'Mr Late never sees anybody in his office when he's actually *in* his office.' He wondered if it would be possible to arrive and leave unseen and never see a soul while he was there. He looked at the window, heavily barred, the drop to the ground substantial, and he sighed deeply. Major Major had the advantage of being a character in a work of fiction. He would just have to find a way to face the world. There was the Visit to think about. To say nothing of the second night of the play, if indeed there would *be* a second night?

He wondered for the umpteenth time how the thing had found its way into the inside pocket of the cloak and where it had come from. After all, such objects weren't freely available in Omeldoum, couldn't actually be bought on the open market. It was later that he noticed the item missing from his downstairs loo.

VI

Late wasn't the only person not relishing the thought of the day. Major Bakheet was sure he'd made the most gigantic blunder in searching the house of Fairfax Gomes-Little and his fears seemed justified when he was summoned to the Minister's office towards the end of the morning.

'Your uncle has been just in touch with me, Bakheet. Apparently you upset one of his senior staff last night.'

Bakheet nodded.

'Your uncle said you knew Mr Gomes-Little. Is this true?'

Bakheet nodded again.

'He said you also knew that he was held in very high regard by the Polytechnic Authorities and particularly by your uncle.'

'That is also true.'

'Then why did you behave as you did? Don't look so alarmed, I ask merely for information.'

Bakheet told the Minister the story of Valentine's trip to the West and his visit to the house of Derek Lomas the morning after Lomas's arrest. He then explained that Valentine had visited Gomes-Little's house.

'Your uncle says Mr Gomes-Little claims that this Westerner – Luko – was trying to kill him when your man arrived.'

'That is also true. We thought it was an act.'

'And now?'

The major shrugged. 'I suppose it could be true.'

'The man who was tailing the Westerner. Is he reliable?'

'Sergeant Mohamed thinks so.'

'Did the Westerner see anyone else?'

'Corporal Abbas says not.'

The Minister tapped his hands on the desk. 'Have you any other leads concerning this damned submission?'

'There is a man we are suspicious of, an Englishman called Charles Digley. He has just returned from the West. We know he didn't carry the submission but we still think he may be involved. And there is another man, an Englishman, out here for a short time. He writes articles in the *Daily Times*.'

The Minister nodded. 'I've read them. All about birds, so he says! Some of these people must think we were born yesterday. Keep a watch on these men, Bakheet. Tell me, did you really think Mr Gomes-Little was involved?'

The major shook his head. 'Not really. But we couldn't take the chance. You can never be totally sure.'

'And now? Is he in the clear?'

'Completely.'

The Minister stood up and smiled at Bakheet. 'You did absolutely the right thing. Don't worry about Gomes-Little. Let your uncle placate him. He's good at that kind of thing. The main thing is this submission. Time is moving on and we must find it. Go to it, Bakheet. I have complete faith in you.'

CHAPTER 8

I

Stephen trembled on the edge of the diving board at the Club pool. There had been a time, he knew, when he would have cut quite a figure – lean, tanned, athletic – and in his more optimistic moments, he convinced himself that such a time could return. But realistically, he had to admit that the bulging pectorals, the roll of fat round the waist that spasmodic attempts at diet and exercise failed to remove, the overall image of size and whiteness reflected in his bedroom mirror, had a depressing permanence about it.

But as he flipped off from the board, and split the water smoothly, the illusion of an ample residue of athletic beauty was quite easy to sustain. He swam a couple of lengths, showered and towelled down. He plastered himself with sun-cream and sprawled out on a towel spread over one of the poolside loungers.

He had a couple of the Stoppard plays with him and picked up *Professional Foul*, realising as he did so that he should be sifting through Gomes-Little's material for the brochure. His eyes shifted uneasily to his briefcase but he had long since discovered the capacity to quell both the Protestant work ethic and the non-conformist conscience it engendered. With no great effort of will, he cast the brochure from his mind and began reading. He needed distraction, something to take his mind off such things as brochures, submissions and rubber penises.

But Stoppard didn't interest him for long and his thoughts turned to the events of the previous evening. Talk around the pool was all about Late and his daring theatrics.

'Can you believe it?!' people were saying to each other in low voices. '*Night of the Stallions* and "a fate worse than death"'! I never thought they'd have the nerve to pull something like that, not in this place anyway. Never thought Andrew Late was that sort of bloke. And John Clifford! Baptist preacher he used to be. Always been a bit strange in some ways, but on matters like that, straight as a die.'

And only Stephen knew the truth and wondered how long it would take Late to cotton on. He could always deny it, of course, but he was sure Late wouldn't believe him. Sooner or later, his mind was bound to turn to Stephen and the blue and white bag with the tin of Harpic.

Then the talk had been of the second performance due to take place the following night. Would there be a repeat? Would they dare? Might they perhaps go even further? Demand for tickets, never particularly great for such offerings, suddenly doubled.

The dramatic reappearance of the penis had for a time taken Stephen's mind off the submission. A nightcap with Alena and Bert had been accompanied by much speculation about Late's most spectacular antic to date.

'He always makes a gigantic cock up,' Alena giggled, 'if you'll pardon the expression. You should have been here for the madrigal evening, shouldn't he, Bert? Not to mention the Gerard Manley Hopkins recital!'

Stephen finished his wine realising that the penis, for all its sensational value, was a mere trifle compared to the document Valentine had foisted on him. He took the submission to his room and, as he read it, the implications of what he had taken on made him tremble with apprehension. In his hand was a document capable of shattering his world into a thousand pieces. He felt like a spy of the late forties suddenly handed the formula for the atom bomb and with it the fear, real and terrifying, that the wrath of the political and military establishment would be turned against him. He had put himself right under the spotlight and just had to pray that nobody turned it on!

Frequently that morning the magnitude of his responsibility had overwhelmed him. Incompetence had dissolved into panic, and several times, like a murderer consumed by his own guilt, he had almost cried out, 'It's me! I've got it!' He couldn't begin to gauge the consequences if he was caught, tried not to picture the faces of his employers in London or that of Late who had asked him to provide 'a bit of ballast'.

He had spent a large part of the morning at the Poly and it had been after eleven when Gomes-Little arrived, pale, chameleon-like, his lenses like small worlds, his movements even sharper and jerkier than usual. He had handed Stephen the draft of the brochure, with instructions to comment on it by the following day. But he obviously had other things on his mind and, with very little prompting, Stephen learned about Valentine's assault and the ransacking of Gomes-Little's flat. Stephen immediately thought of Derek's place, and the ruthlessness of Special Branch. What would the little shit say if he knew that the thing they were looking for was in Stephen's briefcase, right there under his nose? The first quivers of vulnerability hit him as Gomes-Little's lenses suddenly focused on the briefcase and Stephen snatched it up with indecent haste. He didn't feel secure until the submission was locked in a drawer in his bedroom.

After his swim and the feeling of well-being it had generated, he reflected more rationally on the events of the previous twenty-four hours. Valentine's fears had been well-founded and his decision to get rid of the submission had proved wise. Stephen wondered uncomfortably why such an efficient organisation as Special Branch hadn't yet got on to him and comforted himself with the thought it was probably because they didn't suspect him.

His original mission, to find out the truth about Gomes-Little and preside over circumstances leading to his dismissal, suddenly seemed a little puny. Paring the fingernails of a dying man – he remembered Maggie Earl's phrase. Trying to influence the plot of a soap opera while a Greek tragedy vied for possession of the stage. Now he had been given the production notes for the tragedy and doubted whether he was up to the job.

As he lay there soaking up the sun, with altruism and selfishness stepping up their eternal battle for his soul, a tap on his shoulder made him jump.

'Care for a game?' Basil Earl stood there, brandishing a squash racquet. 'My partner's let me down.' He went through the motions of an elegant backhand then looked closely at Stephen. 'You all right, old man? You look as if you've seen a ghost.'

'Do I?' Stephen stared at the squat, balding diplomat and thought what a lucky bastard he was to be married to a woman like Maggie. 'I must have been asleep.'

'Mmm.' Earl stared at him. 'Guilty conscience, I shouldn't wonder.' Stephen didn't know whether he was joking. The Aid Secretary's attempts at humour were so like his normal conversation that it was impossible to separate them. 'Well?'

'Well?' Stephen was perplexed. Was Earl asking for a confession? 'I've nothing to feel guilty about.'

Earl snorted. 'I didn't mean that. I meant what about a game of squash!'

'I think I'll give the squash a miss, thanks all the same. Wouldn't give you much of a game, I'm afraid.'

'Too bad. Not as good as I used to be. Finding it hard to stay in Division I these days, with all these young Aid johnnies about. I'm off to UK tomorrow. Anything you'd like posted?'

Stephen thanked him and said he'd try and have a couple of letters ready by the evening. He thought about posting the submission. That would be a coup, getting it out with the British Aid Secretary! But where would he send it? The newspapers? Impossible. If it went to one of the liberal papers, it would be submerged in the welter of stuff from the work of Amnesty International and such organisations. And if it went to one of the others, they wouldn't publish it. What, publish the rantings of a group of Marxist sympathisers against the authority of a strongly pro-Western Government? Not on your bloody nelly, sir, with respect. He began wondering if the submission had any value, save as another offering from Fate to keep his survival instinct from going stale. Perhaps he should just dump the thing. At least it would be easier to get rid of than the penis! Papers were forever blowing willy nilly through Omeldoum. Not many Easterners could read English anyway. It could even be burnt.

Then he remembered Valentine's trust. To Valentine, the submission had been a matter of overwhelming seriousness. He, Stephen Talbot, was his chosen emissary. Valentine and Derek were in gaol because of the submission and he was thinking of shredding it! What a conscienceless bastard he could be! Altruism made a rare incursion into the ranks of selfishness and he immediately felt better. What a pity he didn't think noble thoughts more often! It made him feel good, like having a healthy meal, giving the body a work-out, reading the thoughts of great men: all well worth the effort if you could be bothered to do them.

He came rapidly to earth. It was all very well giving the soul a lift but that strange, ethereal entity was bugger all use when it came to dealing with the practicalities of life. He watched a stream of perspiration emanate from the hillock of his left nipple, wondering absently whether it would have the momentum to reach the valley of his cleavage. The spiritual uplift he'd experienced should have cleared the jungle, bequeathed to the more physical aspects of his being a clear solution to his problems so that he would have known indisputably what to do with the document that lay under lock and key in Alena's flat.

Not a bit of it. The soul, having been purged, left the mind to do its own dirty work, wouldn't soil its hands on nasty things like submissions. He thought hard and realised there was only one thing to do. He towelled and dressed and set off again to the Green Grange.

II

The previous day Maggie Earl had gone to see Charles Digley as arranged. She still wasn't sure how it had happened. Charles had been sitting on the edge of the bed and had risen as she entered. She had reproached him for not resting and he had smiled in his inscrutable way and said he felt better. It was impossible to avoid his eyes. She had said that as he was better, there didn't seem much point in her staying but as she moved to the door, he followed her, catching her arm.

'What do you think . . . ?'

The utterance remained unfinished. He had pulled her to him and tried to kiss her. She had pushed him away, feeling the maleness of him beginning to overpower her. And suddenly she wasn't struggling, suddenly she was responding with a passion that matched his own, her nails clawing at his flesh, her dress around her waist as he eased her on to the bed.

She hadn't known it could happen so quickly. One minute she had been on the verge of leaving, the next she was engaged in a violent act of love with a man she hardly knew. 'Not recommended therapy, this,' she had managed as he mounted her and penetrated, all in one movement it seemed. And then, as she felt the thrusts of his body, she looked wild-eyed at the faded turquoise walls, the cobwebs, the barely moving fan, and screamed her ecstasy to the heavens, feeling that at last she had caught up with life.

She had dressed quickly afterwards, subdued by the enormity of what she had done and felt. Charles had watched her as she tried to smooth out her dress. She had a sudden feeling of being used, of being a receptacle for the passion of a man in an advanced stage of frustration.

As she had been, she realised. But for her it was different. For him, no doubt, it had been a common occurrence, a ritual fuck, mingled perhaps with some twisted political motive, the rape of privilege by the deprived. But as she was about to leave, he came to her.

'Don't go yet.'

For the first time since the act she looked at him.

'I must.'

'What'll you tell them?'

'About what?'

'About where you've been?'

'They know where I've been. Basil knows I'm treating a patient.'

'All right. About what you've just done?'

'Is there any need to tell them anything?'

He nodded. 'It's in your eyes. And there's a stain on the back of your dress.'

She pulled her dress round. There it was, a large dark patch, a stain of him.

She laughed. 'I'll have to sneak in, then, won't I? Change my dress before anyone sees.'

'And your eyes? What about those?'

She shrugged. 'Ignore them, I suppose. Basil was never very good at eyes.'

She pushed him away as he tried to kiss her. 'I really am going.'

'Will you come tomorrow?'

'If you want me to.'

'I need another treatment.'

She snorted. 'After that little performance, I'm not sure there was anything wrong with your back in the first place.'

He smiled. 'It's not my back that needs the treatment.'

She smiled back, and promised to return the next day.

III

Basil had come in just before supper. She had changed her dress, fingering the dried deposit before putting it in the wash. She had showered energetically, feeling a new respect for her body.

They had eaten in semi-silence, Basil making his usual banal comments about squash, the Tujanians, the Club, but giving up when the most she could manage in reply was the occasional monosyllable. He had looked hard at her once and she had lowered her eyes, still feeling Charles inside her. She was sure it must show but after a second he had carried on eating. She'd been right, he wasn't very good on eyes.

Later, as she lay in bed, the enormity of what she'd done again overwhelmed her. Thankfully, Basil had been too tired to make demands. She couldn't have faced it and had begun mumbling things about headaches a couple of hours before. The Chargé d'Affaires had popped round on business – something about a video surveillance system – she didn't pay much attention. He had stayed for a drink and the conversation had turned to the situation in the West which they discussed dispassionately, like a chess problem. 'Damn you!' she wanted to cry out. 'There are thousands dying out there and to you it's just an academic exercise.' She felt again the firm thrusts of Charles, the thrusts of injustice into the womb of indifference. Except she had never really been indifferent.

She stood outside them awhile, nodding politely as she listened to the well-worn prejudices and saw the faded walls, the cobwebs, smelled his maleness, before becoming aware that they were looking at her and jerking a response. A little later she pleaded tiredness and retired to the bedroom where she could be alone with her deliciously wicked thoughts. And later still, as Basil lay snoring beside her, she lay with her eyes shining and her body alive in every nerve.

IV

'I wish we could lock the door.'

They were lying on the bed in the Green Grange. Charles had been tidying the room when Maggie arrived. He had smiled, taking her by the shoulders and searching her eyes.

'What are you looking for?'

'I want to see if it's still there.'

'And is it?'

'More so.' He kissed her and led her gently towards the bed as she kicked off her shoes.

Their lovemaking was less frantic, more controlled and exploratory. Afterwards they lay there, feeling the heat from each other's body.

He got up and pulled a chair in front of the door.

'Just in case. But don't worry. Nobody ever comes in here.'

She leaned on her elbow and looked into his eyes.

'They stone people for adultery here.'

'That's for men. Women are put in a sack of wildcats.'

'Have you ever wondered what kind of society we're supporting?'

He turned away. 'I know what kind of society we're supporting. A society that treats more than half its citizens as second-rate, that treats its women as possessions, its deprived people as criminals – or worse. If this was happening anywhere else the world would be up in arms. But because it's happening here, what happens? Fuck all!'

She turned his head towards her. 'Let's not get too serious.' She kissed him to silence his protests. 'Let's enjoy this first and get serious after.'

'Do you know what you're doing?'

She nodded slowly. 'It's what I've been waiting for for a long time.'

'I didn't mean . . . You know where I've been, what I might have been up to.'

'I don't understand.'

'I've spent six months mixing with Africans. Mixing with African girls,' he added with deliberate enunciation. 'And here you are having sex with me without protection.'

The TV advertisements leapt to her mind. She felt a surge of panic at the implications of what he was saying. She looked at his body, its leanness suddenly sinister. 'Oh God!' She leapt from the bed. How could she have been so careless, so naive?

He followed her. 'Relax.'

'Relax! How can you tell me to relax when you've just told me . . .'

'Shh.' He put a finger to her lips. 'What have I told you? Only to be more careful before you go rushing into these relationships.'

'Then you haven't . . .'

He shook his head. 'I know not to take risks.'

She looked away. 'You're a cruel bastard.'

'What, for making you think that I might have AIDS? I'd be a lot more cruel if I'd fucked you knowing I *had* got it.' He pulled her towards him. 'I had to shock you to warn you. You've got to be more careful. If you go around screwing every stranger who makes a pass at you without taking precautions . . .'

Her eyes flashed. 'I don't exactly make a habit of this, you know.'

He took her hand. 'I'm sorry. I just thought, you know, yesterday, everything happened so quickly.'

She nodded. 'I know. Quite a speed to enter the sordid world of adultery.'

'I could hardly believe it.' He felt aroused again at the thought.

'A bit like *Last Tango in Paris* wasn't it? That scene always excited me. I never thought it *could* happen in real life. Particularly to me.'

'I'll get some butter next time.'

She shook her head. 'I do draw the line somewhere. Anyway, most of the butter round here is rancid.'

'What a shame.' He pulled her back towards the bed. She pushed him on to it and pressed her body against him as they kissed. She levered herself away from him and ran her lips slowly down his body, enjoying the taste of him while he let ecstasy take over. She suckled his nipples, running her tongue round them and then down over his abdomen with its line of dark hairs. His penis was close to her lips, and she cupped her hand gently around it.

At that moment, there was a noise at the door and Stephen Talbot's head entered the room.

V

The Land Rover was now operable and Stephen trundled along the increasingly familiar road to the Green Grange, having decided to hand the submission to Charles. Charles knew the West, and was committed to its problems. Stephen had spent the best part of his life avoiding the quicksands into which the submission showed every possibility of leading him. Charles's name had been mentioned by Valentine. Charles was the man for the job.

He cursed as he realised he'd left his briefcase at the Club. He had no clear idea of where the various strands of this visit were leading but one thing he did know was that, puny a task though it had begun to seem, his main job was to get rid of Gomes-Little. Assuming the Union decided in the little shit's favour, getting rid of him meant keeping in with him, undermining him from the inside. And keeping in with him involved doing the things he had been asked to do, like reading the draft of the brochure and commenting (favourably) on it. He could hardly do that with the bloody thing abandoned at the Club.

The recent spate of bizarre events had caused him to neglect his Polytechnic brief. He'd seen little of Alena, considering he was dossing down in her flat, and even less of Gomes-Little. His behaviour was that of a man for whom the Polytechnic was an intrusion into the other, increasingly outlandish, aspects of his life and he was pleased when he remembered he'd arranged a boat trip with Alena and Bert later that afternoon.

The portals of the Green Grange loomed as depressingly as ever and he made his way through the dark halls to Charles's room, knocking briefly before trying the door. There was some impediment and he pushed harder. A second later, he popped his head round the door to be confronted with . . . what?

Initially, his mind refused to come to terms with the visual stimuli it was receiving. A man and a woman were on the bed in a position of some intimacy. The woman shot up in a panic, grabbing a cloth to cover herself, but not before Stephen had registered the startled gaze, the small firm breasts, the dark triangle between her thighs. The man . . .

But Stephen saw no more. Muttering a heartfelt 'Sorry, folks', his head withdrew. He stood outside, cringing with embarrassment, very close to the spot where he had found the phallus. A part of his brain responded to the irony of another erect penis appearing in the same vicinity as the previous one though, with all due respect to Charles, the second apparition in no way measured up to the first.

Except that it was presumably real and being put to good use! An image of Maggie walking into the Green Grange flashed across his brain. 'You'd be doing a fellow human being a big favour,' he had said. Some favour! He had hoped to humiliate her, call her bluff, had felt the task he was asking her to do would be beyond her mental toughness. He'd thought she'd be too squeamish. Too squeamish! Not only had she treated Charles, she had presumably made love to him, felt his cock inside her, his dirt over her. Tears of envy and embarrassment welled, of inadequacy tinged with self-disgust.

A minute later, Charles emerged, a cloth round his waist and Stephen lowered his head.

'Sorry, I . . .' His voice moved into strangulation mode, his tongue too dry for further articulation.

'I know. There's no lock on the door so I put a chair behind it.'

Stephen managed to speak. 'I never suspected . . .' His arid palate gave his voice a vaguely German inflection. His tongue felt like a foreign body in his mouth.

'It doesn't matter. But Maggie's pretty upset.' He paused. 'Can I ask you a favour?'

Stephen looked up for the first time.

'Anything.'

'Don't talk about it.'

Stephen wondered if he had heard correctly. 'What?'

'Don't tell anyone about this, any of it. You know how that bloody Club would enjoy this kind of thing. To say nothing of the Embassy. Just forget you ever saw it.'

Stephen was astonished. 'I don't make a habit of humiliating people,' he said. But forget he had ever seen it? Stephen felt that the memory of Maggie Earl's hand stroking Charles's penis would be one he took to his grave. And how many more secrets was Fate going to burden him with? He was the only one who knew the contents of Old Joe's luggage, the origins of Late's misfortune with the penis, the whereabouts of the submission from the West, and now this! Exclusive knowledge that in one of the seedier places in town, a scruffy volunteer was having it off with the wife of the British Aid Secretary!

'So what did you want?'

'Mmm?'

'What did you come for? I assume it wasn't just for a bit of voyeuristic pleasure . . .'

'Good God, no. Look, I didn't even know Mrs Earl . . .' His voice tailed off, and he tried to remember what trivial and futile purpose had brought him back to this mauseleum, this fount of all disasters.

He scratched his head. 'Oh yes, you asked me to find out about Derek.'

'Yes?'

'He was arrested yesterday morning.'

'Arrested? By the police?'

'By Special Branch. There's talk of him being deported. I think the Ambassador's on to it.'

Charles snorted. 'The sodding Ambassador. Lot of bloody use he'll be. Do you know anything else?'

'Yes. His place was completely ransacked.'

Charles nodded slowly. 'That figures.'

'There's something else. A colleague of mine at the Poly, Valentine Luko. He's been arrested as well.'

'What?' Charles thought of the submission and buried his face in his hands, as mindful of negligence as Stephen frequently was. While he'd been buggering about with Maggie, Derek and Valentine had been arrested and whole tribes of people were being sold down the river.

Stephen guessed the cause of his distress. 'I saw Valentine before he was arrested. If you're worrying about the document he was carrying, then don't.'

Charles looked up.

'He gave it to me and mentioned your name. That's why I came to see you. Sorry I chose such a . . . er . . .'

'Thank God. So where is it now?'

'Safe. We obviously need to talk but perhaps now's not the best time.'

'Why not?'

Stephen indicated the room. 'You've probably got more urgent matters.'

'Nothing is more urgent than that submission!'

'I know. But I think we should leave it until tomorrow. We need to give it a bit of thought.' Stephen didn't want to miss his boat trip with Alena and Bert, felt he needed a couple of hours on the river to soothe his nerves.

'All right. Tomorrow afternoon at the Club. Four o'clock?'

'Fine. How's the back?'

Now it was Charles's turn to look blank. He suddenly remembered and felt his spine. 'Feels OK.'

'Obviously responded to treatment!' Stephen said as he walked away and Charles smiled as he re-entered the room.

Maggie was sitting stiffly on the edge of the bed, fully dressed, the face she turned to him empty of everything but horror. He put his arm round her.

'Don't worry. Stephen won't say anything.'

She turned to him incredulously. 'Stephen won't say anything! That's hardly the bloody point, is it? Do you remember what we were doing when he poked his head round . . .'

He stroked her cheek. 'Only too well!'

She pushed his hand away. 'I haven't actually done this very often, you know. And I certainly don't want every Tom, Dick and Harry watching me do it.'

'Stephen isn't every Tom, Dick and Harry. He's just a bloke who happened to arrive at a bad time and he's feeling pretty embarrassed about it.'

'A bad time! That must be the understatement of the year.'

'He promised me he wouldn't say anything. We've just had a talk.'

'I'll bet you have. Were you telling him what a good lay I was? Or that you've had better? Or how good it is to fuck an Embassy wife, getting one over the privileged classes?' She burst into tears. 'I feel like a complete bloody whore.'

He held her until her sobs subsided, then picked up a corner of the sheet and dried her tears.

'How's Basil on red eyes?'

'Basil's hopeless on any eyes. Oh, I'm sorry, darling, but I just wanted all this to be so special, didn't want to share it with anybody. And to think that idiot Stephen Talbot actually saw us . . . like . . . like that!'

'I know. Anyway, Stephen brought me some news that I need to give some thought to.'

'Don't worry about me.' She stood up. 'I'd already decided to go.'

'Will you come tomorrow?'

She hesitated. 'Do you want me to come?'

'You know I do.'

'All right.'

Charles suddenly remembered his arrangement with Stephen. 'I can't make it in the afternoon, though. What about tomorrow evening?'

She shook her head. 'You know I can't make it in the evening.'

'Why not? A patient who can only be treated after work? Surely Basil would accept that.'

Now it was her turn to remember something. 'Oh my God. I must dash. Basil's going to UK tonight. I'd completely forgotten.'

His face brightened. 'Then tomorrow night may not be out.'

She hesitated again. 'I'll see. Will you be in the Club tomorrow?'

'Yes, in the afternoon.'

'I'll leave a note in your pigeon hole. And if I arrange something you'd better be there.'

He kissed her passionately. 'Try keeping me away.'

She left, reassured. But as she backed the car out of its hiding place, she remembered Stephen's intrusion and her cheeks burned. She drove away, the embarrassment fading as she remembered the pleasure of the lovemaking. Already she seemed to have shared more with Charles in two days than she had with Basil in ten years. It was true about people and chemistry, that some people were inherently friends and more, while others could never be much more than strangers.

CHAPTER 9

I

In a distant time, a young man had gazed down the embankment in astonishment. There, amidst an assortment of naked bodies, was a turd on the point of excretion. He had watched as the long brown object flopped on to the bank like a giant earthworm. The perpetrator of this act of nature, alerted to the watcher, had turned and waved. The young man found he had stopped in mid-stride and that the object of his attention had been observed by people above as well as below. Later that day he had passed the spot again and laid eyes on the biggest rat he had ever seen, a two-foot monster with gleaming black eyes and sharp white teeth. Evil. Behind him, the forecourt of the Marlborough Hotel had just been lit up and he had retired for a sundowner. An ice-cold beer.

Ten years later, Bert's boat cleft the waters and the lights of the Marlborough Hotel again heralded the approaching night. Now Islamic Law prohibited the public consumption of alcohol. There was no beer on the celebrated terrace, just limon and Pepsi, and trade was thin. Then the terrace had been crowded but that was in another age when Stephen had been on the approach road to life, ready to take it by storm, gather speed, move into the fast lane. Somewhere along the way, both he and Tujan had missed a vital turning.

Still, it was peaceful drifting along on the river, removed from some of the strange sights and experiences that life had recently sprung on him. It was cool too, a welcome breeze blowing from the north. And to the west, a sight to remind him that there were things other than the sordid and the bizarre, and that not all good things disappeared with time. The approaching sunset promised to be magnificent.

Bert was looking for the mysterious yellow legs – binoculars pressed to his eyes, oblivious to all but his obsession. Alena lay back, sipped a Pepsi and gestured towards him. 'There are some forms of madness that are dear and lovable and don't affect anyone else.' Her voice was full of affection, her eyes watering slightly as she looked at Bert.

The boat drifted towards the reeds near the far bank as the first gloom of the afterglow descended. There was little twilight; in half an hour the world would be dark. Alena was about to suggest that they ought to be getting back when Bert gave a low cry.

'There!' He pointed to the shore.

'What, dear?'

Bert clicked impatiently. 'The bird with the yellow legs.' He started the engine and turned the boat towards the reeds. Alena looked at the sky.

'Don't you think it's a little late . . . ?'

But Bert was oblivious, his jaw set, his eyes fixed on the far bank. Alena tried again.

'You've seen it now, love. Why do you want to see it again?'

Bert gave his wife a withering look. 'Will you never understand? I want to look at the markings and other things. It's not enough to see it. I want to find out what it is.'

Alena looked at the sky again and then at Stephen. It was a look that said, In a few minutes it'll be too dark to see the markings anyway. But she said no more and lay back, trailing her hand in the water.

It was now quite dark. The sunset was fading, the great bridges were black against the western sky. A crescent moon partly lit the eastern horizon and threw a sheen of liquid silver across the water. And still Bert thrust ahead, his jaw jutting out like the prow of some Viking man-of-war as the boat reached the reeds and prodded its way through them.

Then Alena screamed.

Bert was undistracted but Stephen looked at her sharply.

'What . . . ?'

'I touched something soft.' She shivered. 'It felt like . . . flesh!'

Stephen scanned the turbulence in the boat's wake. At first he couldn't quite make out the dark shape bobbing in the water. It looked like a small hippo, similar to the pygmy hippos he had seen in Zambia. But as the current swung the object round, he realised what it was.

A body. A black human body, its mouth fixed in a death grin.

Stephen yelled to Bert to turn the boat round. Bert looked back, irritated by this latest interruption.

'What?'

'Turn the boat round. There's a body back there.'

Alena looked aghast. 'Was that what I touched?' She shuddered again. 'How horrible!'

Stephen's face was serious enough to cause Bert to give up the pursuit of the mysterious wader. He turned the boat with difficulty, the propellor getting snarled in the tendrils of the river plants. A few minutes later they drew close to the body, black even against the dark water.

Stephen gestured to Bert. 'Let's get it into the boat.'

Alena was horrified. 'What good will that do?'

'We can't just leave it. It might not even be dead.'

But the weight of the body indicated that it was not only dead but had been in the water for some time. It was the body of a man, naked from the waist up. The two men threw it on to the bottom of the boat and Stephen and Alena looked at each other in disbelief. The face was bloated, the mouth open and the eyes bulged like a fish in the last throes of oxygen starvation but even with these distortions, there was no mistaking that face. The look of concern that he wore in life had gone. It had been replaced by one of terror, eternally transfixed, as Valentine Luko had encountered death.

Alena turned pale as Bert set course for the far shore. Stephen, after making sure that Valentine was in fact dead, felt a wave of nausea. He leaned over the side and retched violently, keeping his head there after the retching had subsided.

As they left the reeds behind, he caught sight of a thicket well out in the river. Marooned there, bobbing in the current, was a familiar object. It no longer enjoyed the public prominence conferred on it by Late but still, like some harbinger of doom, the phallus from Old Joe's luggage refused to leave the scene.

II

They moored the boat and Stephen went to Central Police Station. Like many institutions in Omeldoum, the police station was the city in miniature. Paint was peeling off the walls, files and papers were strewn on every surface, and everything was coated with dust. Even in the inner sanctum, two panes were missing from the window, the glass in the picture of the President was cracked, and the light green desk had been darkened by decades of dirt. A quill pen stood there in a jar, an implement of grace and individuality, but the inkwell next to it was dry. The officer behind the desk wrote with the ubiquitous blue Biro. There was menace in his gaunt features, his thin moustache. He gave out an air of malevolent indolence.

But there was nothing indolent about his colleagues in the adjoining rooms as, at regular intervals, a handcuffed prisoner was dragged past the open door of the office. Muffled screams soon followed as, no doubt, a 'confession' was obtained and another open and shut case could be referred to the state prosecutor.

At the mention of Valentine's name, the manner of the officer on duty changed from languor to alertness. He rummaged about for a report form and when Stephen had completed it, two policemen accompanied him in a

Land Rover to where Alena and Bert were waiting with the body. Then they all went back to the police station.

'So.' The police inspector, polite but distinctly unsympathetic, looked at the three people sitting in front of him. 'Where did you find the body?'

'We've already told you.' Alena, terribly distraught by Valentine's death, was becoming impatient and Stephen motioned to her to keep quiet. He was sure that no suspicion could attach to them and yet, in spite of several requests, they hadn't been allowed to leave. At some point, Stephen remembered that Valentine had been a marked man, that he had been arrested the previous night, and that the police would be looking for his contacts. He froze. They would be after the submission, the document locked up in Alena's flat and which couldn't possibly have been traced to him if Fate hadn't (almost literally) poked its oar in. Here he was, lumbered with the 'discoverer of the body' role, the body in question being that of the one man he wanted no hint of contact with. At the time, he didn't register how bizarre all this was, finding a colleague dead in the river and taking it in his stride. And only briefly did he reflect on the sadness of Valentine Luko's life. All he could think of was his own survival.

They had been in the room for almost two hours when the door opened and Major Bakheet entered. He greeted Stephen with a smile and an outstretched hand.

'Mr Talbot. So sorry to have to detain you like this.' He glanced at Bert and Alena. 'You and your friends.'

'Can we go now?'

Bakheet smiled more broadly. 'Of course. We can hardly keep an important visitor to Tujan locked up. Nor would we want to.' His English was impeccably old-fashioned.

Bert said: 'We've been here for two hours.'

Bakheet nodded regretfully. 'I know. And I apologise again.' He paused and looked intently at Stephen. 'This Westerner you found, you worked with him, did you not?'

Stephen and Alena nodded.

'The thing is, we are sure Mr Luko was an enemy of the Government. He was arrested last night on suspicion of treason. Today, while he was being taken to the remand prison, one of my officers was stupid enough to leave the handcuffs off him. He jumped from the truck as it was passing over Kandede Bridge, then jumped from the bridge into the river. We thought he was trying to escape but it now seems that he might have been attempting suicide.'

Stephen shrugged. 'Escape or suicide. What difference does it make now?'

He felt a surge of anger. Valentine had been a sensitive, intelligent man who six months ago had looked forward to a bright future. Now both he and his family were dead. Senselessly, criminally dead.

'It makes a great deal of difference. You see, if he was prepared to leap to almost certain death rather than be interrogated, it suggests he had something to hide.'

Stephen remembered the muffled shouts and screams from along the corridor. 'Perhaps he was just frightened of your methods.'

Bakheet's smile hardened. 'Innocent men need not fear the Tujanian legal system. Anyway, as I said, you are now free to go. I apologise again for having detained you. Sergeant Mohamed will arrange transport back to your car.'

They were bundled into a Land Rover and driven back to the river. The breeze had died and the shroud of a hot airless night had fallen on the city. Stephen's hand shook slightly as he opened the car door.

Alena's eyes were red from crying. 'Do you believe that bit about Valentine killing himself?'

'Why not? It makes sense.'

'Then you think he did have something to hide?'

'It's possible, I suppose.' Stephen turned away guiltily, uncomfortably aware that Valentine's secret was locked away in Alena's and Bert's flat.

'But why did they keep us there so long?'

When they reached the flat, they found the answer. Bert parked the car as Alena went to open the door. Almost immediately she shouted. Bert rushed from the car, meeting Alena running towards him. Stephen, trapped in the passenger's side, found difficulty in clambering over the gear lever.

'They've ransacked the flat!'

'What?'

'The bastards! That's why they kept us there.'

Bert pushed her aside and ran ahead. Alena turned and followed him, waddling in her effort to walk at speed.

'All my bird books,' Bert was saying as Stephen rushed to join them. 'And all the notes I've made for the book I was going to write.' He sank into a chair. Stephen looked at the desk, drawers open and empty, clothes, papers, objects scattered round the room. It looked very much like Derek Lomas's place a couple of days previously. He made sympathetic noises and rushed into his bedroom. Again, objects were scattered everywhere and the lock on the chest of drawers had been rifled. He tore open the top drawer and looked in.

The submission had gone.

CHAPTER 10

I

Late fidgeted in the arrivals lounge at the airport. It was a few days after the first night of the melodrama and the embarrassment of that occasion was beginning to recede. The Club committee had postponed further performances indefinitely, their pretext being some obscure religious ceremony against whose rites the performance of such a secular piece of nonsense might offend. The real reason remained unspoken and for that Late was grateful.

It was two in the morning and he was at the airport to meet the man from the Foreign Office, out to organise the Foreign Secretary's visit. Anderson Frank his name was. Or was it Frank Anderson? No, he was certain it was Anderson Frank but the telex announcing his arrival had, to say the least, been confusing. Why couldn't these buggers have straightforward first and second names like Andrew and Late? One would have to be totally stupid to convolute that to Late Andrew. But Anderson Frank!

Late had managed to persuade a still cool Ambassador that, as Basil Earl had gone to London, he should be the one to meet this Foreign Office chappie. It was a chance to regain lost kudos and when he closed his eyes after the phone call to the Ambassador, for the first time since the fateful night, the phallus didn't appear. He'd been about to dictate a letter and the absence of the penis from his mind's eye prompted a burst of manic laughter. He opened his eyes to find his secretary looking at him in alarm. It was the look she had given him several times in the last few days, a look that combined wariness, suspicion and distaste in equal measure as if he were a vicar caught interfering with choir boys. He had steadied himself, composed his features and proceeded with the business.

But he felt much better. The situation at the Polytechnic seemed calm. The Union had not yet delivered their verdict on Gomes-Little and the latter was still fuming at his treatment by Special Branch, but the visit of Stephen Talbot had been a brainwave: an old hand, a steadying influence, the staff under control, Alena very much marginalised. As he paced round the arrivals lounge, the memory of the phallus receding and with ample supplies of mouthwash to help him through the difficult days ahead, he felt a surge of confidence.

He didn't expect to wait long. Customs and immigration could take an age, depending on the whims of the officials, but Anderson Frank was no ordinary traveller. He was a VIP and as such would be given VIP treatment. Sure enough, half an hour or so after the plane had landed, a tall, stooped figure emerged from the fortress of the inner airport, flanked by two immigration officers. Late approached him confidently.

'Mr Anderson?'

The figure looked at him. Late smiled.

'Frank Anderson?'

The man returned Late's optimistic beam with a scowl. 'It's Anderson Frank, actually. It's a mistake that's sometimes made. I hoped it wouldn't be made here.'

Late's facial muscles began twitching. He held out his hand, which was taken limply. 'Late Andr . . . er Andrew Late. British Council Representative,' he added. Frank had a wispy mandarin moustache that couldn't be seen from a distance and there was a slight gap between his two front teeth. 'Welcome to Omeldoum.' Late was quite proud of the Tujanian inflection he gave to the name.

'Ah yes, Omeldoum.' Frank made Late's attempt at Tujanisation sound like an incompetent third former trying to impose a French accent on an unquenchable regional dialect. He gave the 'd' a strong dental inflection that Late hadn't heard before and a stream of saliva hit him on the bridge of the nose, shooting out through the gap in Frank's teeth like spray from a punctured hosepipe. Frank glanced around, almost sniffing the air. 'Looks . . . er . . . interesting.'

'It is, it is. Fascinating place.' Late took out his handkerchief and surreptitiously wiped his nose. 'Lots of history, you know.'

Frank turned to him. 'You're the British Council Representative, you say.' Late nodded, beginning to feel insecure. Frank made his station sound vaguely unsavoury. 'I expected one of the Embassy people to meet me.'

Late laughed nervously. He fingered the boil on his neck, and attempted an air of confidentiality. 'Well, as the visit is concerned with Aid projects, and as we administer many of the important Aid projects, the Ambassador felt I should come along. Leaves quite a few things to me actually.'

'Really?' Frank's tone implied that he couldn't understand why the Ambassador should do any such thing.

Late nodded. 'Basil Earl, the Aid Secretary, would be with me but he's . . . er . . . off to UK.'

'I know. I was supposed to meet him but he's not getting there till tomorrow. Funny chap, I hear.'

'Booked you in at the Hilton,' Late went on. 'Driver will take your luggage and I'll take you. The Ambassador will send a car for you in the morning.'

Frank looked round absently as if totally uninterested in anything else Late might have to say and they drove to the Hilton in silence. After depositing his passenger, Late reflected that for some reason he had made a poor impression. It was this thought that was passing through his mind as he went to bed and drifted unhappily into sleep, his earlier optimism completely dissipated.

II

Stephen sat on the terrace at the Club and waited for Charles. He'd hardly slept a wink the previous night, a feeling of utter uselessness taking him to new depths of depression. He had come to Tujan to sort out the situation at the Polytechnic. Not only had he failed to make any progress on that score, he had also been entrusted with a document signed by thousands of people in fear of annihilation and in no time at all had let it fall into the hands of the very people he had been entrusted to keep it from. And the man who had given it to him had, in all likelihood, committed suicide to prevent just such a thing happening!

Self-disgust had rapidly given way to fear. The submission was dynamite. Its contents would destroy forever the myth of Government innocence. All the allegations and anecdotes led to only one conclusion: that in Western Province, a policy of systematic genocide was being carried out. He had paced around his bedroom expecting at any moment the knock on the door, the arrest, the return to Central Police Station, this time to be detained longer, to be taken past the inner sanctum and into the torture chamber beyond.

Dawn came. The grey light peeking through the shutters gradually turned gold and Stephen got up feeling utterly hopeless, utterly without fight. Alena was already in the kitchen making coffee, tired, drawn, casting occasional glances round the flat which she had made a token effort to clear. She looked at him with empty eyes. 'I never thought . . .'

'What?'

'That Bert's articles would lead to . . . this.' She gestured round the flat. Stephen needed to talk to someone about the submission but hadn't the heart to tell her that there was something missing far more serious than bird books.

Several hours later, he was sitting on the terrace still a free man. His briefcase with Gomes–Little's brochure had also disappeared but in the light of his imminent arrest, everything to do with Gomes-Little seemed vastly insignificant. And how was he going to tell Charles that the submission he had assured him was safe was now in the hands of Special Branch?

The entrance gate creaked open and Stephen looked up anxiously, seeing no end to the demons that might soon start leaping around him. A familiar figure waved to him. Late's embarrassment about *Night of the Stallions* had receded to the point where he felt able to appear at the Club. But he still took refuge behind dark glasses and, with his untrimmed beard, he looked like the dictator of some seedy South American republic in an Ealing comedy.

To Stephen, he was a memory from a previous life, a life before the submission, a life of Alena and Gomes-Little, Charles Digley and Maggie Earl with a rubber phallus or two thrown in; the molehills of his past compared to the mountain of his present.

Late came on to the terrace breathing heavily. 'Thought I might catch you here.' He held out the briefcase he was carrying. 'Yours, I think.'

Stephen summoned a semblance of interest as he took the case. 'Where did you find it?'

'Basil Earl brought it to my office last night. Gave him some letters to take to UK. You left it by the pool, apparently. Good of him, don't you think? Nice chap really. You want to be more careful. Things disappear quickly round here.'

Stephen wondered distantly if this was an oblique reference to the Harpic that had disappeared from Late's cloakroom. It no longer seemed a matter of much consequence. Late took off his glasses and his red-rimmed eyes peered anxiously at Stephen. Stephen absently pictured him in a faded uniform, one gold-braided epaulette hanging by a thread, strutting with false certainty before a crowd of cowering peasants.

'Are you all right? You look terrible.' Late's brow suddenly furrowed as a thought struck him. 'Not getting involved in anything . . . er . . . controversial, are you? Things seem to be going well at the Poly.'

'Er . . . no . . . nothing like that. It's just that Alena's flat was broken into last night . . .'

'Of course, of course.' Late had heard about the ransacking of Alena's flat with some relief. It had sort of equalised the score between her and Gomes-Little, made them partners in injustice as it were, both victimised by Special Branch. Late, his post-phallic depression lifting, could almost envisage a pact. All things were suddenly possible. 'Must have been terrible for you all.'

Stephen nodded glumly. Late had lost none of his capacity for stating the obvious; he had no idea just how terrible it promised to be for Stephen.

'First Derek Lomas, then Gomes-Little, now Alena. Didn't know what VIPs I was dealing with,' joked Late, realising immediately that, with Derek in gaol, it was a remark in somewhat dubious taste. His nervousness returned and he replaced his glasses. A millimetre of pus, like the head of a maggot, oozed from the boil on his neck.

Late stood up. 'Must be off.' He brushed three flies away from the boil, smearing the pus over his neck. 'Meeting this Foreign Office chappie, the one who's come to make sure everything's okay for the Visit. He looked with distaste at the pus on his hand, surreptitiously wiping it against the back of his trousers. 'Interesting fellow. You'll meet him tomorrow. Bringing him along to a staff meeting at the Poly.' The left side of Late's face screwed up and it was obvious that underneath his dark glasses he was giving Stephen an enormous wink. 'Keep up the good work!' His face screwed up again.

Stephen watched him go, one of the more obvious molehills. He felt tired and shop soiled. His white cotton shirt was soaked with perspiration and the blue linen trousers he had bought just before he left UK were in need of a wash. He wouldn't be allowed to wear them in prison anyway, he thought darkly. Another wave of helplessness assailed him. For want of anything better to do and to delay the decision about what he was going to say to Charles, he opened his briefcase and took out Gomes-Little's brochure.

Initially, he wondered why Gomes-Little had designed a brochure on the English Language Department so similar to a submission by a few thousand Westerners. The anecdotes of Government oppression, the statistics of deaths and maimings, what had these to do with English Language teaching? It took him a few seconds to realise that this was not Gomes-Little's brochure on the English Language Department at all but a copy of the submission, made by Basil Earl and brought to him by Late for God alone knew what dastardly purpose.

Then the truth, the earth-shattering, marvellous truth, hit him. This was no copy! This was the original! Dumb bastard that he was, he'd locked the Gomes-Little brochure in the drawer in his room; the submission had been in his briefcase and had been brought back to him via the Aid Secretary and the British Council Representative. His unlikely saviours were the cuckold of the person he was now waiting for and a man who had attained recent notoriety for putting sexual aids on public display. Stephen always appreciated life's little ironies, particularly on the rare occasions he benefited from them, and when he greeted Charles a few minutes later, it was with unbounded enthusiasm. What unfathomable labyrinths Fate moved around in! And, contrary to his long-held belief, it did after all have a conscience, believed in a sort of evening out of its favours. Otherwise how could he have benefited from such incompetence? Whoever would have thought the submission would be safer lying unattended by the club pool than locked away in the bedroom of a private home?

Charles returned Stephen's greeting with surprise. This was far removed from the sheepish individual caught in an unwilling act of voyeurism the previous day. He'd expected a contrite Stephen, still feeling the remnants of his embarrassment and worried about the fate of Derek and Valentine. Stephen in fact had almost forgotten the scene at the Green Grange. The embarrassment and bitterness he'd felt when he'd found Charles making love with such a desirable woman suddenly seemed of little consequence. He looked at the briefcase and smiled.

Charles took the seat opposite Stephen and bent forward. 'Where is it?'

Stephen hesitated. In the briefcase on the chair between them was the document that had threatened to blow his world apart. In the chair opposite was the nearest thing to the submission's rightful owner he was ever likely to meet. And yet he hesitated and then, without fully understanding his motives, made up his mind.

'Safe.'

Charles nodded. 'So you said. When can I have it?'

Stephen told Charles about the break-in, the fact that his room had been searched but that the submission hadn't been found.

Charles was amazed. 'God, these bastards really are something! Imagine them getting on to you so quickly! It must have been well-hidden.'

Stephen mumbled incoherently. He had no wish to explain the means by which the submission had slipped through the hands of Special Branch. Perhaps he was too inefficient to come within the scope of their expectations. Their training was aimed at combating shrewdness and cleverness. Gross incompetence was probably beyond their imaginative reach.

'So perhaps I should hold on to it – at least for the time being.'

Charles was doubtful. 'How do you feel about the West?'

'I didn't come here to get involved, if that's what you mean.'

Charles nodded. 'That's why you'd better let me have the submission.'

'Presumably you didn't come here to get involved either.'

'No, but I *am* involved, that's the difference.'

'So am I, now. Valentine involved me.'

'But you don't even know what we hope to do with it.'

'I do. Valentine told me that as well. I also told him you stand no chance. Hardly anybody knows the schedule for the visit. And those that do are being pretty cagey about it.'

'I know that. Why do you want to hang on to it anyway? You realise what would happen if you were caught with it.'

'Only too well.' Stephen glanced at his briefcase. It should have been so easy. 'Just hand it over,' one part of his brain said, 'Give it to him. Don't get involved.' But another part, the part ruled by some mischievous devil of self-destruction, urged him to keep it.

'Look, they've searched me. They won't come again. It was only by chance I got involved anyway.' He told Charles about finding Valentine's body in the river and the evening at the police station.

'So Valentine's dead.' Charles was silent for a few seconds and then spoke quietly.

'All right. Keep it for the time being. You're right, they won't search you again. But can I ask one thing?'

'What?'

'You'll give it to me when I decide what to do with it.'

Stephen nodded. 'Unless I think of something to do with it first.'

As Stephen left the Club, Charles went to the members' pigeon holes. He quickly found the envelope with his name on it; the message was brief.

Come to the house about eight o'clock. I've told the guard there's a patient coming. Limp a little, darling.

x x x

Charles smiled. She was more used to deceit than he would have imagined; the excuse had come naturally to her. He was looking at the note again when he was disturbed by a purposeful clearing of the throat behind him.

A decrepit old gentleman stood there looking disapprovingly at him. 'Yes?'

The old man coughed again. 'Excuse me, old boy, could I just . . .' He pointed to a notice on the wall. Charles was improperly dressed! It was after six thirty and he was standing in the members' lounge wearing a shirt without a collar.

'Sorry. I was just leaving.'

The old man muttered something about keeping up standards and turned away. There was a button missing from his shirt and his flies were half open. But Charles had more important things to think about than the pettiness and hypocrisy of the Club. The submission had arrived safely in Omeldoum and at eight o'clock he was seeing Maggie. The one fly in his immediate ointment was an uncomfortable feeling that he was falling in love.

III

Maggie herself had no doubts. She *was* in love, head over heels, with a man who in one sense she hardly knew at all but in another, felt she had known all her life. He had set her alight, satisfied her in a way she hadn't thought possible, and for the first time in her life she felt a complete woman.

She had seen Basil off at the airport the previous night and had spent the afternoon at a lunch party given by the Ambassador to welcome an official from the Foreign Office. She had been relieved to find that Stephen Talbot wasn't there although the behaviour of the new man soon made her forget her embarrassment at the Green Grange. The Ambassador introduced them and it quickly became clear that this odd-looking character rather fancied himself as a lady's man, particularly a man of attractive ladies whose husbands had recently left on trips to London. He held her hand and her eyes far longer than necessary and the toothy leer that came over his features was obviously an attempt at a seductive smile. His salivary glands emitted a fine jet of liquid when he was angered or aroused. 'Like a skunk's anus,' Maggie thought.

'Full many a flower . . .' the man muttered, looking into her eyes and holding her hand.

'I beg your pardon.'

'Full many a flower is born to blush unseen

And waste its beauty on the desert air.'

Maggie felt a thin stream of fluid hit her just below the left eye. She had the prescience to sway slightly just before Frank's next statement, rather like a boxer moving inside, and the spray passed over her left shoulder. Frank misinterpeted her movement towards him and gestured expansively round the Ambassador's lounge. 'This is certainly the desert air. And you, Mrs Earl, are surely a rare beauty.'

This time she was too late and a fine spray hit her full on the nose. As a seduction technique it left a lot to be desired even if she'd been in the market for a lover and had been remotely attracted to the strange Mr Frank. His eyes roved over her body and she felt a flash of anger at this weird stranger looking at her in a way she wanted only one man to look at her. She turned sharply away, becoming even angrier when, on joining another group, she glanced back and found him still staring and smiling his idiotic smile.

Later, as she was helping herself to food, she felt a pressure behind her and knew intuitively that it was him. His hand lightly traced the curve of her buttocks before she could move away.

'Perhaps we could have a drink some time.'

She eyed him coldly. 'When my husband returns, we shall be pleased to entertain you.'

He lowered his eyes, staring pointedly at her breasts. 'What about before your husband returns? I have a feeling it can be quite boring here at night.'

'My husband will be back well before you leave. And I'm sure you'll have lots of other things to do with your time.'

His eyes moved lower down her body. 'I do have quite a bit of influence in the Foreign Office. I take it your husband is an . . . ambitious man?' He smiled as he saw the look of outrage on her face. 'Don't look so shocked, my dear. It happens all the time.'

A little later, she left the Ambassador's and, as she dropped off the note for Charles, she began wondering what on earth she was doing. She even felt a twinge of sympathy for Basil, at the mercy of such creatures as the odious Anderson Frank, who had asked her more or less directly to open her legs and help her husband up the diplomatic ladder! She sighed, wishing she *could* help Basil's career. It might be some compensation for the acts of adultery she had committed and had every intention of committing again.

IV

An hour or so later Charles arrived at the house and Maggie let him in. He looked around. Subdued lighting, soft music, a bottle of white wine in an ice jug with two glasses on a silver tray – all the trappings of romance in a sophisticated setting. She expected some comment about her privileged lifestyle but it didn't come. He held her eyes for a second before sinking to his knees, lifting her dress and burying his face in the warmth between her legs.

Minutes later they were making love and afterwards, she lay with her head on his stomach as he dozed, caressing his torso, tracing the line of hairs that led like a dark river to the sprouting bush around his penis. Her fingers followed the river to its source and she watched as the budlike organ began to flower. She felt Charles stroking her hair and as her own hand continued its caresses she looked at the body of her lover, the long lean torso, the long lean legs. Everything about him was long and lean. What a contrast to Basil with his stout body, his short neck, his short squat legs, his short squat penis. Charles's penis was swollen in her hand and she marvelled that an organ she had previously found rather repulsive could suddenly become the most beautiful thing in the world.

A little while later, the doorbell rang and Maggie held a finger to her lips and slipped on her dressing gown. Visitors at this hour were rare and she had a horrible foreboding as she went down the stairs. Her fears were confirmed when she opened the door and found Anderson Frank standing there holding a bunch of flowers.

'Mr Frank?' She hoped her voice conveyed the extent of her indignation. What right had this man to intrude on her ecstasy?

The leer hovering around the corners of Frank's mouth became more pronounced.

'I told you I might call on you.'

Maggie took a deep breath. 'And I told you to wait until my husband returned.'

'But it seemed such a waste. You alone at home, me alone in the hotel. Opportunities such as this shouldn't be spurned.' He thrust the flowers at her. 'A gift for a most desirable woman.'

Maggie tried hard to show how angry she was without actually being rude. 'It's very kind of you but I want neither you nor your flowers.'

Frank's look hardened. 'I think I mentioned this afternoon that I am not without influence in the Foreign Office.'

Maggie hesitated, feeling again that strange shaft of sympathy for Basil. How dreadful to be at the mercy of unprincipled idiots like this man! She pictured him in his London Club, sipping a whisky, swopping the latest jokes, unaware of the drama unfolding in his home in Omeldoum. Frank took advantage of her hesitation to slip past her.

'Mr Frank!'

He turned back to her. 'Anderson, please.'

'Mr Frank, will you please leave. I really have no desire to spend any time at all in your company.'

Frank put the flowers on a chair and began pacing round the room in that odd way of his, almost sniffing the air. His movements had a clumsy grace about them, reminding Maggie of the wildebeest she had seen on an East African safari. The clown of the plains! But the possible consequences of Frank's intrusion were in no way comic. The smell of Charles, the odour that had become synonymous with sex, was so strong that she felt Frank must smell it too. He went towards the stairs and Maggie moved hurriedly after him, terrified that her adultery would be discovered and by a man who would have no hesitation in using his knowledge to the full. He turned to her. 'I assume the . . . bedrooms are up there.' He jerked his head upwards, his eyelids drooping in a sudden attack of lust.

She nodded mechanically, petrified that he would insist on going up. He looked around curiously.

'No servants?'

'It's their evening off,' she said and immediately regretted it.

Frank beamed, his good humour returning. 'Good, good.' He noticed the wine and the two glasses and nodded appreciatively. 'So you *did* anticipate a visit.' His eyes moved from the wine to her body, the gleam of lust now very bright.

Maggie felt tired and confused, and terribly exposed in her summer dressing gown. She made another effort to exert control.

'Mr Frank, it's late, you have no business here and, as you can see, I was just getting ready for bed.' Following the direction of his eyes, she was horrified to see that her dressing gown had fallen open. She pulled it together but not before Frank's lust had intensified.

'You really are a most desirable woman.' His salivary glands were now activated and a fine spray landed on Maggie's left cheek. A movement behind him caught her eye and she almost fainted as she saw Charles, a towel round his waist, padding down the stairs.

'Come here.' Frank's voice was growing hoarser by the minute. 'Let's not waste any more time.' Maggie hesitated again, horrified at the approach of Charles and having no idea how to deal with Frank. Frank mistook her hesitation for consent and leered alarmingly. Like a vampire closing in on its next victim, he moved towards her, his hands clutching her buttocks as he buried kisses into her neck. Over his shoulder, Maggie saw Charles take a huge wooden candlestick from the sideboard. She mouthed an emphatic 'No!' realising at the same time that they had little choice. She pushed Frank away as Charles glided towards him.

Frank stood back, presenting a thoroughly disturbing sight, nostrils flaring, eyes rolling, facial muscles tensed as he prepared himself for a conclusive onslaught. His expression changed to one of astonishment as Charles brought the candlestick down on his head and he collapsed in a heap.

Charles bent over him. 'Who is this bastard?' He looked up at Maggie. 'I thought you said you didn't put it around.'

'I don't! And even if I did . . .' – she softened – 'You surely don't think . . .!' She gave a hysterical laugh. 'My taste in men was never quite as bad as that.'

'So, who is he?'

'Some chap from the Foreign Office out here to organise an important visit.' She looked at the figure on the floor. 'God, I hope you haven't killed him.'

Charles felt Frank's pulse. 'No such luck. He'll just have a nasty headache in the morning.'

Maggie felt that nasty headaches in the morning might not be the sole preserve of Anderson Frank. The cloud of scandal loomed. She and her lover semi-naked in her living-room with an important visitor from the Foreign Office unconscious at their feet! The headline writers would have a field day!

She looked at Charles. 'What shall we do with him? He can't stay here.'

Charles stood up. 'Where *is* he staying?'

'The Hilton, I think.'

'Have you got any whisky?'

'Loads of it.'

'Get me half a bottle. And some money,' he shouted as Maggie disappeared.

When she returned a minute or so later, she had the whisky in one hand and a bundle of notes in the other and Charles had gone. She looked with concern at Frank, who was showing no sign of movement.

'Just went to call my taxi,' said Charles, returning. 'Let's have that whisky.'

He poured half the whisky down Frank's safari suit and stuffed the bottle in the diplomat's inside pocket. Then he went to the front door and called the driver. He said something in Tujanian, indicating the inert diplomat, and the man laughed. Charles peeled several notes from the bunch in Maggie's hand and gave them to the driver. Then the two men carried Frank outside and deposited him in the back of the taxi.

'What did you tell him?' Maggie asked when Charles returned.

'I just told him that the Englishman had had a little too much to drink and that we would be very grateful if he could be taken to his room at the Hilton. No questions asked.'

'Darling, you're brilliant,' Maggie enthused. Charles moved towards her but Maggie held him at arm's length. 'Don't you think it might be wise if you went as well?'

'What, when I save you from bastards who try to take advantage of your husband's absence? Surely I deserve better than being slung out as well? Not only that but we haven't had a fuck for at least an hour.'

Her resistance faded as he undid her dressing gown. She pulled off his towel with a sudden urgency as he led her up the stairs.

CHAPTER 11

I

The short walk from the Club to Alena's flat led past rubbish dumps, along roads riddled with pot-holes and with a familiar stench in the air. For Stephen, carrying the document which an hour earlier he had been sure was in the hands of Special Branch, it was a journey through white clouds smelling of roses. He felt like a man who, having been reprieved from the gallows, had been given the freedom of the city and a cheque for a million pounds to enjoy it.

He arrived at the flat with the broadest of grins on his face to find Bert and Alena in sombre mood. One look at their faces brought his fears flooding back.

'Something terrible's happened.' Alena's face was tear-stained and her voice carried overtones of total disaster.

Stephen's eyes widened, storm clouds gathering rapidly on what a minute earlier had been a blue horizon. Such a doom-laden voice could mean only one thing. Special Branch was on to them after all. The charge – treason? murder? – made little difference. Only the possibility of being dragged to that torture chamber in Central Police Station could have produced such gloom.

'What?' He dreaded the reply and felt a sudden urge to defecate. Surely the submission was *in* his briefcase? Surely he hadn't been mistaken! He fumbled with the catch and the briefcase fell from his hands, spilling its contents on the floor.

Alena took a deep breath. 'You won't believe it,' she said and Stephen, on his knees, looked up.

'The Union.'

Stephen glanced at the papers with relief. 'What about them?'

'I just can't believe it. They've decided the gnome can stay! Oh Stephen, isn't that just the most awful thing that could have happened?' She burst into tears.

Stephen, gathering together the papers from his briefcase, was stopped in his tracks. The most awful thing that could have happened? He thought of being caught in possession of the phallus, of being arrested with the submission, of having his tongue plucked out and his genitals burnt in the torture chamber, of festering in Omeldoum gaol like Derek Lomas, days and weeks running into months and years, time interminable without variety or hope. For the second time that day, relief overwhelmed him and he started laughing.

It began quietly, a little giggle puncturing the corner of his mouth. When Alena looked at him querulously and Bert suspiciously, the giggle became several loud guffaws until he exploded in uncontrollable mirth.

'I was just thinking,' he spluttered. 'Gomes-Little is like – ha ha ha – is like – ha ha ha ha ha ha . . .'

'Is like what, Stephen? God, what's the matter with you. Don't you see what this means??'

'Gomes-Little!' Stephen roared anew. 'Gomes-Little is like the black – ha – ha -ha – fingernail of a . . . ha ha ha ha ha ha ha – dying – he he he – man!!!'

It was then that Alena snapped and Bert decided that Stephen was no longer welcome in their home.

That night he took up the option of a room in the Hilton. He wasn't really sorry although he regretted the circumstances of his moving out. Bert had seen his outburst as a terrible betrayal of Alena. Stephen had made a few half-hearted protests before realising that leaving the Collingwoods' fitted in neatly with his ploy of siding with Gomes-Little. He was mortified by the look in Alena's eyes as he left and for a moment almost confided in her. He stopped himself just in time. Alena had many qualities; the capacity to keep her mouth shut wasn't one of them.

The following morning, as he enjoyed a full English breakfast at a table overlooking the pool, his over-riding feeling was gratitude to Bert for insisting that he left the flat. The luxury of a good night's sleep in efficient air-conditioning had been followed by morning tea served on a silver tray, and the eggs, bacon, sausages and sundry accompaniments he was now enjoying were a distinct improvement on Alena's bean stew and infinitely preferable to the prison fare that for long hours the previous day had seemed an even money bet.

He had checked in about nine thirty, promising himself a much needed early night. On the verge of falling asleep, he'd been disturbed by the head porter and another Tujanian carrying a stricken European into his room. Stephen had shot up as the light went on, his fears of the earlier part of the day returning. And the condition of the creature being carried didn't immediately reassure him. The man looked like someone who had escaped from a torture chamber only to fall head first down a mine shaft. Stephen's protests had produced a series of loud and profuse apologies from the Tujanians during which he gathered that they had brought the man to the wrong room.

He remembered the incident as he tucked into another plateful of fried delicacies. He had heard stories of European down-and-outs living in the back streets of ex-colonial cities, shadowy figures, marooned in limbo by the march of time. Surely the creature carried to his room the previous night must be such a person. He had looked like a man who should have been dumped in the underground car park with the street kids rather than been carried to a room in the city's best hotel.

Stephen shrugged, brushed a few crumbs from his lap and shoved another forkful of bacon and egg into his mouth. White down-and-outs weren't his problem. He had bigger fish to fry. He looked across at the pool where two or three bikinied beauties were already preparing to soak up the sun, spreading towels on Lilos, rubbing sun cream on exposed skins. How tempting they looked, and how easy Stephen found it that morning to see himself as the international lover. The Union's decision had cleared the debris, removed all possible reason for procrastination. He, Stephen Talbot, British Government Consultant, was now cast as the Fulfiller of Destiny, the Arrow of God, and that morning he felt absurdly suited to the role: tastefully dressed, thoughtfully diplomatic, not bad-looking in a 'middle-age-is-just-around-the-corner' sort of way, the greying at the temples more a mark of distinction than of age.

Two of the bathers came to the bar beneath the breakfast terrace and helped themselves to fruit juice. Distance and fading eyesight had lent enchantment and he had a vague feeling of wonder that life's capacity to shatter illusions could still surprise him. The two women below were more like semi-arthritic prunes than the bathing beauties he had mistaken them for. Certainly too old and dried up for a man of destiny like himself, though perhaps not for the creature who suddenly appeared in the doorway.

Stephen looked at the figure leaning against the doorpost with a shock of recognition. The wild hair, the gaunt face, the safari suit straight out of the laundry basket – it was the man dragged into his room and out again the previous night. The man yelled at a waiter in Tujanian and Stephen felt uneasy. Europeans who spoke the local language always made him feel insecure. But he quickly relaxed. If this man had spent the last thirty-odd years cooped up in some hovel in a back street of Omeldoum, naturally he spoke Tujanian. In fact it was doubtful if he spoke anything else. Stephen watched, fascinated and somewhat confused, as the man slouched after the waiter and sat at a neighbouring table. If he *was* a 'poor white', what was he doing breakfasting in the Hilton and behaving as though he owned the place?

II

Anderson Frank had woken in the middle of the night with his head throbbing and the room full of a familiar smell. His concern that he couldn't identify the smell quickly gave way to the much bigger concern that he could remember nothing at all about the end of the previous evening. He remembered visiting the delectable Maggie Earl and her responding to his advances after an initial and perfectly understandable coyness. She had let her dressing gown fall open, revealing the most delectable . . . and she had raised no objection as his hands had felt her beautifully rounded buttocks . . . But then . . . everything had gone blank. He turned over and cried out in pain as the back of his head touched the mattress. He felt the spot and his fingers came into contact with a lump the size of an egg. He frowned. Something very strange had happened to him, something that had to do with this lump on his head and the pounding in his temples. He was certain he and Maggie Earl hadn't made love – unless she had ravished him in his sleep. He certainly *felt* ravished, though less by Maggie Earl than by a tribe of overweight Amazons!

Curiosity as to how he had ended up lying on his bed caused him to stagger downstairs to the foyer. His questions met with a resentful silence until his insistence finally produced a response from the head porter, the man who had supervised Frank's arrival the previous night, and in whom the principles of the good Muslim were in conflict with the discretion of the loyal employee.

'You must be careful here.'

'Careful?' Frank gingerly felt the lump on the back of his head and winced. 'What do you mean, careful?'

'People who consume . . . bad things . . . must be very very careful.' The tone implied that 'being careful' extended not only to an awareness of the possible legal consequences of consuming 'bad things' but also to a respect for the sensibilities of the local population.

'Consume bad things? You mean alcohol!' Frank was incensed. 'I haven't touched a drop of alcohol since . . .'

He looked at the man and was amazed to see he didn't believe him. 'Dammit, man, I'm telling the truth!' The indignity of the situation suddenly hit him, a distinguished member of the Foreign Office, a vital spoke in many a diplomatic wheel, visiting Tujan on a mission of international importance, discussing his drinking habits with a night porter at 2.30 in the morning! He drew himself up to his full height and scowled.

'I don't like your tone, my man. I'm reporting you to the management in the morning. Now, what's your name?'

Frank reached into his inside pocket for his notebook but no notebook emerged. What did emerge was a half bottle of whisky which he stared at in astonishment. Not even Late's unhappy sorties into inside pockets had produced a greater shock. Now he realised what the smell in his room had been. The porter gestured disapprovingly to the front of Frank's safari suit. That too smelled of whisky. Frank looked from the porter to the whisky and back to the porter. Somebody round here was going crazy and the only person it could possibly be was . . .

With this disquieting thought, his head started to spin and for the second time that night he fell to the floor. The porter called his mate and again they carried the diplomat into the lift and deposited him on his bed where this time he stayed until morning.

Frank sat at the breakfast table still feeling distinctly queasy and could manage no more than a croissant and a cup of black coffee. He was just about to go back to his room when he remembered that the British Council man was picking him up and taking him on a tour of some of the institutions the Foreign Secretary would be visiting. He groaned and while he was contemplating the morning which stretched before him like a desert of discomfort and boredom, Late breezed into the Hilton.

Late was in a thoroughly good humour, savouring the news from the Polytechnic that Gomes-Little had been cleared. He bounced up to Frank, smiling broadly.

'Morning, . . . er . . .'

Frank looked up at him and frowned. He had quickly identified Late as someone who would scotch any enthusiasm he might otherwise feel for this brief the Foreign Office had lumbered him with and he responded to Late's breezy entrance with a glum expression and glazed eyes.

Late helped himself to a coffee and sat down. 'Thought I'd come a little earlier than planned. Take you round a couple of Government departments before the meeting at the Poly, give you a chance to get the feel of the place.' He looked at Frank for some reaction. 'Doesn't that sound a good idea?' he asked doubtfully.

Frank nodded unconvincingly. This was getting worse and worse. Did this idiot really think a tour of Government Departments should sound like a good idea? His head felt as though it had a lunatic drummer inside it and here was a man proposing a tour of Government Departments and expecting him to react as though he'd been invited to an orgy!

Late's confidence wavered as he looked at Frank's face. 'We should be off soon,' he managed, but as Frank's head sagged towards his coffee cup, his voice tailed off and he looked round. To his surprise he saw Stephen sitting a few tables away.

Stephen had seen Late enter the dining room and he watched in amazement as Late joined the down-and-out. Perhaps the Council was sponsoring local charities – Salvation Army Homes or whatever the Tujanian equivalent was – although Late had never struck him as the type to have much time for such institutions. Late waved to him and called him across.

'Stephen!' Late bounced up from his seat. 'Thought you weren't staying here.'

'I wasn't until last night. I thought it better to move out of Alena's . . . under the circumstances.'

'Very wise, very wise. Good decision,' Late muttered, like a football commentator passing his opinion on a referee. He turned to Frank. 'Can I introduce you? Stephen Talbot, Frank An . . . er . . . Anderson Frank.' Stephen's outstretched hand was shaken limply. 'Stephen's our English Language Consultant at the Polytechnic. We shall no doubt be seeing you later, Stephen. Fairfax has invited us to look in on the staff meeting.'

'Invited who?'

'Mr Frank and myself. We think it's important that Mr Frank gets the feel of the place and meets as many people as he can as soon as possible.'

Stephen looked at the figure still scowling into his coffee with a total incomprehension as to what he could possibly have to do with a Polytechnic Staff Meeting.

'You mean . . . Mr . . . er . . . Frank will be coming with you to the meeting?' Perhaps the odd-looking man had applied for the job of caretaker.

Late laughed. 'You're very slow this morning, Stephen. Must be all this luxury living. Of course Mr Frank will be coming with me. He's the man I told you about yesterday.'

'Told me about yesterday?' Stephen looked at Frank who was still contemplating the inside of his coffee cup. 'I'm sorry, but . . .'

'Don't tell me you've forgotten.' Late turned to Frank. 'You'll have to forgive him. He's had a lot on his mind recently.' He turned back to Stephen. 'Mr Frank is from the Foreign Office. He's been sent out to make sure the Foreign Secretary's visit is a success!'

CHAPTER 12

I

'So what do you think of Fairfax?'

Late looked across the lunch table at Frank. They had just returned from the Poly staff meeting and Late had suggested lunch at the Club. He was feeling inordinately pleased with life. Without that meddlesome bitch, Alena Collingwood, the meeting had been a remarkably good-humoured affair. Thank God she would soon be on her way. The letters had been dispatched and all that was needed now was the written consent of London. With the evidence against her, that should be a formality. So the Poly situation was normalised, he'd backed the right horse and God, after all, was in his heaven. He cheerily acknowledged a couple of acquaintances, wavering slightly when he remembered the penis but quickly regaining his equilibrium. Never again would he allow morose thoughts to cloud moods of optimism. He even seemed to be making a better impression on the peculiar man sitting opposite.

'Mmm?' Frank prodded one of the barely identifiable components of the mixed grill he'd ordered and wished he'd eaten a bigger breakfast.

'I was just asking about Fairfax Gomes-Little.'

'Well?'

'What do you think of him?'

Frank shrugged. 'Seems all right. Finger on the pulse, hand on the tiller, that sort of thing.' He shoved a piece of something that looked like sausage into his mouth and looked with irritation at Late, seeing not the highpowered head of an important British institution that some people – particularly Late himself – occasionally saw, but a neurotic individual with food in his beard, a nauseating mouthwash on his breath and a boil on the side of his neck.

Late nodded. 'Yes, a good man . . . A good man,' he added contemplatively. 'Had a bit of trouble at the Polytechnic, though.'

Frank muttered something through a mouthful of rubbery fried egg. Why had he let Late bring him to this God-awful club? It put the tin-hat on a tedious morning. To get here they'd hit every pothole in creation and Late had parked the car so far from the entrance that they'd had to walk miles along hot, dusty streets with little black beggar children besieging them at every turn. Frank hated beggars. He hated them like he hated anything that gave the slightest jolt to the privileged hedonism to which he'd devoted his life. Beggars gave pinpricks to a conscience that had long since hibernated. But at least his headache had gone and the lump on his head had subsided. During the morning, he'd spent a lot of time thinking about the previous night. He concluded that he must have been attacked and wondered whether to mention it to Late. He decided against it, realising he would be asked about the circumstances before the attack. His mood improved when he thought of Maggie; other occasions would arise when they could resume their unfinished business.

'Still, it's all sorted out now.' Late beamed across at Frank, feeling that he might even get to like his strange-looking companion. He followed Frank's gaze towards the half-naked bodies lounging in a variety of postures by the poolside and saw a gleam of interest that neither he, the Polytechnic staff nor half a dozen under-secretaries had been able to produce. 'Perhaps a turn in the pool after lunch?' he suggested.

Frank nodded as a couple of brown bodies emerged from the changing rooms. He was sure that one of them was Maggie Earl. 'Not a bad idea,' he agreed and Late's optimism soared. 'A turn in the pool.' He rolled the phrase round in his head. He certainly knew how to handle people, how to home in on their pleasures and desires, to identify precisely what they wanted. 'A turn in the pool.' He looked around with the serenity of a man in complete control of his destiny.

A sudden gust of wind scattered newspapers and lifted tablecloths. Late, startled from his mood of self-congratulation, looked up at the sky. The bodies by the pool rose hurriedly, wrapping towels and *kikois* around them.

'What's happening?' Frank suspended a forkful of liver and fried egg a few inches from his mouth as another gust swept through the Club.

'Looks like a *haboob*.'

Late viewed the onset of one of the dreaded sandstorms with all the enthusiasm of a werewolf contemplating the full moon. A colleague had once told him they were the worst weather phenomena he had ever experienced and Late had found no reason to disagree. Hot sand swirled in the atmosphere, blocking every crack, filling every orifice. So much for his inspired suggestion. A turn in the pool now would be like bathing in warm consommé. He watched as the sky darkened and the club became a flurry of activity. Waiters hastily gathered up tablecloths and plates, mothers grabbed offspring and headed for the changing rooms and Late fidgeted in his seat. 'I think we'd better be off,' he said, his optimism vanishing with the light.

Frank couldn't help thinking that Late was making a mountain out of a climatic molehill. All this fuss about a bit of sand! It was true what everyone said, he thought. Keep a chap out in these places for too long and he loses all sense of proportion.

For himself, the climate was part of the essence of a place. And the essence had little to do with starving Westerners or little black beggar children or even things that went bump in the night. These were changing phenomena, shifting continually in the kaleidoscope of time. The essence was the land, the artefacts of history, and – he looked up at the darkening sky – the climate. *His* mind presented the broad panacea of the diplomat, far removed from the narrow, pinched consciousness of the little man sitting opposite. Still – he looked at the remnants of his mixed grill – that was, after all, why some led and others followed.

He popped the last piece of lamb chop into his mouth and chewed thoughtfully. 'I feel one never really knows a place until one's experienced both the best *and* the worst that it has to offer. *God Almighty!!!*'

The last exclamation had nothing to do with Frank's philosophy of travel. He had bitten hard on a piece of bone and a filling the size of a crouton had been dislodged from one of his upper molars.

'What's the matter?' Late's concern about the *haboob* was diverted by the anguish in Frank's voice.

'Filling come out. Bit on a piece of bone.' Frank fished around in his mouth, producing both the filling and the bone and displaying them like an angry witness showing exhibits in court. He poked his tongue into the cavity and the pain forked through his head. He looked at Late with loathing. 'Why did you bring me to this God-awful club?'

The first grains of sand were swirling in the atmosphere and Late realised action was called for. 'We'd better get you to a dentist,' he said unhappily, standing up and frowning at the sky.

'A dentist! Here?'

Frank had travelled for years in third world countries, cocooned in the air-conditioned, duty-free world of first-class flights and ambassadorial privileges. He knew there was a world outside, but had rarely experienced it – his philosophy of experiencing both the best and the worst that a place had to offer had never really been put to the test. The worst a place had had to offer up to now had been an absence of smoked salmon at a cocktail party, or drinking warm gin and tonic on a hot night in some outpost of Empire when the fridge had broken down. Tujan showed disturbing signs of completing his education. The lump on his head sustained in mysterious circumstances the previous night was distressing enough. But a Tujanian dentist! Frank couldn't begin to imagine what Tujanian dentistry might be like. The concept was beyond his comprehension, to be filed away alongside

Finnegan's Wake, the theories of Wittgenstein, the promotion policy of the British Council, as a subject for greater minds than his to grapple with. It was part of that other world that he took on trust, the world of power cuts and petrol queues and food rationing, the world he had heard about but didn't really believe in, the world beyond the looking glass of Frank's reality.

'Yes. Tujanian dentists are first rate. Look.' Late opened his mouth to reveal gold molars, pulled down his bottom lip to display gleaming white incisors. Several years before, he had embarked on a dental reclamation job at British taxpayers' expense and the result was a testimony to dental engineering in the third world. He had hoped the removal of some of his mouth's less wholesome furnishings might also improve his breath, but the rancidity remained to sully the visual effect, as if the Taj Mahal had been built downwind of a sewer.

Frank, for whom the invitation to examine the inside of Late's mouth had provided neither reassurance nor enlightenment, cried out again as pain jagged around his head, and Late went to phone the dentist. Actually he was getting rather tired of this chappie from London who seemed to pour scorn on all his efforts.

'The dentist can see you in twenty minutes,' he said as he rejoined his companion. He looked again at the sky. 'Come on. We must get moving.'

It was very dark indeed as they walked back to Late's Land Rover. Frank climbed in warily, still holding his face.

'Mind that pothole!' he yelled as they set off and, as Late swerved to avoid the crater, Frank was hurled against the door. His headache was back and as pain shot from his tooth and did a comprehensive tour of his head, the whole of his cerebral apparatus felt on the verge of breaking into a million pieces. Another pothole bounced him against the roof and he was relieved when the vehicle stopped and Late pointed through the driver's window.

'Do you want me to come with you?'

'I think I'm old enough to go to the dentist by myself,' Frank said, as he attempted a dignified departure.

'I'll pick you up in an hour,' yelled Late as Frank walked shakily towards the gate Late had indicated.

II

Stephen emerged from the Council buildings to see papers being blown from the nearby skip. His musings on the morning and his astonishment at discovering that the 'down-and-out' in the Hilton had in fact been a high-level diplomat were cut short. A *haboob* was advancing from the north, a tidal wave of sand filling the sky. Dust was swirling in the air and overhead the sun was a small silver disc.

Gomes-Little woke from his customary post-prandial snooze, pulled on his dressing-gown and lit a cigarette. Then, although it was early for such indulgence, he poured himself a large whisky. Outside, the wind was howling and he was aware that a *haboob* had started. He was as fond of *haboobs* as the rest of Tujan's population but that afternoon not even an earthquake could have dampened his spirits.

He picked up three letters from his coffee table and smiled. Two were letters to Alena Collingwood copied to him. One was from the Polytechnic authorities, the other from the British Council. His smile broadened as he looked at them.

He went over to his computer installed on two large tables in a corner of his living room and ran his hand lovingly over the monitor. This was his toy, his mistress, his constant companion. No deviant contemplated the acquisition of a new sexual aid with greater satisfaction than Gomes-Little contemplated the addition of a new piece of software to his informational arsenal. He switched the machine on and programmed it. Then he selected a disk from the several dozen methodically stored. On the management screen, underneath two files labelled 'PAL COUP INI' and 'PAL COUP DEV' he opened a new file with the title 'PAL COUP ABOR'. In this he typed the copies of the two letters he had received that morning and at the bottom of the second letter, he typed in large letters

THIS SUBJECT IS NOW TERMINATED

He then turned to the third letter. This was from the Polytechnic Teachers' Union and was addressed to him. As he looked at it, he punched the air in an untypical display of emotion. He finished his whisky and, after a second's hesitation, poured himself another. Alena Collingwood had been dealt with. It was now time to bring the rest of those bastards to heel!

The beggar outside the house of Mustafa Badawi wrapped his *djelabiah* round him and prepared to face the *haboob*. He was, in fact, no ordinary beggar. Underneath the dirty *djelabiah*, his clothing was smart, and in one of his pockets was an identification card. Lance Corporal Abbas of Special Branch was on another assignment, keeping watch over one of Omeldoum's most notorious political figures, Mustafa Badawi, leader of the Communist Party of Tujan. Abbas's instructions were to report on all visitors to Badawi's house.

Abbas had been at his post for almost three days and Badawi had received no visitors at all. The monotony of his task soon bored him and he regretted that the neighbourhood had no compliant Western girls to provide a few hours of distraction, completely forgetting the pledge made during his previous mission.

Earlier that afternoon, the sky had darkened and Abbas had cursed. Being stuck out in a *haboob* wasn't a prospect he relished and there seemed little point in it anyway. Badawi had received no visitors during three days of good weather. They were hardly likely to flock here now there was a sandstorm to contend with.

He took out his radio and was just about to report that he could see no point in continuing his vigil when a vehicle jolted to a halt, one of its front wheels resting in a huge pot-hole. A strange-looking man in a safari suit emerged from the passenger's side, holding his face and remonstrating with the driver. The vehicle drove off and Abbas watched with quickening interest as the man crossed the street and made his way to the house of Mustafa Badawi.

Alena Collingwood hardly noticed the *haboob* as she drove from the Council offices to her flat. She parked the car and picked up the two letters lying on the seat beside her. Before leaving the car, she read them again, blinded by sand and tears.

Bert greeted her as she entered the flat. She said nothing, just thrust the letters at him and turned away, her body convulsing in great sobs. And as Bert looked at his wife and read the letters, a feeling came over him that in later years he could only describe as madness.

Cocooned in their haven of ecstasy, Charles and Maggie made love. And afterwards, as the wind raged outside, Charles wondered how to broach the subject he knew they had to talk about, and Maggie thought of Basil's return and the hopelessness of the future.

The Club put up its shutters and the street kids fled to the underground car park as the *haboob* intensified and the invasion of the sand began in earnest.

III

Late sat in his house. He had closed his shutters but could do nothing about the gap under the door. He'd asked his workers to repair it but, useless buggers that they were, they'd said they couldn't find it. Couldn't find it! It was wide enough to accommodate a troupe of limbo dancers, never mind a few million grains of sand! He looked at his watch and realised that it was time he picked Frank up. Steeling himself, he went out to the Land Rover.

The receptionist greeted him as he entered.

'Mr Late.' He smiled selfconsciously at this girl who had access to all his dental secrets.

'Er . . . is Mr Frank with Dr er . . .' He gestured towards the dentist's surgery.

'Mr Frank?' The girl looked puzzled.

'Yes. The . . . er . . . gentleman I phoned about earlier this afternoon.'

'Oh yes, I remember. He never came.'

Late blinked. 'Never came?'

She shook her head. 'We thought . . . with the *haboob* . . . No one has been here all afternoon.'

Late was confused. Of course Frank had come. He'd seen him walk through the dentist's gate. He felt an impulse to look behind chairs, under tables.

'If he does come, I'll tell him.' The receptionist smiled reassuringly as Late sneaked a quick look behind a chair before returning home. Settling down with a glass of home brew he frowned. Where the hell could Frank have got to? he thought as he drifted into a light sleep.

He was disturbed by a loud and persistent knocking. He shot to his feet, opened one of the shutters, and peered out. The sand razored into his eyes and he closed them, but not before they had registered the figure at the door. Frank stood there, head bowed like the hero of some second-rate desert epic and something told Late that whatever emotions Frank was experiencing at that moment, contentment with his afternoon wasn't one of them. He cleared his throat, had a quick pick at his boil and, assuming what he hoped was his most businesslike expression, he went to the door.

IV

Frank had had a thoroughly unnerving afternoon. The lost filling had been followed by the idea of Tujanian dentistry and as he staggered through the gate indicated by Late, he hesitated. Dentists in any society were cultural outcasts, dealers in sharp pain and steep bills, one of the necessary evils to which nature in the unholy mess it had made of providing adequate biting equipment had subjected us. What kind of man voluntarily spent all his working life looking into other people's mouths? Judged by any reasonable standards, dentists were a race apart, different in kind to men like doctors, lawyers, diplomats. And a Tujanian dentist! Frank shuddered. He thought of the pot-holes and wondered how a country that couldn't even maintain its roads could produce anyone capable of handling a dentist's drill. Frank's knowledge of the anatomy of his skull was at best hazy. What was to stop the drill in the hands of a half-baked practitioner missing its target, going clean through the roof of his mouth and embedding itself in his brain? His hesitation lasted for several seconds and it was only another surge of pain that stopped him turning back.

He opened the door of what he assumed was the waiting-room and peered in. The room was occupied by half a dozen patients, all of them female. Frank wiped the sand from his eyes and blinked. The ladies looked at each other and began laughing and Frank was reassured. Tujanian dentistry couldn't be so bad if it produced such a relaxed atmosphere in the waiting-room. None of the women showed the slightest sign of tension and the eldest rose and offered Frank a seat. He thanked her and sat down. 'I assume this is the waiting-room,' he said.

The women giggled again and Frank felt a little irritated. 'Bloody silly creatures, women,' he thought. 'Make a perfectly reasonable statement and all they do is giggle.' He looked at each of them in turn. They weren't bad-looking, not any of them, and three of them were really quite beautiful, particularly the one who looked the youngest. Rather a stunner, in fact, with olive skin and big doe-like eyes. And it was certainly pleasant finding himself with a bunch of attractive women after spending the day with that British Council idiot.

Within minutes, Frank had forgotten his tooth and was leering round, indulging his fantasies. For years, his agenda had included making love to a forbidden woman. Muslim women were just about as forbidden as you could get and here he was sitting in a dentist's waiting-room with six of them, all forbidden, all indisputably female.

The youngest rose and left the room, returning a few minutes later with several small glasses of tea on a tray. She handed one to Frank who took a sip and smiled.

'Hot and sweet, rather like you, my dear.' The girl's smile changed to a look of surprise as a fine spray hit her just below the right cheekbone. She declined Frank's offer of a seat on his lap and took the chair next to him.

Frank was in ecstasy, so consumed with desire that he had completely forgotten why he was here. The hot sweet liquid seeping into the cavity refreshed his memory and he cried out in pain. The women looked concerned and Frank turned to them, trying to regain his composure. But his query, 'Will the dentist be long?' produced the most prolonged bout of giggling to date. This time it was the eldest who rose and left the room.

Frank, momentarily phased by the pain and the reaction to his question, resumed his advances to the girl at his side. He placed an arm round the back of her chair, and brought his face very close to hers.

'You are a very desirable woman,' he began, in what he hoped was his most seductive voice. 'I really feel that you and I should . . .'

But Frank's plans for the creature by his side remained unarticulated as the eldest woman returned accompanied by two men. Frank's regret that his overtures would have to be abandoned was balanced by relief that help for his stricken tooth was at hand. He looked up at the two men. 'Which of you is the dentist?' he asked hopefully.

The response from the two men was altogether more alarming than a bout of giggles. The older gestured to his companion, a broad man whose muscles bulged beneath his tight shirt. The next second Frank found himself lifted by the armpits, taken through the door, and hurled into the street.

V

'You what?'

Frank glared at Late as if he had just emerged from a home for odious reptiles. 'I went to the wrong house. You directed me to the wrong house. I've never felt such a fool in my entire life.'

Frank was pacing frenetically round the room, his head focusing on Late like a death-ray. Saliva was spraying in all directions and Late bobbed and weaved in an effort to avoid it. 'Why the hell didn't you come with me if there was any doubt?'

'It was you who said you could find it,' Late said, his customary sense of injustice this time on firmer ground. Mentally, he warmed to his theme.

'You were the stupid bastard who went into the wrong house, not me,' he wanted to say. 'How many dentists have you known offer you tea? And how long did you sit there like an elephant's prick before you realised something was wrong? Two hours! Two bloody hours! I've met some pope's testicles in my time but you, my shitty-arsed friend, take the fucking biscuit.'

Aloud he said: 'So, how did you . . . er . . . get back?'

'Taxi.'

Late tried an encouraging smile. 'Well, at least there was . . .'

'It broke down halfway!'

'Pardon?'

'Broke down! Stopped working!! Refused to function as a means of transport!'

'Perhaps it ran out of petrol,' Late said helpfully.

'Or it ran out of petrol. What's the bloody difference? I tell you I've never had such an afternoon in my entire life . . . *Argggghhhh!*'

'I take it that the tooth hasn't been filled,' Late ventured.

Frank's eyes exuded neat venom. 'Well as I've been nowhere near a dentist and not many teeth have been known to fill themselves . . .'

'Then we'd better get you to the dentist. Fast,' Late said leaping into action. He led a still muttering Frank out to the Land Rover. They were just about to enter when a figure emerged from the mist and asked for a few words with the gentleman in the safari suit.

VI

Lance Corporal Abbas had waited a long time for the strange-looking Englishman to emerge from the house of Mustafa Badawi. The *haboob* had intensified and he sank lower into his *djelabiah*, comforted only by the fact that such a long stay could mean only one thing: the man and Badawi had something pretty important to discuss. He wasn't even surprised when Badawi emerged with one of his sons dragging the Englishman by the collar and hurled him into the street. 'A good ploy,' he thought. He'd come across it often. Only recently, that man Gomes-Little had been acting out some ridiculous farce with the Westerner who'd committed suicide. Then he remembered that Major Bakheet had told him that the attack on Gomes-Little had been genuine and for a second he had doubts. But this was different. An Englishman in the house of Tujan's leading communist! For a whole afternoon! He went round the corner to where his taxi was waiting and asked the driver to follow the man who was walking unsteadily down the main street.

CHAPTER 13

I

'What?'

After several phone calls, Late had located the Ambassador at a cocktail party at the German Embassy.

'Mr Frank, sir. I'm afraid he's with Special Branch.'

'With Special Branch?'

For a second, the Ambassador was puzzled. Then light dawned. 'Well, he's entitled to visit Special Branch if he wants to. We're not his keepers, Andrew. No doubt he wants to check on some points of security.' The Ambassador maintained his patience with an effort. 'Don't worry about it.'

'No, sir,' said Late who had been looking for a moment to get a word in edgeways. 'Mr Frank isn't visiting Special Branch.'

'But you just said . . .'

'No, sir, I said he was with Special Branch. I'm afraid he's been . . . arrested.'

'Could you repeat that, Andrew? The *haboob* must be interfering with the line. For a moment I thought you said that Mr Frank had been arrrested.'

'That's right, sir, I did.'

'What?'

'Just now, sir. A Lance Corporal Abbas accused him of being in collaboration with Mustafa Badawi, the communist, and took him away for questioning.'

'In collaboration with Mustafa Badawi the Communist?' The Ambassador's mind refused to come to terms with the information being fed it. His thoughts slipped back to a minute or so previously when he had been nibbling snacks, sipping white wine and chatting to the delightful wife of the German Ambassador. Late had again catapulted him into the middle of a bad dream.

'Yes, sir. ' Late recounted the events of Frank's afternoon and by the time he had finished the Ambassador was shell-shocked.

'So how did Mr Frank get into Badawi's house?'

'I've explained that,' said Late. 'He thought it was the dentist's.'

'Yes, I know. But why was he there?'

'A filling had come out of his tooth. A very large filling,' Late added, like a man giving the conclusive piece of evidence in a murder case.

'What I mean is' – the Ambassador enunciated his words carefully – 'how did he get to that area at all? Who took him there and then allowed him to go to the wrong house?'

Late replied in a very small voice, 'I did.'

'You!' The Ambassador exploded. 'Good God, I might have known it.' He slammed the phone down, leaving Late staring unhappily into a dead mouthpiece. 'How unfair life is,' he thought. 'This bloody idiot from the Foreign Office gets himself in the shit and even that is my fault. The bloke was supposed to be competent, with diplomatic skills and organisational ability. So far he's shown little capacity for organising the escape of stale air from a colander!'

It was a minute or so before Late realised that no arrangements had been made with the Ambassador for retrieving Frank. He was steeling himself to phone again when the Ambassador, his mood dark as he kissed goodbye to excellent white wine and flirtations with charming German ladies, pre-empted him.

'I'll pick you up in twenty minutes,' he barked. 'And be ready!'

II

Charles woke from a brief sleep and looked at Maggie dozing beside him. What had started as a distraction had now become the central feature in his life and he was uncomfortably aware that his obsession with Maggie was blinding him to his responsibilities. Thousands were denied anything remotely resembling what he was enjoying, through starvation, mutilation, rape, oppression, by being treated worse than cattle. How many Westerners had lost people they loved as much as he loved Maggie? Food, tents, clothes, deliverance from death was what the world hoped to offer. The emotional suffering, the hell of being alive when family and friends were dead, this was something different.

He leaned over and kissed Maggie's shoulder. Her eyes opened and it was a second or so before she registered where she was. She snuggled against him in relief.

'I was having the most appalling dream.'

He stroked her hair. 'Tell me about it.'

'You were making love to me . . .'

'Oh thanks! That does wonders for my ego . . .'

'Listen! We were in Basil's office. And we were just . . . you know . . . when Basil came in and caught us.'

'And then?'

'You kissed me on the shoulder and I woke up. Thank God.'

Charles was silent for a moment. 'Basil comes back tomorrow, doesn't he?'

She nodded, her heart somewhere near her feet. For such a short squat man, Basil was casting one hell of a shadow.

'Have you seen anything more of that idiot I knocked out the other night?'

She shook her head. 'No. And I shouldn't think I'm likely to except at official functions.' She laughed. 'I wish I could have seen his face the next morning. Let's hope he thought the bump on his head was his punishment.'

'For what?'

'For being a lecher.'

He put his hand under the sheet and began stroking her. 'I hope all lechers don't get such punishment.'

She shook her head, feeling the familiar tremor. 'The handsome ones get rewards.'

She returned his caresses, her desire intensifying as she felt his penis grow. After a few minutes she flung the sheet aside and mounted him, riding hard through her first orgasm until she felt him come. And still she rode, past fulfilment, past desire almost, aware of Basil's dark shape engulfing them and terrified of their bodies coming apart.

After a while, he eased her from him and she gave a little whimper, still clinging to him.

'Does Basil know the schedule for the Visit?'

'What visit?'

'I understand there's a pretty important person coming to Omeldoum in a week or so.'

'Oh, that. Yes, I think so. All the top Embassy officials would know it. That's the reason Anderson Frank's here,' she added.

'What?'

'That idiot you knocked out. He's here to organise the visit.'

Charles thought of Frank's body lying at his feet and cursed. There might even have been a copy of the schedule in his pocket, perhaps the very pocket where he'd put the whisky! He beat his head in frustration.

Maggie looked at him.

'You're getting very serious, all of a sudden. Why all this talk of Basil and schedules?'

'So Basil would have a copy of the schedule?'

Maggie sighed in exasperation. 'Don't go on about Basil. We'll have to think about him soon enough.'

'Where would he keep it?'

'What?'

'His copy of the schedule.'

'In his office, I suppose, at the Embassy.'

Charles was silent for a moment before plunging in. 'Can you get in there?'

Maggie nodded. 'Of course.'

'How?'

'Basil leaves me his keys when he goes away.' She added quietly. 'He trusts me.'

'Could we get in and look for it?'

'If we wanted to. What's all this about?'

This was the moment Charles had dreaded, the moment when, unless he was careful, Maggie would feel that all his attentions had been calculated. He told her about the submission from the West and the hopes resting on this document that had taken courage to compile and even greater courage to smuggle into Omeldoum.

'So it's vital that we give this submission as much publicity as possible. We thought if we could present it to the Foreign Secretary . . .'

He tailed off and the chill he had feared bit into Maggie's heart. She pulled the sheet round her and turned away. Charles took her shoulders.

'I know what you're thinking, and it's not true. Our relationship started because of what we are, not because of what you could do for me. But now you *can* do something for me. Or for those poor sods in the West at any rate.'

Maggie was doubtful. 'I can't do it, Charles, not to Basil. Not anything else. Look how I'm betraying him already. Isn't this enough?'

He could feel her heart pounding.

'For me it's more than enough. And it would be easy to forget about everything else. But I can't forget what's happening in the West. And if I can do something to help, I have to do it. Don't you understand?'

She nodded slowly.

'So can we get into Basil's office?'

She nodded again.

'He returns tomorrow, doesn't he?'

'Yes'

'What time?'

'Early morning.'

'Then we'll have to do it tonight.'

III

The security guard was closing the Embassy gates behind Late and the Ambassador when he saw Mrs Earl driving towards them. Like all the local employees, he had a lot of time for the wife of the Aid Secretary. Not only did she treat them with respect, she was also a beautiful white woman and fed the fires of many a fantasy.

Maggie got out of the car and went to sign the book. 'Just going in to do some work for Mr Earl, Suleman. He comes back tomorrow and I shall be in hot water if it's not done.'

'Hot water, yes.' Suleman smiled. He had no idea what she was talking about. Mrs Earl could have said anything and he would have smiled. He looked beyond her to the car and his smile faded. 'There is someone with you?'

Maggie glanced back. 'A friend of Mr Earl's. He's going to help me.'

'You have help. That is good.' Suleman's smile was back. 'All right, Mrs Earl, that is all.'

Maggie thanked him and returned to the car. She turned to Charles as she drove through the gates.

'That wasn't so bad, was it?'

'Piece of cake. Good job the guard fancies you.'

'Suleman? Oh, that's ridiculous!' He thought how unaware she was of her startling attractiveness.

A few minutes later they were walking through a deserted Embassy to Basil's office, Maggie knowing the codes to each security lock. They locked the office door behind them and Charles began searching through the papers on the desk.

'I think it'll be locked in one of the drawers,' Maggie said, holding up a bunch of keys. An elfin impulse came over her and as Charles went to take the keys she pulled them away.

'Payment first,' she said, a strange excitement surging through her.

'What? Oh, let's get on with the job in hand.'

Maggie blushed and felt slightly ridiculous. She meekly handed over the keys and Charles started checking the drawers. After a while he pulled out a slim beige file and gave a cry of triumph as he read through the top document.

'This is it.' He waved the document in front of her face. 'This is it!'

He sat at the desk and began copying details of the schedule. When he had finished, he locked the file back in the drawer and faced Maggie.

'Now.'

'What?'

'Payment. But I think this' – he waved the copy of the schedule – 'is worth more than one or two kisses.' Maggie's excitement was unbearable as he closed on her.

'Remember your dream?' he said, unbuttoning his shirt.

She nodded, her throat dry.

'The only difference is now there's no chance of Basil disturbing us, is there?'

She shook her head as he reached her. He undid the buttons down the front of her dress. Her nipples were hard and the thought of where they were made her weak with lust.

Charles pointed to the document again as he took off her dress. 'That's something special.' He kissed her breasts and began taking off his clothes. 'I think it deserves payment in full.'

IV

The Ambassador and Late sat in silence as the Princess carried them to the offices of Special Branch. Initially, the Ambassador had hardly recognised Late whose habitual resemblance to a Cypriot terrorist had changed dramatically to one of the Irish variety. His beard and bushy hair were red with sand, the blue eyes wild and panicky, and the fact that he had forgotten to use his mouthwash did nothing for his sagging confidence. Occasionally, he felt impelled to speak, to say something – anything – to relieve the oppressive silence. But one look at the Ambassador's profile stifled the words in his throat and he picked obsessively at his boil. The Ambassador, for his part, found it difficult to hide his contempt for the man at his side. The fellow was a cretin, a blot on the intellectual structure of the British careers system. Not only that, he was a distasteful cretin, with a suppurating boil that he couldn't leave alone. And – the Ambassador realised with a start what the smell in the car was – he had bad breath!

So both passengers were relieved when the chauffeur turned into the offices of Special Branch although the Ambassador had little idea of what he proposed to do, and Late realised that whatever turn events took during the next few hours, it was unlikely to reflect well on him.

The Ambassador explained their business and they were shown into Major

Bakheet's office. He shook hands sombrely with the Ambassador and more offhandedly with Late, who was beginning to feel familiar with the desire for the earth to swallow him up. The Major addressed the Ambassador, glancing across at Late whose lips twitched as he attempted a smile. 'Could we discuss this in private? I mean without er . . .'

The Ambassador nodded. 'Of course.' Nothing would please him more than to have an opportunity to snub publicly the man who had accompanied him. 'Andrew, wait outside for a moment . . .'

Late did so, feeling a sort of finality as the door clicked behind him. The heavy beige panels mocked him, the final affront to his dignity, the indisputable evidence that, whatever feelings he occasionally had to the contrary, when it came to the mainstream of events, he was stranded forever in a backwater.

Twenty minutes later the Major and the Ambassador emerged, accompanied by the Minister for Internal Affairs. The Minister had acknowledged there had been a misunderstanding. A dreadful mistake had been made arresting such an important visitor to Tujan and those responsible would certainly pay. The Ambassador pleaded leniency, feeling nothing could begin to compensate for the loss of his evening – the chilled white wine, the flirtatious chat, to say nothing of the journey to Special Branch with the British Council Representative.

Late attempted a smile. 'All's well that ends well,' he ventured.

'It should never have begun in the first place,' growled the Ambassador.

The Minister nodded. 'Visitors to Tujan need a lot of guidance to begin with,' he said and the Ambassador gave Late another telling look.

Late coughed. It was so obviously the cough that precedes an utterance that the other two looked at him. He had pulled a bunch of tickets from his pocket and was holding them out beseechingly to the Minister.

'We're putting a film on at the British Council next week. It would be a great honour if you could attend.'

He smiled and simpered and the Minister took the tickets tentatively as though he suspected they might be hiding a small dog turd.

'What day next week?'

'Wednesday. 7.30 at my residence.'

'Next Wednesday.' The minister sighed as Late gave a ticket to Major Bakheet. 'There is a football match I want to see that night. If I don't come, you will perhaps understand.'

'Of course, of course.' Late was the soul of understanding. The four men stood there awkwardly, Late wondering what they were waiting for but not wishing to ask in case the answer was obvious. In fact, the answer *was* obvious. Ten minutes later, a bristling Anderson Frank appeared, accepting the Minister's repeated apologies with less than good grace and completely ignoring Late. They drove away in silence and the Ambassador told his driver to drop Mr Late at the end of his road. It was the final insult. He walked several hundred yards in sandy darkness, kicking out at a couple of street dogs that snapped at his ankles before closing the door behind him and sobbing in humility and frustration.

CHAPTER 14

I

Maggie watched the video, feeling the bottom drop conclusively out of her world. Twice she tried to leave but Basil maintained a vice-like grip on her wrist and forced her head towards the screen. He was breathing heavily, his eyes bulging, his face even redder than hers. She was in a state of shock, too numb to pursue any of the thoughts that had initially crowded in. Gradually, as she watched, the shock began to subside and a feeling of intense weariness overcame her as if she had been living beyond her emotional means and no longer had the energy to feel anything.

Early that morning, she had met Basil at the airport, feeling panic as her conventional peck on the cheek had been returned with interest. After a few hours sleep, he had left cheerfully for work.

If she was surprised by his return mid-morning, the change in him surprised her even more. In all the years she had known him, Basil had never changed very much. Good-hearted in a jingoistic way, always the first to buy a round of drinks, offer lifts in his car, give a tenner to a friend down on his luck. It was this generosity that had first attracted Maggie and as it was accompanied by a certain robust masculinity, she had convinced herself she was in love with him. It had taken several years and the arrival of Charles for her to realise that what she felt for Basil was nothing like love.

But the Basil she had known and resented for years wasn't the Basil who returned to the house that morning. This was a different Basil, a Basil of tense facial muscles and pent-up anger. She had realised immediately that he knew. She spent the next few minutes discovering how he had found out.

Basil put the video on pause. On the screen, the picture flickering slightly, Maggie lay naked across a desk. Charles, also naked, was above her, parting her buttocks and preparing to mount her from behind. How could she have been so stupid as to have forgotten the video surveillance? Basil had told her that it had been installed – or she had heard him discussing it with someone. All the acts of love they had so carelessly indulged in were there on the tape. Gradually the initial horror changed to numbness and she just watched and felt nothing.

Basil turned to her, his fury barely under control.

'Have you been having an affair with this . . . man?'

She felt an uncontrollable urge to laugh. She wanted to say, 'Does it look as if we've been playing tiddlywinks?' Instead she uttered a barely audible 'Yes'.

Basil exploded. It was as if he had wanted her confirmation of the act before accepting the evidence of his own eyes, as though he had hoped for some other explanation, however implausible, for the actions on the tape. Hearing her confession removed the last vestige of doubt and he began pacing the room like a caged tiger. The questions when they came were staccato-like, direct and unambiguous.

'How long has it been going on?'

'What?'

'You know bloody well what.' He gestured violently to the screen. '*This!*'

'A couple of weeks.'

'Who is he?'

'Just a man . . . I treated for back trouble.'

'Back trouble!' Basil gave a humourless laugh. 'Is that what you call it nowadays? Bloody back trouble!'

'Basil . . .' Maggie tried a reasoning tone.

'I can't bloody believe it.' He glared at the screen before dragging Maggie out of her chair and forcing her head towards it. 'Look what a whore you are! *Look!*'

Maggie looked and saw, not herself, but another person, a performer in a blue video so far removed from the rather prudish, distant woman she had always been that she couldn't believe it was her.

Basil grabbed her and shook her so violently that her head swam. He restarted the video, watching in perverse fascination as Charles had violent intercourse with her.

'Look at that! My wife! *My bloody wife!* What was he doing, brownholing you?'

Maggie shook her head mechanically. 'We didn't . . .'

'Why not? It's about the only bloody thing you didn't do.' He looked again at the screen. Maggie was now on her knees in front of Charles. She rushed to the set.

'For God's sake, turn it off!'

'*No!*' Basil dragged her away. 'I like to watch my wife behaving like a whore. Makes me realise what I've been missing all this time.' He looked at the screen in mock admiration. 'Splendid performance. What a lot of dirty little tricks you know. I never knew you had it in you.' He laughed hollowly at the pun.

Maggie came to her senses sufficiently to have a further worry.

'Who showed you this?'

'*Nobody* showed me this. I check the video every time I go back to the office. So don't worry. Nobody else's seen your antics . . . yet. Though I don't know how I'm going to keep it from the Ambassador.'

Maggie was aghast. 'You mean you'd show this to . . .'

'In case you've forgotten, there was also a small matter of a breach of security before all . . . this.' He gestured violently towards the screen. 'Before the breach of your marriage vows, before you started playing the whore of Babylon, you and your . . . boy friend . . . interfered with a top secret document.'

'Oh God.' Maggie had completely forgotten the schedule.

'So not only do you let this pervert into my office and into your cunt, you also let him get his hands on a top secret document. So, yes, the Ambassador will have to know.' He looked at the video. 'I should think you'd enjoy the top brass seeing what a little raver you are.'

Through her confusion, Maggie was dimly aware that the schedule would now be changed and that the information copied by Charles was now worthless. How completely they'd messed it up! She thought of the passion of the previous night, how excited she'd felt, how her sexuality had poured from her, how after years of frustration and repression she'd suddenly felt the complete woman. How sour it had all turned!

Basil switched the video off and turned towards her. There was another unfamiliar look in his eyes as he began removing his clothing.

'Basil, what . . .'

He grabbed her and flung her on the carpet. 'If you can behave like a whore with . . . him . . . you can behave like one with your legal wedded husband.' He pronounced the last phrase with heavy sarcasm.

Maggie bit her lip in horror but after a token resistance she lay back, all the fight knocked out of her. And as Basil fucked her with a savagery she hadn't thought him capable of, she found herself responding, crying out as he brought himself to a climax and left her gasping on the edge of an orgasm that a few minutes before she would have found unimaginable.

II

What Stephen Talbot would have made of the video, God alone knew. He had, after all, been given something of a preview that afternoon in the Green Grange and his embarrassment had been spiced with more than a little envy.

But although Stephen knew nothing of the video, he was quickly informed of its consequences. The previous day, Charles had left him a note arranging a time when he could hand over the submission and Stephen had looked forward to this with relief, delighted that Charles had decided on a course of action. But at the meeting, Charles had told him that his plans had changed although he hadn't explained why, and had asked Stephen to hang on to the submission a little longer. And so, just when Stephen hoped that he could give Gomes-Little and the Poly his full attention, the document from the West was dumped firmly back in his lap.

Alena Collingwood knew nothing either of the video or the submission. And even if she'd known, it is unlikely she would have cared. Her world had fallen apart several days earlier when she had received the letter from Late informing her of the Council's decision to terminate her contract. So Basil's view of the video as the ultimate obscenity was not one she would have shared. For her the ultimate obscenity was the presence in positions of influence of men like Andrew Late and Fairfax Gomes-Little, men who could play politics with people's lives.

But she had a greater worry even than that. On the day she had received Late's letter, Bert had left the house. And he hadn't been seen since.

Two men who might well have found the video very much to their taste were Major Bakheet and Anderson Frank. The Major, pious and puritanical in public, spent a large part of his spare time drooling over the sirens of the hard-core world who disported themselves on the TV screen in the private room reserved for his most intimate acquaintances. Major Bakheet had a blue video collection to rival the best. However, for several weeks his collection had remained untouched and it is unlikely that at this particular juncture in his life he would have spared more than a glance for the antics of Maggie and Charles.

The Major was perplexed. In the process of trying to find the submission, he had arrested one expatriate, apprehended two more, thoroughly searched the belongings of a further three and heard that his prime Western suspect had fallen to his death while escaping arrest. While his star had escaped unscathed from most of this, it had fallen substantially since his department had detained a high-ranking member of the British Foreign Office. It had now become a matter of extreme personal urgency for him to locate and destroy this damned document and all who were associated with it. But the submission remained as elusive as ever.

The video would have been right up Frank's street, and seeing Maggie in the lead role would have confirmed his hopes about her tendencies and her availability.

But Frank also had other things on his mind, not least the several affronts to his dignity during his first week in Tujan. Here he was, a vital cog in the British diplomatic machine, sent to Tujan on important business of state, and within days he'd been knocked unconscious in the house of the Aid Secretary, lost a massive filling from his tooth, spent a couple of hours chatting up the wives of a communist before being hurled into the street, and finally dragged the Ambassador out of a cocktail party on a filthy night to explain to some mickey mouse major that he wasn't a terrorist. Now the Ambassador had told him that there'd been a security leak at the Embassy and the schedule for the Visit would have to be changed. In addition, the dentist, when Late had finally got him there, had done a miserable job on his tooth, leaving jagged edges and a permanent taste of cloves in his mouth. In the face of all this, even the insatiable concupiscence of Frank had temporarily lost its edge.

In theory, the person most likely to be interested in the video other than the two participants and the solitary viewer was the Ambassador. He would certainly have been the first witness to the frolics in Basil's office had he not been extricating Frank from Special Branch. For the video surveillance was the Ambassador's baby. He had commissioned it at great expense and in the face of considerable opposition, arguing that Tujan with its civil war and civic unrest was a major security risk, one that needed to be guarded against with a top class system of internal surveillance.

Initially, he had planned to check the machines himself every morning to see if the automatic switches had been activated but he decided to delegate this task although he still retained responsibility for the videos of all personnel on leave. So only his trip to Special Branch had prevented his checking Basil's video on the morning in question.

Not for the first time recently, the Ambassador was puzzled. When Basil had reported to him that his copy of the schedule had been stolen, the Ambassador's face had lit up. A security breach had occurred and his decision to install the video system would now be vindicated. As he asked Earl to show him the tape, he basked in self-congratulation. Thanks to his foresight, they would see the crime and perhaps identify the culprits as well.

It had taken him a few seconds to cotton on to what Earl was muttering about. What was he saying? The video had broken down and had recorded nothing at all? The Ambassador couldn't believe it. 'Nonsense!' he heard himself saying. 'Bring me the tape.' So Earl had brought him a tape and the Ambassador had spent hours going through it. But never once was the dreary pattern of the surface broken by anything resembling a recording.

To the Ambassador, the capacity of the system to detect breaches of security had become more important than the breaches themselves. With heavy heart, he had instructed an engineer to examine the system and had been even more perplexed to find there was nothing wrong with it. He checked the visitors' book for the evening in question; only the name of Maggie Earl was entered. He questioned Basil who informed him that Maggie had gone to the office to collect some work he'd asked her to finish. There was something in Earl's tone that made the Ambassador look at him more closely. He had certainly taken the theft of the schedule to heart. He looked as if he hadn't slept for days and there was a wildness in his eyes that the Ambassador hadn't seen before.

But the Ambassador had more important things to do than speculate about the mental health of someone who, whatever his intellectual limitations, had always been a perfectly adequate Aid Secretary. He decided that perhaps the people who had objected to the surveillance system had been right. This had been its first real test and it had failed dismally. Perhaps it was, after all, a gigantic waste of taxpayers' money

If the Ambassador had known that his system had not only recorded the breach of security, but had provided evidence of pretty extreme adultery as well, acting as spycatcher and private eye all in one as it were, he would have jumped for joy. But he didn't know this and, unhappily for him, no one would ever tell him.

CHAPTER 15

I

The garden of Andrew Late's house was alive with people gathered for the showing of *Professional Foul* and the host looked down from his balcony before joining them. He was again resplendent in his white *djelabiah*, and felt a different person from the dejected soul who had cut such a sorry figure at Special Branch and who had slunk back to his house that night like a rat to its hole.

It was the finale of Late's cultural season and, after two or three of the events that had preceded it, he desperately needed an evening that progressed according to plan. The madrigal evening when the recorders had failed to materialise and the audience had endured unrelieved the vagaries of a contralto from the French Cultural Centre had been bad enough. But even this had been eclipsed by the Gerard Manley Hopkins poetry session when the guest reader had succumbed to laryngitis half an hour before he was due to deliver the first sonnet. Late himself had stepped bravely into the breach only to find the verbal eccentrics of the Welsh cleric way beyond his control. A kind of aphasic dyslexia had set in and his frustration at being able to do little but flounder on the margins of articulation found its outlet in a sudden hatred of all things Welsh. As yet another tongue twister from the ludicrously titled 'Windhover' eluded him, he made a mental note to cancel 'Under Milk Wood' which he had provisionally scheduled for the next cultural year.

So even forgetting *Night of the Stallions* (as if he ever could!), Late's recent ventures into the field of entertainment and culture had not been conspicuously successful and it was with some trepidation that he had decided to go ahead with *Professional Foul*.

However, as he looked at the crowd below and sprayed his mouth with an extravagance usually reserved for Italian tenors, he was glad that he had. This evening would restore his reputation as a culture buff, a man discerning enough to present aspects of the great British tradition to a waiting world and who still held hopes that some day he might be asked to do so in a slightly more pleasant environment than this sand-ridden shit-hole.

He looked at the little talk he had prepared on Stoppard and found himself inordinately pleased with it. Informative without being tedious, erudite without being obscure, forceful without being dogmatic, concise without being omissive – he congratulated himself on having struck exactly the right note. The audience would leave having had their knowledge of contemporary British theatre considerably extended.

Below were the usual expatriates, interspersed with a smattering of Tujanian academics and administrators. The Ambassador had pleaded a prior engagement, for which Late was grateful. But Frank was there, fresh from his confrontations with dentists, security chiefs and irate communists. Late wondered if his experience at Special Branch had chastened him, lowered his self-esteem, taken the wind out of his sails a little. Not in the least, judging from the way he was expounding to a group that included Gomes-Little, Stephen Talbot and the Earls. Late noticed that the Earls seemed a little removed from their usual cheerful selves. Probably received some bad news, he concluded. Even the lucky bastards at the Embassy must occasionally have houses in Belgravia that burned down, investments that went bust, elderly relatives who died naming the local cats' home as their sole beneficiary. Basil and Maggie looked as if any or all of these calamities could have befallen them and for a moment Late pondered. But psychology, either of the social or the individual variety, had never been his strong point and within seconds his attention had been diverted.

He suddenly became aware of a pair of dark eyes turned upwards and found himself drawn to them like a rabbit to a snake. He shuddered. There was something profoundly disturbing about those eyes as they bore into him. Focusing on the face behind them, he recognised the Minister for Internal Affairs, the man he had encountered at Special Branch and who had said something about a prior engagement.

With an effort, Late tore his gaze away and was about to descend into the garden when he saw a figure in jeans and tee-shirt coming through the gates. He frowned. The man must have come to the wrong house. Bearded, unkempt, dressed like a refugee from an Oxfam shop – Late felt a surge of indignation. Who did this individual think he was, gatecrashing a British Council cultural evening!? He was on the verge of yelling to his head servant to have the man thrown out when he suddenly remembered who it must be. Digley, Charles Digley. Late always made a point of inviting at least one of the lower forms of Aid life to these Council evenings even though he hated them and all they represented. Dirty, long-haired creatures, the lot of them! He recalled the judgement of an aging representative during his early days with the Council:

'Volunteers? Bunch of bloody commies more like. All they do is smoke pot and shag the locals. Still, while they're doing it here they're not doing it in England. Nor living off the Government. We must never forget that, Late.'

Late never had. Yet he had still acquired a reputation for magnanimity and frequently congratulated himself on his ability to subordinate personal feelings to the demands of office. He looked at Charles's jeans and tee shirt with distaste. Why couldn't the buggers at least take the trouble to dress properly if they were going to turn up?

In fact, Charles had thought for a long time about turning up. In normal circumstances, he would have refused to be party to Late's tokenism but these were not normal times. He was in a state of total confusion, guilt about the submission mixing uneasily with an intolerable longing for Maggie. He had decided to come because it was likely that both Stephen and Maggie would be here. These were the two people he had to see though for vastly different reasons, and as he entered the garden, he scanned the crowd anxiously.

Late came downstairs just as a large figure dressed in a low-cut bell-tent appeared and Late flashed a smile of gratitude.

'Dolores!'

'Andrew!' She gave him a peck on the cheek. Her dress was scarlet and would almost certainly have been indecent on anyone else. There was something comfortingly asexual about Dolores's breasts. He took her arm.

'Good of you to come,' he murmured. 'Haven't seen you for ages.' His gratitude to the large woman knew no bounds. In a world of fickle people ruled by malicious fates, Dolores could always be relied on to be in the right place and say the right thing. Within seconds he had changed his mind.

'Yes, not since *Night of the Stallions*. By the way, whatever happened to that magnificent prop you produced so spectacularly?'

Late spluttered. An image he thought he'd exorcised leapt back into his mind.

'Really Dolores, I . . .'

Late glanced at Dolores who was looking straight at him.

'Well?'

'I don't, er . . .' He suddenly saw Stephen break from the group he'd been talking to.

'Stephen!' Late whisked Dolores towards him. 'Have you met Dolores?'

Stephen nodded. 'We met in your Land Rover.'

Dolores smiled at him. 'The Harpic man.'

'Harpic man?'

'Your little bit of shopping.'

Stephen coughed and the embarrassment of the journey in the Land Rover came back to him. He couldn't keep his eyes off Dolores's breasts in what was a purely objective appraisal.

'If you'll excuse me . . .' Late fluttered, hesitated, and was gone, and a reluctant Stephen found himself paired off with Dolores. He followed her meekly to the group that included the Earls and Anderson Frank.

In spite of the ravages of the previous few days, Maggie was still looking devastating in a plain white cotton dress, the gauntness of her features emphasising her beauty. Basil stood on the fringe of the group, eyes darting around like those of a frightened but dangerous animal. Since seeing his wife performing such a variety of sexual acts, one of the facilities that had deserted Basil was the ability to make polite conversation. Or any conversation, come to that. He was stumbling around on the edge of sanity, consumed by a mixture of lust and jealousy, one minute wanting to kill her, the next minute feeling he couldn't wait another minute before ravishing her.

Every night after he had fucked her, he would sneak downstairs for another look at the video, full of self-disgust at the lengths to which lust was driving him. A few minutes viewing suppressed his disgust and rekindled his desire, a further few set it ablaze and he would rush back to the bedroom and force himself again on his distraught and wary wife.

For her part, Maggie felt she was in a disintegrating boat with rapids ahead and crocodiles all round. Since the discovery of the video she had eyed Basil as one might eye a killer dog, never more worried than when he was sitting quietly watching her. Her distress was compounded by a desperate urge to leave and spend the rest of her life with Charles, but Basil gave her little chance to see anybody. She had managed to write a note telling Charles that Basil knew and that their efforts to get the schedule had failed. She told him about the video and Basil's rage, but omitted to mention his lust.

She had left the house for less than twenty minutes to slip the note into the Club. When she returned, Basil had been waiting at the gate, eyes blazing. He had struck her so hard that she had gone down seeing stars. And now, two days later, they were at Late's, displaying an edginess that was apparent even to the limited sensibilities of their host.

Stephen and Dolores joined the group just as Frank, already on his fourth glass of wine, put his arm round Basil's shoulders. 'If I might say so, Basil, I think your wife is . . .'

Whatever Frank thought Basil's wife was disappeared in the explosion of sound that heralded the projectionist's first trialling of the film. Late looked up in alarm and shot over to the projector. For God's sake, nothing must go wrong tonight!

If Frank had been more sensitive to atmosphere, he might have realised that his present line of conversation wasn't going down at all well with Basil. But Frank was in his element. He had an audience, he had consumed plentiful quantities of wine and he fancied Maggie Earl as he had fancied few women before. In such circumstances, the proximity of a husband had rarely deterred him. Most husbands had viewed the attentions of the odd-looking Frank as mildly amusing. Only someone whose reason had totally deserted him could have felt threatened by Frank.

Frank brought his face closer to Basil's.

'I visited her one night while you were in UK.' He moved towards Maggie, resting his hand on her arm. 'Quite a night it was too, if my memory serves me right.'

Frank's memory, of course, didn't serve him at all, right or otherwise. His overriding impression was of opportunity lost, his only recollection was of Maggie's breasts briefly exposed. At the thought of this he began stroking her arm. His erotic musings were cut short by Maggie pulling away and his wrist being locked in a grip that threatened to cut off the blood to his hand.

'TAKE YOUR HANDS OFF MY WIFE!'

Basil's voice boomed through the gathering and all conversation stopped. Heads turned slowly in the direction of the voice and Late, bending over the projector and giving frantic instructions to the projectionist, went rigid. What was this latest threat to his social pretensions? Looking up, he saw Basil, the tried and trusted Basil, the man who could always be relied on to do the right thing and who no one could ever remember losing his temper, turning to his wife, jerking his thumb in the direction of Frank and bawling in a voice that grew louder with each successive syllable,

'SO THIS IS SOMEONE ELSE WHO'S FUCKED YOU!'

'Basil, please.'

The gathering was now completely hushed. Whatever his other failings, Late certainly had the capacity to attract the most compelling scenarios. The guests watched spellbound as Frank took his cue. Initially nonplussed by this outburst from Basil, he decided it was time he exercised some control. A realisation had dawned on him that Basil wasn't taking his advances to Maggie kindly. But he wasn't a diplomat for nothing. Coping with such situations was part of his training, the essence of his art. He smiled and put an arm round Basil's shoulders, adopting the avuncular tone which rumour told him he was particularly good at.

'Now, Basil,' he soothed, 'I don't really think we need to make any more of this, do you?'

Basil swung round and addressed him in a voice which allowed for ambiguity in neither meaning, tone nor volume.

'PISS OFF!'

Nothing in Frank's diplomatic training had prepared him for such a moment. There he was, a high-ranking member of the Foreign Office, almost certainly the most important presence at a gathering that included several distinguished expatriates and Tujanians, being told to piss off by a man several grades his junior. It was time he exercised some authority.

'Now look here, Earl . . .' he began.

But he got no further. Basil stepped back a pace and with one swing of his forearm brought his right fist into contact with the side of Frank's face. Frank went down as if poleaxed and Late almost joined him.

'Come on!'

Basil grabbed Maggie by the arm and dragged her towards the gate. On the way they passed Charles who made as if to intervene. Basil screamed like a dervish and again leapt into action. Another blow from his right fist left Charles in a position similar to that of Frank but this time it wasn't enough for Basil. He leapt on his victim and would no doubt have killed him if Maggie, showing surprising strength, hadn't pulled him away. Basil's voice boomed out again as Maggie dragged him off into the night.

'WHAT IS THIS? A CONVENTION OF ALL THE MEN WHO'VE SCREWED YOU?'

Behind them, there was total silence. All eyes turned to Frank, prostrate on the floor, blood trickling from his mouth, and then to Charles, who had struggled to his feet and was staring into the darkness where the Earls had disappeared. It was a scene that Late had experienced only in nightmares. Worse than the madrigal evening, far worse than the poetry reading, even worse than *Night of the Stallions*.

Suddenly, the projector thundered again and the tableau leapt into life. But Late didn't know what to do. He'd almost forgotten why all these people were here. He was on the verge of following the Earls out into the night and never coming back when a large, red fairy godmother took over. Dolores began ushering everyone to their seats, summoned two servants to carry Frank to the guest room, ensured that drinks were served, snacks finished, and the film ready to start. Late stood there, simpering his gratitude, feeling that if he tried to speak, only a babyish gurgling would come out. Here he was again, trying to show British culture to the world and what had the world seen so far? An Embassy official assaulting two fellow guests (one of them a high-ranking colleague), and accusing them, in rather earthy language, of making love to his wife. He might as well be promoting football hooliganism for all the good his recent efforts were doing his career.

The film was a poor copy. The sound was fuzzy and the picture blurred and Late, having been instructed by Dolores to 'sit down and enjoy it', found it impossible to do so. Damn the Council! Why couldn't they send decent copies to these far-flung places. Hadn't he got enough troubles without this?

How could he expect the audience to forget the scene between Frank and the Earls when what they were now experiencing resembled a muffled conversation in a Siberian winter?

But he needn't have worried. At the start, most of the audience were too astounded to concentrate on the film, feeling that in terms of pure theatre, Tom Stoppard could only come a poor second to Andrew Late. And by the time their adrenalin had regularised, the quality of both sound and picture had improved.

In the guest room, Anderson Frank opened his eyes and wondered what he was doing in mountainous terrain. Two huge peaks reared up on either side of him with a deep valley between. Behind them the sky was red. But everything seemed upside down.

Dolores looked down at him. She wiped his brow and, following the direction of his gaze, realised that the neckline of her belltent had sagged even lower. Frank raised his eyes and saw the face of a woman. He smiled weakly and Dolores smiled back. He tried to remember what had happened and began muttering a question. Dolores stroked his cheek.

'Relax, honey, you've had a nasty experience.'

Frank relaxed. He couldn't quite remember what the nasty experience was but if it meant waking up in a strange bedroom with a woman bending over him exposing gigantic breasts and calling him honey, it couldn't be so bad. It was the stuff of fantasy even though he wished this particular fantasy didn't look quite so much like two women rolled into one.

Still, he had never been one to look a gift horse in the mouth. He leered foolishly, but as he raised a hand to grab one of those monstrous mammaries, the leer faded and he lapsed back into unconsciousness.

Below, *Professional Foul* was well under way. By the second reel, the only doubts were about the weather. The wind was getting up and another *haboob* threatened. Late sat shell-shocked, unaware that, as the film progressed, Ibrahim Masoud was again fixing him with his dark reptilian eyes. Well before the end, the Minister rose and left.

Gomes-Little registered little of the film. He was preoccupied with the Polytechnic and his efforts to produce a satisfactory brochure before the visit. Stephen had told him that he had lost his copy and this annoyed him. A consultant should set better standards. Still, now Stephen was no longer under the influence of the bitch Collingwood, perhaps they could form a better working relationship.

In the seat next to him, Stephen thought about the scene he had just witnessed. He couldn't understand why Basil, who had obviously found out about Maggie's affair with Charles, had decided to take it out on Frank as well. Could his assertion that Frank was 'somebody else who'd fucked her' possibly be true? Stephen's hopes rose. Surely he must be higher on the desirability scale than Frank. And if so, perhaps there was a chance . . .

His face fell. Whatever her taste in men, Maggie had never given the slightest indication that it included him. And judging by the way Earl had dealt with Frank and Charles, perhaps it was no bad thing.

His thoughts turned to the little man by his side. There was a perkiness about him which Stephen found intensely irritating. And he seemed to have grown. His fawn gaberdine suit almost fitted him. Stephen had no idea how to get rid of him now the Union had failed them. He couldn't even give it his full attention, not with the submission still on his agenda. Perhaps he should just abandon the idea, tell London that there were insufficient grounds . . . But that would mean abandoning Alena, tolerating injustice. He couldn't do it.

In spite of his worries and the onset of another *haboob*, Stephen quickly became absorbed in the film. He found himself amused and interested, and finally concerned. But it was only at the end, when it was revealed how an incriminating document had been smuggled out of Czechoslovakia, that a thought struck him. He remembered how the submission had escaped Special Branch the night Alena's flat had been searched. He remembered what Alena had said about Gomes-Little's briefcase.

A few minutes later the film ended and Stephen murmured a few pleasantries to the people about him. But he was preoccupied with his thought, a thought which on first analysis seemed to present solutions to both his problems. And as the sand swirled and he said goodbye to a haunted-looking Late, his expression of thanks for the evening was one of the few that was completely genuine.

CHAPTER 16

I

Late was woken up the following morning by the telephone ringing beside his bed. He had slept miserably, aware that the previous evening couldn't have got off to a worse start. Yet again his personal demon had struck; yet again, an evening he had hosted would be remembered for all the wrong reasons. Perhaps in future he wouldn't have events, he would just have 'happenings': invite people along and wait for the fun to start.

Still, at least the quality of the film had improved in the second reel and the audience seemed to have enjoyed it. And if anyone held him responsible for Tujan's appalling weather or the behaviour of two supposedly responsible Embassy officials, then there really was no justice in the world. What irked him more than anything was that he hadn't given his little talk on Stoppard. Perhaps he would publish it in the Council newsletter.

He picked up the receiver.

'Late here.'

'Pity you're not,' thought the Ambassador darkly at the other end of the line.

'I've just had Ibrahim Masoud on the phone.'

'Oh.' Late tried to inject his response with the enthusiasm he knew was expected whenever a Tujanian name was mentioned. Ibrahim Masoud? The name was unfamiliar. Probably some nomadic poet wanting to commandeer the Council premises for an evening of fifth-rate doggerel. Or perhaps the manager of a team of traditional dancers – thousands of years of Tujanian culture allegedly encapsulated in the wild gyrations of what was loosely described as dancing.

'I'm afraid he wasn't at all impressed with your choice of film last night.'

Light dawned on Late. Ibrahim Masoud. Of course! The Minister for Internal Affairs, the man with the black mamba eyes. He experienced a familiar sense of foreboding as he tried to sound as casual as possible.

'In what way, sir?'

'Well, according to Mr Masoud, the film contained a nude woman.'

'Nude woman?' Late was astonished. Could they have been watching the same film?

'Yes. Apparently right at the start there was one of those girlie magazines fairly prominently displayed.'

Late sighed. 'It was only a magazine . . .'

'Makes no difference, Andrew. This is a very strict society in which public displays of prurience have no part. I thought I'd made that clear after that last disaster of yours, at the Club.'

Late sighed again. The Ambassador made it sound as if keeping track of Late's engagements should be left to the social equivalent of a seismologist. 'Is that all?'

'Far from it. You know that Mr Masoud's son is studying for a degree in Applied Linguistics and Phonetics at Leeds University.'

Late, of course, knew no such thing. 'I had heard rumours . . .' he blustered.

'I also understand from Mr, Masoud that one purpose of the film was to make fun of such disciplines.'

'A very minor purpose, sir, I think . . .'

'Minor or not, it was there. Mr Masoud is very proud of his son and took great exception to the worthiness of his chosen profession being called into question in such a way.'

'And that's still not all,' the Ambassador continued as Late tried to interject. 'Mr Masoud also said that another theme was the attempt of certain individuals to carry out subversive activities against a particular government.'

'That would just about sum up the . . .'

'And that the film viewed these activities sympathetically.'

'Yes, sir. It was a very authoritarian government.'

The Ambassador took a deep breath before continuing in the most censorious tones. 'You realise, do you not, that Tujan is currently not the most stable of places?'

Late couldn't work out whether a 'yes' or a 'no' was the expected response to this so he kept quiet.

'And that a film such as the one you showed last night could easily encourage disaffected citizens to attempt revolutionary activities against the Government.'

Late was silent, awed by the range of possible objections to the film he had chosen.

It was a few seconds before he realised the Ambassador was still speaking.

'. . . even worse than these objections.'

Even worse? What could be even worse? His memory gave him a violent jolt.

'I know what you're going to say, sir, but I'm afraid I could do nothing about that.'

'Do nothing about what?'

'The fight between Mr Frank and Mr Earl.'

'Fight between Mr Frank and Mr Earl? I know nothing about a fight between Mr Frank and Mr Earl.'

'You mean Mr Masoud didn't tell you about it?'

'Not a word.'

Late was more surprised than ever. He pondered on the mentality of a man who could complain about a woman's boobs, twice removed as it were, while finding the sight of the British Aid Secretary running amok not worth a mention.

'So what was the other thing?' he said at last.

'You invited Mr Masoud to see this film that night when we were at Special Branch. Quite insistent you were, as well.'

'Well, hardly insistent, sir . . .'

'And Mr Masoud expressed doubts about whether he would attend as he had tickets for a World Cup qualifying match the same night.'

'Yes, sir.'

'Well, he decided that, rather than risk offending the head of an important British Institution, he would give the football a miss.'

'Very good of him, sir, and I told him so,' Late said, wishing like hell that the Minister had gone to his bloody football match.

'Again, I understand that a vital strand in the plot of the film is that the main character is intent on seeing a World Cup qualifying match but circumstances force him to miss it.'

'Well, hardly a vital strand . . .'

'Vital or not, you do see what Mr Masoud's driving at?'

Late thought, but could see nothing. Was he not as intelligent as in his better moments he judged himself to be? Was he even more dense than he felt in moments of acute self-doubt?

'Well, almost, sir, if you could just . . . er . . .' Late tailed off, articulation deserting him.

'A character in a film misses a World Cup qualifying match through force of circumstance. A member of the audience also misses a World Cup qualifying match by coming to see the film.'

Light was beginning to dawn, but it was light falling in a vacuum. 'I see that sir, but I still don't . . .'

'The minister thinks you chose the film deliberately.'

'Deliberately?' Late was confused. All his films were chosen deliberately.

The Ambassador must really have a bad impression of his films if he felt they were chosen by some 'pin in a list' method.

'Yes. To make fun of him!'

Late was now literally open-mouthed. 'Chosen to make fun of him?' His self-esteem asserted itself and he spluttered with indignation.

'Does the Minister also feel I wrote the script and organised the production?'

'That attitude, if I may say so, Andrew, is probably responsible for the mistakes you made yesterday evening and which has led to the other recent mistakes which you seem constitutionally incapable of avoiding.'

'All right, sir.' Late realised that with his recent track record it would be unwise to protest too strongly. 'What do you suggest I do about it?'

'I suggest you write to the Minister and apologise.'

Late's spirit asserted itself again. 'Apologise? But I've got nothing to apologise for.'

The Ambassador paused for a moment feeling that perhaps a quick summary of his talk 'How to behave in a Foreign Land' might not be out of place. He launched into it.

'When will you realise, Andrew, that we are not here as individuals. We are here in a foreign country, coming to terms with a foreign culture as representatives of Her Majesty's Government. As such, it is our duty to ensure that we do not offend against that culture *under any circumstances* even though we may not always be sympathetic with the values it represents. I can only hope for your sake that future excursions into the field of public entertainment are far more sensitive than this one was. Do I make myself clear?'

Late put the phone down. There would be no future excursions into the field of public entertainment, sensitive or otherwise. He couldn't believe it. A film chosen for its intellectual content had come over as a lewd, lampooning piece of subversion specially selected to take the piss out of one member of the audience. Mechanically, he got out of bed and wandered to the bathroom, only to find the door locked. Locked? Now who the hell could . . . ?

Belatedly he remembered Frank was in the house and that it was probably this goon who was blocking the evacuation of his bladder. It was very nearly the last straw. He could go to the downstairs loo but dammit all, why should he?

He slouched back to his bedroom and began composing the apology to the Minister. As he wrote, tears of frustration ran down his cheeks and through his beard, falling in splashes on to the writing paper.

The Ambassador felt a little uncomfortable after his phone call wondering if he had perhaps been a bit unfair. Late was a fool, there was no doubt about that, but a fool more sinned against than sinning, more accident-prone than anyone he had ever met. The man did his best; it was just that his best was lamentably short of good enough. The very thought of Late was enough to make the Ambassador's hackles rise.

And what was all this nonsense about a fight between Frank and Earl? Surely it was something else Late had got wrong.

He phoned his secretary and asked her if she knew anything about it. After some hesitation she replied that, yes, apparently there had been a bit of trouble between Mr Frank and Mr Earl, but she hadn't heard the details.

The Ambassador groaned. More problems, more difficulties. He was seeing both Frank and Earl later that morning about the Visit. Now there would have to be something else on the agenda. Two Embassy officials fighting at a public function! It beggared belief. And why couldn't London have sent him someone more suitable than Anderson Frank? He thought of the grotesque Frank, the wild-eyed Earl, the bumbling Late; he looked at the sand swirling outside his window and a note on his desk from his security advisor warning that political unrest might soon develop into something more serious. He groaned again and ran a hand through his silver-grey hair. Could anyone have faced the most important two weeks of his career with outside influences so inauspicious?

CHAPTER 17

I

By day, Omeldoum is a city in a hurry. It starts before sun-up, with the booming mullahs calling people to prayer. It proceeds peacefully at first, with menials making their way to work and the donkey man calling from street to street peddling his goat's milk. There is a warmth in the air as the street dogs stir and an occasional vehicle appears. *Gaffirs* rouse themselves, store away their beds, and sweep the dust from their little patch of pavement while in the alleys and underground car parks, the street kids stagger on to matchstick limbs like freshly-born ruminators of the African plains, bracing themselves for another round in the struggle for survival. The ferry from the Island of Doum groans beneath its cargo and makes its way to the mainland where fruit and vegetables are loaded on to handcarts and pulled away to the central souk.

By the time Stephen was making his way down the main street, the skirmishes of early morning had exploded into fully-blown battles. Heat and life had caught up with the city, and the plan suggested by *Professional Foul* was beginning to take shape in his mind.

The Land Rover had again refused to start, and so he decided to walk the few kilometres to the Polytechnic. He passed skips overflowing with rubbish and festering with cats who contested pickings with the now lively street kids. Hands grey with dirt stretched out to him; he dispensed small change and hurried on, crossing roads that through years of heavy weather and light repair hardly resembled roads at all, passing money changers plying their illicit trade, nodding to pavement hawkers selling everything from cameras to bootlaces, batteries to trousers, gold watches to chewing gum.

And above, through the haze of the *haboob*, the silver disc of the sun cast an eerie light on a city wearied by its haste but unable to stop, carried along by its own momentum. Haste was its only purpose and it led unfailingly to jams, bottlenecks, cars parked three abreast or bumper to bumper, the cacophony of horns betraying impatience, aggression, assertiveness on a never-ending journey to God knew where. The taxis disentangled themselves from the mêlée, wending their way like yellow crabs along the debris-strewn shore of the city.

And over all was a sort of blind faith, the faith that if you journey often enough you may one day arrive, that at some unspecified future date things will unaccountably come right. The traffic, the people, impulses through the nervous system of what? An indifferent Fate?

For the people who stepped blindly from pavements and diced with death in the traffic, Fate was far from indifferent. Fate, in the form of God, was welded to their lives. If it was God's will that they suffered yellow death in the maelstrom of taxis, so be it. His will be done.

Stephen walked on, sweat soaking his shirt, marvelling at the faith of these downtrodden people; at the optimism of the man building his mountain of grapefruit in the souk day after day; at the street hawkers eking out an existence selling chewing gum and shoe laces; at the street kids who, scattered here and there like troupes of scavenging monkeys, managed against all odds, to survive; marvelling above all at the people from the West, setting out, like Christian, on the trek to the eternal city. And what was their eternal city? This maggot heap of decay, this ragbag of humanity, this new Jerusalem of heat and filth and dust.

He passed the great mosque and crossed over the traffic island near the old Moonlight Club where he had once downed half a dozen whiskies in the company of a Tujanian general and watched a peroxided blonde uninspiringly take her clothes off. He found the memory extraordinary. For half an hour he walked, speculating on the present and the past, realising that for thousands he had seen that morning, the present and the past were all they had. He'd seen nothing (because there was nothing) to feed dreams or fantasies. For these people there was nothing in the future but the future, at least not in this world.

But for him there suddenly *was* a future, immediate and urgent. And as he thought of his plan, he thrust aside his reflections on Omeldoum life and strode purposefully towards the Polytechnic.

II

A few hours earlier, just as the first ferry was leaving the island, another man had risen and joined the crowd waiting to be taken to the mainland. Risen is putting it strongly as he hadn't slept for three nights, not since the day his wife had told him that her job was lost and her career in tatters. At that moment, images flitted across Bert Collingwood's brain – the dead Valentine, his lost bird notes, the treacherous Stephen Talbot, the vindictive Andrew Late, Special Branch, Fairfax Gomes-Little. And suddenly his mental balance left him.

Later Bert admitted that he had gone mad. At the time, as he walked out of the flat, he felt simply confused, needed to think things out away from Alena and the all-pervading presence of the British Council.

A few hours later he found himself on Doum island. The nights were warm and he made himself a bed among the leaves and the sugar cane. The islanders smiled and welcomed him, gave him lentil soup and bean stew. They recognised in his eyes the look they saw in one another's, the look concerned above all with survival. But there was another look there, one they had occasionally seen before in the eyes of a mad mullah or in the eyes of the wild man who ranted up and down the streets of Omeldoum. This other look muted the welcome they gave him and caused mothers to tell their children to give the little Englishman a wide berth.

Bert stayed on the island for three days. He ate little and drank less. He felt safe, insulated from his previous life by the stretch of water separating him from the city. But he didn't sleep. He lay awake on the warm Omeldoum nights staring at the sky, identifying stars – Sirius, Orion's belt, the Plough. And the planets. Up there was Jupiter, king of the seven moons. And Bert looked and thought, and reached for a stone he had found by the river. With this he honed the knife he had bought in the souk, quietly and skilfully, hour after hour for three nights, until the merest touch brought a spot of blood to the surface of his skin. The first light of a sand-laden dawn was in the sky as he boarded the ferry. And as the boat creaked beneath its load, Bert sat among the cabbages and waited.

III

Stephen walked the last few yards to the Polytechnic, suddenly riddled with self-doubt. In the last day or so, the Polytechnic had become engulfed in a sea of sewage and he picked an uncertain way through it. At one point, his left foot slipped and he swung his arms like a hyperactive tightrope walker, just managing to avoid a substantial baptism. A man passed him with a swerve worthy of an international rugby player and Stephen envied him his sure-footedness. He reached the Polytechnic gates musing on life's infinite capacity to present difficulties.

Early that morning his brain had been clear. As he had set off from the hotel, he had revelled in his brilliance, believing that perhaps the optimism of his parents all those years ago had not been misplaced. Perhaps they had after all conceived a genius.

But by the time he reached the compound he was certain that his head

contained nothing more than the brain of an optimistic half-wit. His plan
needed too many of the commodities his life had always lacked – planning,
organisation, commonsense. Not to mention luck.

The *haboob* was again gathering intensity and the compound was deserted
as Stephen walked trancelike towards the Department, recognising the feeling
spreading from his brain as a major crisis of confidence. The silver sun
gleamed overhead as he climbed the steps to Gomes-Little's office. At least
if Gomes-Little was there he could have a chat about the brochure, offer the
constructive criticism the little shit allegedly wanted, wheedle his way further
into his confidence, lay a firmer foundation for his suddenly nebulous plan.
Yet when he thought about it, his new plan necessitated hardly any contact
with Gomes-Little at all. The time for sham allegiances could well be over.
He no longer needed to be nice to Gomes-Little. But he did need the help
of Alena or Bert.

He knocked on the door of Gomes-Little's office and poked his head in.
A second later he was sprawling on the floor, the door was slammed and a
hunched figure turned to face him. Something glinted in the figure's hand.

As Stephen looked up, shock was replaced by fear. It was Bert who had
hauled him into the room and flung him across the floor, but a Bert who
had somehow gone wrong. The muscular tensions in his face were different,
as though he wasn't Bert at all but some demented twin brother, some Mr
Hyde to the real Bert's Dr Jekyll. And he suddenly knew why. The crouched
figure with the contorted face threatening him with the terrible knife was
off his head. Utterly and completely off his head.

Stephen had no idea what to do. For the first time in his life, he knew
physical fear. Cold, bowel-loosening fear. He wanted to cry out, to blubber,
to bawl. His whole life flashed before him, images of his mother's death, his
growing up, and then Omeldoum – the phallus, the submission, the bloated
body of Valentine, Maggie Earl's hand round Charles Digley's penis. Finally
a plane was crashing and only he was left alive. His knees buckled and he
tried to scream. But all that came out was a croak. The present refocused
and the figure was advancing. Instinct told him to get behind the desk.
Outside there were sounds of traffic, distant voices and a motorcycle
stopping, sounds from beyond the grave. In the office, the silence was eerie.
The figure advanced until only the width of the desk separated them.

The figure mouthed the word 'traitor' which Stephen sensed was the
prelude to an attack.

'Bert, I have a plan,' Stephen managed in a hoarse voice that echoed strangely
in his head and didn't sound like him at all. 'Bert, for God's sake *listen!*'

Bert snarled his reply. He crouched and the knife glinted.

William, the old departmental print boy, enjoyed an occasional visit to the Department. He had been dismissed when Gomes-Little took over but now had a pleasanter job with a motorbike thrown in. No child was more proud of a new toy than William of his motorbike. He had initially come back to the Department to show it off and, having discovered that Gomes-Little was rarely there, had popped in from time to time to chat to his friends and hope for pickings from philanthropic expatriates.

But never had a visit been more opportune than the one he made that morning. As he poked his head into the room, William's toothless grin froze. Bert looked towards the door and for a second his concentration wavered. Stephen saw his chance. Summoning all the expertise gleaned from five minutes of fourth form boxing thirty years previously, he launched himself over the desk and into a right hook. As Bert turned his head back, Stephen's fist landed plumb on his jaw. Bert stiffened and fell in one slow movement and Stephen, shaking like a nervous jelly, slumped into a chair. William stood like a statue, unable to believe his big white eyes.

IV

It had been quite a day for would-be pugilists. Basil had woken a few hours earlier to find Maggie feigning sleep beside him. He had fucked her furiously before reflecting with pride on the way he had despatched those two creatures the previous night. Although he had attacked Charles with murder in his heart, it was the right cross to Frank's jaw that had given him the greatest pleasure. For years he had endured the elitism of the Foreign Office. Many of his colleagues were pleasant enough but there were sufficient Anderson Franks around to cause more than the occasional resentment. There would be few times in his life when he had opportunity, excuse and inclination to hit someone as objectionable as Frank. His manhood, he felt, was on the way to being vindicated.

Thoughts of his manhood led to thoughts of its major physical manifestation from where it was a short step to thoughts of his wife. And when his thoughts turned to Maggie these days, it was with one activity in mind. Not only was his lust uncontrollable, it demanded instant gratification. He felt that even if he fucked her ten times a day for the rest of their lives, her sexual account would still be overdrawn. He rolled her over and inserted his penis into her from behind. His lust was insatiable and he was soon driving into her like a wild animal.

Maggie went weak as she felt Basil push her on to her stomach. It was no time at all since his last onslaught and she wondered how much more of his frenzy her body could take. The thrust of him inside her was a feeling she had come to know well in the last few days and she lay numbed by it all, letting Basil have his will, panicked only by the thought that Basil's lust was obliterating all previous experiences. She had forgotten what it was like to make love to Charles. As she lay there, enduring the initial thrusts, she felt like a prisoner trying to remember what it had been like to be free.

They never spoke about these times. They just happened. Every time Basil had an impulse they happened, and Basil's impulses were becoming increasingly frequent. And in particular they never spoke about the final act of these sessions when Basil's thrusts always took her from resentment to arousal. She couldn't identify the point at which endurance became enjoyment. She only knew that at the end her involvement was as intense as his, her gasps indicating that Basil had fucked her to yet another orgasm and as they lapsed away from each other, she cried silently for what she saw as a complete betrayal of her feelings for Charles.

When they weren't making love, Basil stayed firmly by her side. Frequently, her longing for Charles became intolerable but after her one attempt at communication had produced such a violent reaction, she was afraid to try again. Slowly, the realisation came that it might be days before she saw Charles. She might never see him.

V

Meanwhile, what of the recipients of these acts of pugilism? Charles was waking up in the Green Grange, the ache in his jaw not nearly as grievous as the one in his heart. He felt heavy, unmotivated, only half alive. A dull feeling of guilt passed through him as he realised another day had gone, another thousand people had probably died, and, with the Visit rapidly approaching, he was no nearer presenting their case.

At lunchtime he went to the Club, hoping Stephen would be there. Stephen was the one person who might help him do something about the submission. But it wasn't only that. Stephen knew about him and Maggie and was someone he could talk to who would understand both his guilt and his desire.

But Stephen wasn't there. The Club was sandstrewn and deserted.

VI

Frank's evening at Late's had again ended prematurely, the blow from Basil coupled with the effects of several large glasses of wine rendering him *hors de combat* and he had spent the night in Late's spare room. The view of the twin peaks of Dolores had revived him momentarily but the lapse into unconsciousness as she prepared to pour herself over him had lasted until dawn. Late himself had retired with the uncomfortable feeling of having a cuckoo in the nest.

Frank woke shivering, his head throbbing, wondering if he had contracted malaria. Surely headaches of this proportion coupled with uncontrollable shaking must indicate the onset of some lethal disease. And where the hell was he?

His brain slowly brought events into focus. He was shivering because the air conditioner was on full blast and he had kicked all the clothes off. And he was in the guest room of that idiot Late, brought here under the guidance of a large woman with mountainous breasts. The memory of Dolores produced a familiar stirring in his loins, but a flash of pain in his head caused it to disappear. It was while he was wondering why his headache should cause his sex drive to vanish that the main event of the evening came back to him. He'd been attacked, clubbed down by that bloody Aid Secretary. He fingered his jaw and found an acute tenderness at the point where he'd been hit.

He went to the bathroom, aware that very soon he would have to do something about the Foreign Secretary's visit. He had to change the schedule for a start. At that moment he felt in no fit state to change his socks. He was horrified when he looked in the mirror and saw one side of his face dark and swollen. As far as he could remember, he and Maggie Earl had engaged in nothing more than a mild flirtation – worse luck! He looked again at his right cheek. If this happened to *all* members of the Foreign Office who took a fancy to another man's wife, there wouldn't be a diplomat around who didn't look as if he'd gone ten rounds with the heavyweight boxing champion!

He swallowed a couple of aspirins from Late's medicine cabinet and washed his face. The towel was coated in sand, specks of which got into his eyes and did nothing to improve his mood. Someone tried the bathroom door, knocked loudly, tried it again, and walked off. The mutterings told him it was Late. Too bloody bad. Let the idiot wait. One way or another,

Late seemed to be associated with all his problems. The only thing he'd been right about were these bloody sandstorms.

He sat on the toilet, reflecting that his philosophy of enjoying both the best and the worst that a place had to offer had failed every Tujanian test. The odds were too heavily stacked on the side of the worst in Omeldoum: beggars, communists, Special Branch, dentists, plus the fact that some demon had apparently decreed that he should be knocked unconscious at regular intervals. Add to this the ubiquitous bumbling of this British Council idiot and weather conditions that would have tried the altruism of Lawrence of Arabia, and his feeling that Tujan couldn't be judged by normal standards was, he thought, perfectly reasonable. Nothing good could ever come out of the place and he just wanted to be shut of it. He poked his filling tentatively. The damn tooth was still painful.

He went back to his bedroom, hearing something on the way that sounded like crying. God, if anybody should be crying it ought to be him! He lay on the bed remembering that he had an appointment with the Ambassador at ten. A minute later he was asleep.

Late sat at the breakfast table, one hand fingering his boil, the other picking grains of sand off his watermelon. He was well into another dreadful depression. He wondered what madness felt like and whether it occurred when spirits that were as low as they could go were asked to sink lower. However hard he tried, nothing good or creditable ever resulted from his efforts. In Omeldoum, he was locked in a perpetual duel with Fate and there could be only one winner. He would have been surprised had he known how closely his thoughts at that moment resembled those of Frank.

In this mood, what he wanted more than anything was to be alone. He had hoped Frank would vacate both bathroom and breakfast table before he emerged, but although he heard the bathroom door being opened, he listened in vain for the sound of Frank leaving his bedroom. Now, having beaten Frank to the breakfast table, he desperately wanted to be away from it before the diplomat appeared. He felt he had nothing more to say to Frank, or to anyone for that matter. Even his instinct for self-preservation had gone. He no longer cared whether he was preserved or not. When Frank did appear a few minutes later and made his faltering way to the table, Late gave him the look that a shattered vampire hunter might have given Dracula as he watched him yet again rise from the grave.

VII

The Ambassador was sitting at his desk feeling increasingly irritated. He had been waiting twenty minutes and neither Frank nor Earl had put in an appearance. He spent his time alternately looking at his watch and reading a letter that had been left at reception. He was musing for the third or fourth time on its contents when Earl appeared, looking remarkably spry and cheerful. And not a word of apology for being late!

The Ambassador glanced meaningfully at his watch as Earl sat down but the Aid Secretary, usually so quick on picking up nuances, was oblivious to this one and the Ambassador gave it up. At least Earl looked happier today.

The Ambassador cleared his throat. He thought it perhaps wise to broach the subject of the previous evening's fisticuffs before Frank appeared, to get Earl's view privately.

'Er . . . It's a bit . . . er . . . tricky, Basil, to . . . er . . . say what I want . . . I understand there was something of a set-to last night . . .'

Basil looked at him brightly. 'That's right. I punched that fucker Frank on the chin.'

The Ambassador coughed again. That fucker? He'd never heard Earl use such terms before, wasn't even aware that he knew them.

'So why did you punch that . . . er . . . Mr Frank on the chin? It doesn't sound a very diplomatic thing to have done.'

'Oh, he annoyed me. Fancied his chances a bit with my wife. I think he wanted to screw her. Imagine, a shirt button like that thinking he could . . .'

'Yes, quite. I think that's enough for now, Basil. I can't say I'm over-impressed with your behaviour, though. Or your language,' he added to himself.

Basil shrugged. At that moment, he didn't care whether the Ambassador was over-impressed or not. He was glorying in his new-found manhood, this ability to have intercourse with his wife as much as he pleased and to punch people who had offended him more or less as it took his fancy. There was still that volunteer in the background but in general he had managed to keep Maggie glued to his side. For the first time since his return from UK, life seemed worth living. A week ago the Ambassador's 'I can't say I'm over-impressed with your behaviour,' would have sent shivers down his spine and prompted days of soul-searching. Now he had more important fish to fry. He had looked into the face of Hell. After that, the Ambassador's disapproval seemed a shade trivial.

'You realise that Mr Frank will be here' – the Ambassador looked at his watch – 'Well, half an hour ago, in fact. I want the two of you to shake hands, apologise and forget whatever it was that caused the problems last night. We can't afford to waste any more time. The schedule has to be re-ordered and everything prepared for the Foreign Secretary's visit.'

And so ten minutes later, when a scowling and unapologetic Frank arrived, he was surprised to find Basil on his feet with his hand extended. The Ambassador was delighted. So Basil had listened to him. He knew his Aid Secretary was made of sound stuff. 'Good man!' he mouthed to him, 'Good man!'

But Basil's bonhomie had little to do with gratifying the Ambassador. In fact, he registered the bruise on the side of Frank's face with a great deal of satisfaction, regretting that he couldn't give him one on the other side to match. He'd suddenly realised that time was moving on and that in an hour or so, Maggie, whom he had left having coffee with the Transport Manager's wife, would be on her own. And the last thing he wanted was to give her the chance to slip off for a quickie with that bloody volunteer.

As the Ambassador started talking about the schedule, Earl's brain went into overdrive. Within minutes he had reorganised it in such a way that while sticking broadly to the concept of the original, each place was visited at a totally different time. The Ambassador smiled his thanks. Basil had always been something of a favourite with him. He had seen in him a kindred spirit, a man destined to rise not through any great intellect but by dint of his personality, the fact that he could get on with people. That was why he had been alarmed when Basil had behaved so completely out of character. Basil attacking people? Surely not! That bugger Late must have put something in his drink!

But it was all over now. Basil had shaken Frank's hand as though he meant it. And he could fully understand Basil's jealousy, not to mention Frank's interest. Maggie Earl was a tasty morsel. He himself had often . . .

But he left that line of thought and concentrated on Basil. 'Well done, Basil. That took' – he looked again at his watch – 'just over half an hour. An excellent piece of work. I'm sure you agree, Mr Frank.'

Frank nodded, trying to work a smile on to his morose features. 'Well, gentlemen, I think that will be . . .'

The Ambassador had barely finished before Basil was out of his chair and scooting at full speed through the door, out of the Embassy and into his car. As Frank got up to follow him, the Ambassador called him back.

'Before you go, Mr Frank, there's something I must discuss with you.'

Frank turned back, scowling. 'I suppose you've heard about that business last night at the British Council . . .'

'I have, yes, but . . .'

'Well, if it's all the same to you, I'd rather not discuss it. Being assaulted in public by a junior colleague is not an occurrence best served by idle chitchat. I shall be making a full report, of course.'

'I was going to say that I have no wish whatsoever to discuss it. Your behaviour is up to a point your own affair. I can't say it pleased me, but, well . . .'

'Then what is it you want to discuss?'

The Ambassador motioned Frank back to his chair. 'I'm afraid something rather serious has come up.'

Frank took one look at the Ambassador's face and sat down.

'Serious?'

The Ambassador nodded.

'Well? Are you going to tell me what it is?'

'Yes, yes, of course.' He picked up the letter he had been looking at before the arrival of the two men. 'There's been an assassination threat.'

'Really.' Frank was unimpressed. 'Well, surely you can't think it means anything. In these situations you're bound to get the odd loony wanting to make a name for himself. And usually if they intend to try anything like that, the last thing they'll do is give you warning.'

'Yes, I know. I just thought you'd better be told, that's all.'

Frank smiled. 'Well, as the man in charge of the Visit, I suppose I should be informed of anything connected with it. But don't worry, I'm sure our distinguished visitor will be quite safe.'

The Ambassador nodded. 'I'm sure of that as well.'

Frank looked at the Ambassador, puzzled.

'You are?'

The Ambassador nodded again. 'Yes. You see, the threat isn't against the Foreign Secretary.'

Frank sighed in exasperation. 'If the threat isn't against the Foreign Secretary, why are you telling me about it?'

'For one very good reason.' The Ambassador handed Frank the letter. 'The threat is against you.'

VIII

Stephen and William bent over the prostrate form of Bert as he regained consciousness. Stephen was prepared to hit him again if he showed any sign of aggression but the knife had been taken from him and the eyes that opened had lost their wildness.

Stephen spoke quietly. 'Bert, listen to me. I'm still Alena's friend, do you understand?'

Bert nodded uncertainly.

'And I can't stand Gomes-Little and have been sent here to try and get rid of him. Is that clear?'

Again Bert nodded, this time more surely.

'So, if we help you up, will you sit quietly and listen to what I have to say?'

William and Stephen helped Bert into a chair and Stephen asked William to fetch three drinks. William looked doubtful.

'It's all right.' Like Basil after he had flattened Frank and Charles, Stephen felt in control, capable of coping with any situation. He turned to Bert.

'So why were you waiting with that knife?'

'I wanted to kill Gomes-Little.' He hesitated. 'Or Late. Or you. It didn't make much difference.'

'Thanks a lot! You mean you bracketed me with Gomes-Little and Late?'

Bert shrugged. 'Things are a bit clearer now. But you seemed to have changed sides. You've seen more of him than of us, and then the way you laughed when Alena told you that he wasn't being kicked out.'

'Look, you know Gomes-Little. Confront him and there isn't a chance. You've all tried that. The local staff tried it. It didn't work. I thought I'd stand a better chance if I gained his confidence, pretended to be his friend.'

'So why didn't you tell us?'

'I . . . didn't think Alena could keep her mouth shut.'

'All right. But that still doesn't explain why you laughed when she told you about the Union.'

'I'd got so much on my mind that day . . .' He told Bert about the submission and how relieved he'd been that Special Branch hadn't got hold of it.

'But surely you could have told us about that. Why didn't you trust us? Particularly if that was the reason they broke into our flat.'

'I just felt the fewer people who knew the better. Even now I'm not particularly happy about you knowing.'

Bert rose and walked across the room, feeling his face where Stephen's fist had connected. Stephen watched him warily but he showed no sign of his earlier aggression. When he turned he was smiling.

'I think I must have been a little crazy.' He hesitated. 'Can you . . .?'

'Well?'

'Can you forgive me for what I tried to do?'

'Forget it. Let's not waste any more time fighting among ourselves. How's Alena?'

'I don't know. I haven't seen her for a few days.'

'You mean you left her alone in the state she must be in?'

'I just had to get away.'

William came back with three Pepsis and Stephen handed one to Bert. 'Drink this. Then we'll get you home. And I'll tell you and Alena about my plan to get rid of the little shit once and for all.'

IX

'An impressive piece of work.'

Gomes-Little looked at Stephen and smirked. It was two days after Stephen's confrontation with Bert and he had used the time profitably. He had taken Bert back to a relieved Alena and explained his plan to them. All he needed from Alena was her briefcase, a telephone call on the morning of the Foreign Secretary's visit, and for her to keep her mouth shut! He'd left a note at the Club for Charles telling him not to worry, he'd worked out what to do with the submission. Then he went through Gomes-Little's brochure.

The atmosphere in the department couldn't have been more different. In spite of the *haboob*, a few members of staff were there and – a sight almost as rare as Halley's comet – Gomes-Little sitting at his desk! It was obvious the Visit was getting close – the little shit was pulling together the strands of his professional life and trying to weave them into something substantial. The brochure was the most substantial strand of all.

'I think so.' Gomes-Little smirked again. 'But you've taken so long getting back to me on this, I'm afraid I pre-empted your approval and went ahead with the printing.'

Stephen nodded. 'Everything's been a bit hectic recently. You heard about Valentine, I suppose.'

'Yes. Mind you, after what he tried to do to me, any sympathy on my part would be somewhat false. So, you approve of the brochure?'

'What more do you want me to say?' thought Stephen. 'That it should be short-listed for the Booker prize?'

'As I said, an impressive piece of work.'

'I have the cover here.' Gomes-Little produced a binder from a desk drawer. It was in red and blue with activities radiating from a central photograph of a smiling Gomes-Little. The writing was in English with a Tujanian translation.

Gomes-Little pointed to the photograph. 'I thought it was a good idea to personalise it a bit, give it a suggestion of intimacy. I know I haven't been here long but I couldn't really work out how else to give it the touch I was seeking.'

'I bet you couldn't,' Stephen thought again. 'Pomposity spiced with vanity and a large helping of megalomania. Couldn't be more appropriate.'

'Very effective. I like it.'

Gomes-Little positively beamed.

Stephen hesitated for a second. 'Do you think I could have a copy?'

'Of the cover?'

'Well, preferably the whole brochure but failing that, the cover will do. For my memorabilia.'

'I didn't realise you were sentimental. I took the liberty of having a few extra binders produced. I anticipated something of a demand. The contents aren't back from the printers yet. When they are I'll give you the whole thing. In the meantime,' he produced a cover from his drawer and handed it to Stephen, 'have this on the house!'

'Thanks.' Stephen looked at the cover and thought how hideous it was, in concept, design, function. But it would serve his purpose.

'The contents should be back from the printers tomorrow,' Gomes-Little said. 'Then we'll put it all together and hand out copies to the Polytechnic management and any involved expats. I don't think many institutions will be better prepared than we are.'

Stephen nodded, delighted at how well his own plan was developing. A few more 'i's' dotted and 't's' crossed and the mechanism for wiping the smile from the little shit's face should be well and truly in place.

CHAPTER 18

I

On the day of the Foreign Secretary's visit to the Polytechnic, Stephen woke early and went over his plan, mentally ticking off the items before checking the contents of his briefcase. Then he showered, shaved, and went down to breakfast.

Frank hadn't been in the hotel for several days. After hearing of the assassination threat, the diplomat had persuaded a reluctant Ambassador that it would be wiser if he moved into the official residence. And there he'd stayed, maintaining the lowest of profiles.

The *haboob* had cleared sufficiently for the Foreign Secretary's plane to land and the previous day the visit had taken in the agricultural campuses spread round the outskirts of the city. It was Frank's first public appearance since he had learnt of the assassination threat and he spent much of the time conjuring up demons in the hot brown mist that still shrouded the city. Initially he had taken up a position next to the Foreign Secretary, where he was surrounded by security men, until the idea dawned that one of the security men might well be the assassin. He had slid nervously away, only to slide back again when he realised how exposed he was.

The Ambassador watched all this with growing irritation. A threat on one's life wasn't something to be taken lightly but, dammit all, the man had been sent to organise the Foreign Secretary's security and to ensure that the Visit suffered from no major liabilities. The only major liability was Frank himself! He lamented the fact that Basil wasn't there, but Basil, horrified at the prospect of leaving Maggie alone for a whole morning, had pleaded illness and cried off. The worst thing about Basil not being there was that the Ambassador had had to take his place. He had planned to give these outlying campuses a miss. Still, the Ambassador had reservations about Basil he wouldn't have had a week ago. A man who could use the word 'fucker' and talk about his wife being 'screwed' was perhaps not the model of reliable conformity the Ambassador had always considered him. The only good thing was that the unrest in the city hadn't erupted into the predicted violence.

The Ambassador spent much of the day mopping his brow and putting on his diplomatic face. This consisted of a slight furrowing of the forehead and a knowing and sympathetic smile. Behind this façade, he was yearning for his air-conditioned cocoon at the Embassy. If this was the real Tujan, he had no wish to experience too much of it. He mopped his brow again, flicked sand out of his eyes and wondered about the wisdom of providing aid to such outlandish places. It would all be so much easier if Frank could exercise a modicum of self-control. Trying to provide a bridge between the Foreign Secretary and these semi-literate Deans was bad enough in itself without having Frank flitting in and out like an incompetent member of a ball relay team.

In his bedroom that night, Frank sat in a chair, his pillows arranged in the bed in the shape of a body. He sipped whisky and jumped at any sound, real or imagined. It was several days since the threat on his life and so far no attempt had been made to carry it out. Now there was only one day left. Twenty-four short hours and he would be on the plane, never to return.

He stood up and looked at himself in the mirror. His eye was black and his cheek had turned a dull yellow. He would certainly have the question of Earl to deal with when he returned to London, to say nothing of Late. Violent instability and complete idiocy had no place in such organisations as the Foreign Office and the British Council. He wondered for the thousandth time about the assassination threat, finding comfort in the thought that only important people received such threats. They were the price of success, he thought ruefully, one of the emblems of fame.

But he would soon be safe. Twenty-four hours seemed a very short time until he remembered that the act of killing could take no time at all. Hands trembling, he poured himself another whisky and settled warily in his chair, eyes fixed on the door, ears alert for the slightest sound.

II

The English Department was in a state of nervous expectancy when Stephen arrived at the Polytechnic. The Tujanian staff were all there, the men looking uncomfortable in suits and ties. The day was hot, the air still full of sand from the *haboob*. Stephen slipped the briefcase he was carrying behind a cupboard just before Gomes-Little emerged from the inner sanctum bristling with self-importance. He strutted around, barking orders, checking little details before belatedly noticing Stephen.

'Ah.' He looked at his watch. 'I thought you were never coming.'

'It's a quarter to nine, Fairfax. You said the proceedings didn't start till nine thirty.'

'I did, but you can never be sure. Anyway, I want to run through the brochure with you.'

'We've already gone through it twice. Surely now it's published . . .'

'I want to check it through again. This is an important occasion for the Department. Nothing must go wrong.'

'An important occasion for you,' thought Stephen, reflecting on the importance of the next half an hour or so to his own plans.

Gomes-Little pulled the brochure from his briefcase and slowly turned the pages. Stephen watched as the work of the Department rolled before his eyes – teaching materials, intensive courses, examinations, copies of the Unit magazine – Gomes-Little claiming credit for things that had happened long before his time and which, until recently, he had probably never heard of. The presentation, however, was faultless.

'As I said before, an impressive piece of work.'

'I think it will convince the Foreign Secretary that the money Britain sends to Tujan isn't entirely wasted.' He put the brochure on his desk.

Stephen looked at it in alarm. 'Why are you leaving it there?'

'It may as well stay there until the dignitaries arrive.'

Stephen found it difficult to hide his dismay.

'Is it safe there?' he blustered. 'I mean, it might be stolen.'

'Stephen, really. Surely your opinion of our importance is hardly so inflated that you think my brochure, excellent though it is, would be of any interest to a thief?'

Stephen looked glumly at the brochure lying on the desk. If it stayed there, all his plotting would be up the spout. But he could hardly put it back in the briefcase himself and he had less than ten minutes if the phone call he had arranged was on time. The next second he jumped as the phone rang. What the hell was going on?

Gomes-Little picked up the phone and listened, nodding as he did so. 'The Ambassador,' he explained, replacing the receiver. 'The meeting is to be in the Principal's office. Frank wants to keep the security as tight as possible by cutting down movement to a minimum. We're to meet there in twenty minutes.' He went to the door and passed on the message to the staff. His voice was surprisingly deep and resonant, like music with an impressive bass coming from a pocket-sized speaker. Stephen gestured towards the brochure.

'Don't forget that.'

'I wasn't about to,' Gomes-Little said stiffly. He returned the document to his briefcase and Stephen hoped his relief wasn't too obvious. The next minute the telephone operator came into the office.

'Telephone call for you.' His tone bordered on the insolent. None of the support staff had any time for the little man.

'Well, transfer it!'

'Your extension is broken.'

'Nonsense. I've just had a call on it.'

'I know. But now it is broken.'

Gomes-Little clicked in annoyance and went out of the office. The operator winked as he followed Gomes-Little down the steps. The telephone exchange was in the next block but one and Stephen had ample time to carry out phase two of his plan before a seething Gomes-Little returned a few minutes later.

Stephen looked up innocently. 'Anyone I know?'

'Alena Collingwood! Phoning to say she would have to miss this morning's meeting because she's sick! I told her she was missing the meeting because she wasn't bloody well invited! When will she realise that she no longer has any business at all in this place?'

'Some people are slow learners,' murmured Stephen. He glanced at his watch. 'Come on. We don't want to be late.'

III

The scene was the one Gomes-Little had played over and over in his mind like a favourite record. Notwithstanding threats of student protests and a strong anti-government mood in the country, everything was proceeding according to plan. There, in Mustafa's office, next to Gomes-Little, addressing him in friendly, understanding tones, was the British Foreign Secretary. Next to the Foreign Secretary stood a beaming Ibrahim Masoud. The Principal and Bakheet were to the left of the Foreign Secretary. Major Bakheet was there, in control of security. And to the right and slightly behind the Foreign Secretary was the Ambassador.

Gomes-Little smiled winsomely at the dignitaries. He had rarely been so close to a dignitary before and he was finding the experience exhilarating. At last, he felt, he had found his niche, his rightful place in the order of things. Rubbing shoulders with the successful and the famous was where he belonged, certainly more than any of the other members of the entourage; more than the strangely cowering Anderson Frank, more than the unpredictable Basil Earl, far more than Andrew Late who recently seemed to have lost his grip on events completely, infinitely more than that simpleton, Stephen Talbot; more than any of them the limelight fell naturally on him.

He had organised the day to perfection, even persuading the Tujanian staff to wear suits and ties. He himself was dressed in a charcoal grey suit ('comfortably loose' was how he would have described it) with a starched white shirt and primly knotted tie.

With the demeanour of a headmaster organising a group of unruly students, he paraded the staff before the dignitaries and one by one they confirmed Gomes-Little's opinion of himself and his work in the Department. Stephen wondered if they were the same people he had spoken to that day in Alena's flat and several times subsequently at the Poly. Perhaps he was wasting his time defending the virtue of such creatures. Here they were, presented with the perfect opportunity to protest and showing no more inclination to criticise Gomes-Little than mourners at a funeral would to speak ill of the corpse.

The British entourage was strange enough to have caused the Foreign Secretary to ponder on the kind of subspecies currently representing the interests of the Old Country overseas. The Ambassador was attempting to portray the sangfroid for which people in his position were reputedly famous. His eyebrows were going up and down like those of a snooker player attempting a critical pot and he was vacillating between reassuring smiles to the Foreign Secretary and worried glances behind him. And who could blame him? For there, among Tujanian politicians, academics and security men, stood Andrew Late, Anderson Frank, and Basil Earl.

Late, that morning, had assumed his full Fidel Castro look. He nervously fingered his boil, fearful lest the wrath of Ibrahim Masoud fell on him for the imagined slights suffered during the showing of *Professional Foul*. Frank was to his left, his natural stoop having degenerated to a crouch since he'd learnt about the threat on his life, the dark glasses hiding the bruise around his right eye but doing nothing for the swelling on his cheek. For him, what was happening in front was of little consequence. What was happening behind and to the side was of far greater concern. There, in all probability, lurked his assassin, the unknown assailant who, before the proceedings were over, would almost certainly try to kill him. As this thought entered his head, he gave a little whimper of fear.

The group at the front started and the Ambassador looked back in annoyance. He saw Frank, like a schoolboy subjected to frequent irritation by a mischievous colleague, sneak a quick look behind him and the Ambassador silently cursed. He began wishing the unknown assassin would carry out his task, and quickly!

Basil, standing behind Frank, was consumed by far more obsessive matters than Frank's life or death. A feeling of disquiet had been with him from the moment he had realised that he would be expected to accompany the official party on its visits. The previous day he had feigned illness but today the Ambassador had been insistent. 'No excuses today, Basil, not even death. This is the big one and we must *all* be there.'

Earl had listened to this with sinking heart. Maggie would be on her own. For the first time since his return from UK, she would have an opportunity to see Digley and indulge in any dirty little act that took her fancy. He had disconnected the distributor on her car but suspected that nothing short of manacling her to the Embassy railings would stop her seeing Digley that morning. He stood helplessly in the Principal's office, a soul in utter torment.

So, just as Gomes-Little was talking to the Foreign Secretary and preparing to present his brochure, at least two members of the entourage were in the grip of morbid fantasies. But, unlike Frank's, Earl's fantasy was based on precedent. And as it happened, it wasn't far wide of the mark.

IV

Meal times had become one of the several ordeals Maggie had to face in the course of a day. Basil's appetite for sex was matched only by his appetite for food and he tucked into hearty breakfasts while she sat at the opposite end of the table like a reluctant girl from an escort agency, picking at pieces of toast, her body aching from Basil's unremitting attentions. What disturbed her most was the sudden realisation of how much Basil needed her. For years, he had treated her as a possession, never asking her opinions, informing her only of that which she needed to know. They had never talked, never laughed, never been anything but two people sharing the same house and the most impersonal of sexual relationships. It was this apparent disregard for anything she might stand for that had led to her contempt for him, a feeling she had assumed was mutual. The last few days had convinced her otherwise. She was now uncertain, unsure of what she felt or what she should do. She was certain of only one thing: that as soon as the opportunity came, she would have to see Charles again.

At breakfast on the morning of the Foreign Secretary's visit to the Polytechnic, Basil ate nothing. A car from the Embassy called for him at 8.45 and he left reluctantly. They both knew where she was going and what she planned to do but it didn't matter. As soon as Basil had disappeared, she dressed quickly and, although her car wouldn't start, she was soon in a taxi, bouncing from pot-hole to pot-hole on the way to the Green Grange.

She paid the driver's inflated price without a murmur and ran along the corridor to Charles's room. Charles was about to go out. Within minutes she was naked on the bed. It was as if they'd never been apart.

CHAPTER 19

I

The Ambassador contemplated the expatriate members of his entourage and vowed that never again would he allow himself to be lumbered with such strange underlings. There was Gomes-Little in a suit two sizes too big for him, a ventriloquist's dummy of a man, Late looking like the dictator of some disreputable republic, Frank in fugitive mode, and Earl unaccountably giving the occasional moan and looking as out of place as an all-in wrestler. At least Gomes-Little, for all the imprecision of his tailor, seemed to be rising to the occasion.

After a few exchanges with the Foreign Secretary, Gomes-Little reached into his briefcase and pulled out the brochure which he handed to the distinguished guest, swelling visibly as he did so. The Foreign Secretary opened it and Stephen held his breath. For what seemed an eternity, the Foreign Secretary studied the document and Gomes-Little was unable to keep the smugness off his face. He looked expectantly at the dignitaries, convinced that favours couldn't be long delayed. The honours list beckoned. An OBE perhaps. Perhaps even a knighthood!

Then the Foreign Secretary turned to Ibrahim Masoud:

'What is this supposed to be?'

As the Minister looked at the folder the Foreign Secretary held towards him, his jaw dropped and his mouth stayed open. Only the restraint developed by long years of diplomacy prevented him from snatching the folder out of his distinguished visitor's hand.

'I think that is the wrong document, your majesty,' he stammered, his forms of address failing him in the confusion of the moment. He moved to take the folder from the Foreign Secretary but a hand, brooking no argument, restrained him.

'Wrong document or no, I should like to have a look at it.' The Foreign Secretary was silent for a moment, flicking over pages. 'Yes, I should certainly like to have a *good* look at this.'

Gomes-Little's smile had frozen as he realised that the document in the Foreign Secretary's hands was not the one he had prepared with such care. Unaccountably, it was something different and this something different didn't seem to have pleased the Minister by the Foreign Secretary's side who had fixed Major Bakheet and his uncle with one of his infamous stares. The Foreign Secretary looked at him.

'I don't think this is the wrong document. In fact, it couldn't be more right. Thank you, Mr Gomes-Little, for using this occasion to give me a document of even greater value than a brochure on the work of your Department.'

Now it was Gomes-Little's jaw that gaped as he tried to make sense of the Foreign Secretary's words. To the rear, Late picked at his boil and cowered as Ibrahim Masoud's eyes swept the group like searchlights on a gun tower and Stephen could hardly control his elation. The submission was finally in safe hands and the man responsible for putting it there was the man the Poly Management had entrusted with the running of their English Language Department. He almost literally jumped for joy.

Frank, still twitching uncontrollably, was only vaguely aware that events at the front were not proceeding quite as planned. He was the first to hear the distant shouts and chants in the compound, the first to react as the noises grew louder.

A demonstration was taking place and attention was suddenly switched from the Foreign Secretary and the document he was holding to the noises outside. A crowd of banner-waving students had gathered, protesting about the War, the policy in the West, the denial of human rights, and British Aid. The Minister looked at the security men and at Mustafa before turning to the Foreign Secretary.

'I think we must leave, your majesty,' and the Foreign Secretary nodded. The Minister went to reclaim Gomes-Little's brochure but again the Foreign Secretary restrained him.

'I'll hang on to this, I think.'

The Minister went unhappily to the window.

'This looks serious.' Major Bakheet looked warily at the Minister who viewed him and the crowd below with equal disdain. 'Just a bunch of communist adolescents,' he sneered. 'We can deal with it in two minutes.' He turned to the Ambassador. 'Who is responsible for the Foreign Secretary's safety?'

'It's the gentleman you arrested. He's just . . .'

The Ambassador scanned the group but could see no sign of Frank. In a fit of exasperation he yelled at Late, who jumped. 'What has happened to Mr Frank?'

'I d-d-don't . . .' stammered Late and Stephen interrupted him.

'He shot off down the fire escape as soon as he heard the noises outside.'

The Ambassador clicked in annoyance. Cowards as well as fools were coming out of the Foreign Office these days, it seemed. He turned to the Foreign Secretary. 'Don't worry. We'll get you out of here safely.'

The Foreign Secretary clasped Gomes-Little's file and smiled.

'I'm not worried. In fact this looks like being a very worthwhile visit.'

Ibrahim Masoud heard this and winced. The document they had searched for had finally appeared, presented right under their noses by one of the men classified by Special Branch as completely in the clear! Somebody would pay for this and no mistake!

As the security men ushered the party down the stairs, Stephen hung back until the room was empty, wanting to tie up all the loose ends. The briefcase lay where Gomes-Little had left it. If he returned it to Alena, Gomes-Little would never know the truth but Stephen hesitated. Perhaps he *should* know the truth. Let him know how he had been trapped and who had done the trapping! He left the briefcase where it was and was running down the stairs when the first shots rang out.

II

In the Green Grange, Maggie and Charles lay quietly on the bed.

'So you're going back?'

He nodded. 'It's the least I can do.'

'I thought you said Stephen Talbot had the matter organised.'

'He did. In fact, if his plans have worked out the Foreign Secretary should have the submission by now. But that doesn't excuse me. It was just lucky Stephen was here. The submission was my responsibility and I've been here a month and done sod all.'

'You've made me into a complete woman. That's not sod all. And what can you do if you go back?'

'I don't know. Anything.' He looked at her. 'Come with me.'

'What?'

'Come with me.'

'To the West?'

He nodded. 'Together we could really do something to help those poor buggers.'

Maggie was silent, stunned by the magnitude of the decision facing her. So she could have Charles, but under what conditions? Would there be time for them in a place of such constant demands?

'I don't know. I want to spend the rest of my life with you . . .'

'But not in Western Tujan, is that it?'

'It's not just that. There's something else . . .' He waited. 'Oh, how do I explain? It's . . . Basil. Until the last week I never thought he needed me.'

'He'll get over it.' He took her shoulders. 'You're worth better than Basil.'

'I don't know whether I can build happiness on someone else's misery.'

'What about the misery in Western Province?'

'I don't know the people there.'

'What difference does that make? You don't doubt their suffering, do you?'

'No, but I don't know them personally. I haven't seen their grief.'

He shook his head, more in surprise than anything else. He had thought that if he could make love to her once more, she wouldn't refuse him anything.

'You're married to a violent man. Who knows what he might do.'

She turned to him. 'Charles, if you love me, stop this. I want to come with you, you must know I do. Do you think I'd hesitate if . . .'

'If I was going anywhere but the West.'

She felt like slapping him. 'That's a hurtful thing to say. It's Basil. I've told you, I can't stand his pain.'

Charles turned away. 'And my pain? Can you stand that?'

III

The party from Mustafa's office hurried across the compound to the waiting cars, the Ambassador looking back before getting into the Princess. What had happened to Frank? 'Mr Frank!' he yelled. 'Mr Frank, we're leaving!'

There was no reply and no sign of the man from the Foreign Office. Gunfire was echoing round the compound and soldiers were dodging from building to building. He abandoned thoughts of Frank and ordered his chauffeur to drive to the Embassy.

IV

At the first sign of trouble, Anderson Frank broke from the official party. He heard one of the students shouting something about the distinguished visitor and decided that his only chance was to run for it, completely forgetting that there was a visitor in the Principal's office considerably outranking him in distinction. He scooted down the back stairs and into the compound. A few seconds later the shots started and he didn't need much to persuade him that they were aimed at him. Like a headless chicken, he ran in mazy circles round the compound, instinct finally taking him towards the English Language Department, the only place on the compound with which he was at all familiar. And as he shot into the storeroom, he was spotted by a man waiting in the offices upstairs.

V

Since his return to sanity, Bert Collingwood had felt an overwhelming debt of gratitude to Stephen. It was natural and right that he should be Stephen's accomplice in his plan. And the plan was so ingenious that Bert had felt humbled in the presence of a superior intelligence. He could identify birds; that was almost all he could do. A propensity to win the visitors' tennis tournament at the Hilton didn't really count. The other entrants were either geriatrics or cripples, or geriatric cripples. Apart from that he was nothing, dependent on his wife for his subsistence, a kept man. A kept birdwatcher, in fact, someone who spent hours identifying yellow-legged waders in the river while Tujan was going collectively mad and thousands were dying.

So when Stephen revealed his plan, Bert gave it his wholehearted support. It gave him something to get his teeth into. It might even get rid of Gomes-Little and save Alena. More important still, it might keep him sane.

On the day of the visit, Bert felt incredibly excited. Stephen had put him on Alena patrol, instructing him to stay near his wife and ensure that she made the vital telephone call and kept her mouth shut.

But he needn't have worried. Alena's hormonal cycle was at its monthly low. Not only did she see no hope of the plan succeeding, she scanned the distant horizon and saw not a ghost of future employment. As for the demise of Gomes-Little, even if she'd seen him shot in the head, she wouldn't have believed it until she'd examined his brain and had ballistic evidence that the piece of metal lodged there was indeed a bullet. But she went along with the plan and made her call, after which Bert, unable to contain himself any longer, set off to the Polytechnic to await developments. The sewage had been cleared and the only disturbing feature of the journey was the large number of soldiers patrolling the route, a result, no doubt, of the increased security for the Foreign Secretary's visit.

The students on the main gates eyed him disapprovingly and informed him that there might be trouble. Soldiers with light machine guns languished in the background. He made his way to the English Language Department and went into Gomes-Little's office. Here, a week or so previously, he had tried to kill Stephen but that was like a memory from a previous life. Now he was interested in other things, or rather one other thing, and a quick search of the office revealed it.

The briefcase was hidden behind the filing cabinet, not a particularly good hiding place, he thought, until he remembered that Gomes-Little would have no reason to suspect anything amiss. He opened it and inspected the file that was inside, feeling the tingle that he usually associated with the sighting of a rare bird. In his hands was the brochure about the work of the English Language Department. So if the briefcase with the brochure was here, the briefcase with the submission must be . . .

While he was contemplating this happy fact, disturbances started in the compound and he went to the window. The place was suddenly crawling with students, waving banners, hurling stones. More disturbing was the appearance of the soldiers he had seen by the gate. Like a pack of street dogs, they had raised themselves from languid insolence to snarling aggression, firing warnings as the students milled around the science block and marched towards the admin. buildings where the meeting with the Foreign Secretary was taking place, the warnings failing to disperse them. Other men with guns appeared and formed a shield round the students.

Bert watched all this with growing concern. Then a man emerged from the admin. block, running like an Olympic sprinter who has lost his bearings before disappearing like a dart into the storeroom below. It wasn't often one saw white men in suits and ties running around the Polytechnic like demented chickens and it took Bert a minute or so to realise that the man below felt himself to be in danger, a not unreasonable conclusion when trapped in a compound with bullets flying around. Bullets flying around! Bert felt he had yet to realise the full significance of all this. But what he did realise was that the man would be safer upstairs in the office. He went down the stairs and into the storeroom, calling meekly, 'Is anybody there?'

There was no reply and he peered around the dusty interior. Four or five cupboards pushed tightly against the wall were firmly padlocked and obviously held no fugitive. In the corner, just away from the wall, were four piles of teaching materials, coated with dust. Behind them, he found a scrawny figure, on his knees, his head in his hands.

'Excuse me.'

The figure started violently and a strange face peered up at him, eyes wild, nostrils flared, teeth bared beneath a wispy moustache.

'Excuse me. I think you would be safer upstairs.'

The figure glared and moved his lips in an effort to speak. A strangled gurgling came out which Bert eventually identified as 'Leave me alone.'

'I think upstairs is better,' persisted Bert but the figure shook his head.

Something came crashing through the window and there was another volley, this time very close. Both Frank and Bert jumped and Bert went to look out.

The next minute the door was wrenched open. 'Don't let anyone in!' screamed Frank, leaping from behind the papers and hurling himself at the figure who entered the storeroom.

VI

Stephen stood hugging the wall of the admin. block, a sudden fear replacing the elation he had felt in the Principal's office. This was more than a student protest being put down by a beleaguered government. Artillery fire had started outside the Polytechnic and a grenade exploded barely fifty feet away. He suddenly felt a searing pain in his eyes and flung himself to the ground. Tear gas! Another grenade exploded nearby and he struggled to his feet and began feeling his way along the wall, knowing that he had to get to the safety of a building. But the discomfort in his eyes was increasing and he could hardly see a thing.

He headed towards the English Language Department, running headlong into the wall of the classroom block which was closer than he had realised. The air was now free of tear gas and there had been no shots for several seconds. Through watery eyes, he made out the outline of the Department and he pressed himself against the wall, taking deep breaths as he prepared himself for a final sprint.

He thought of climbing the outside stairs to reach the sanctuary of the first floor but decided to wait in the downstairs storeroom until his eyes had cleared. He opened the door and peered into the darkness. The next second he was hauled into the room and thrown to the floor.

Two men crouched over him and as his eyes became accustomed to the gloom he saw who they were. One was Anderson Frank, the man who had disappeared from the official party barely five minutes before. The other was a figure Stephen was becoming familar with in these surroundings. He thought back to their last confrontation and the hair on the back of his neck stood on end. Then the figure helped him to his feet and spoke.

'Stephen! Thank God!' And Stephen realised with relief that Bert Collingwood had not lapsed back into insanity.

CHAPTER 20

I

Throughout the day, Omeldoum reverberated to the sound of gunfire. The respective parties from the morning's affairs at the Polytechnic had managed to find their retreats. The Tujanians had escaped to their homes, the Ambassador's party had reached the Embassy. There was some concern for the safety of the Foreign Secretary; the airport was closed and there were fears that the war from the West had spread to Omeldoum. In the privacy of his bathroom, the Ambassador wrung his hands in frustration. He couldn't imagine that any member of the diplomatic corps had ever experienced such a traumatic few weeks, and now, to top it all, a major attempt to overthrow the Government right in the middle of the most important visit of his career.

He checked the roll call of his party, noting with a distinct lack of concern that Frank and Talbot were missing. Pity Late and Earl weren't missing as well!

In another part of the building, Late sipped a gin and tonic and tried not to breathe on anyone. The Ambassador was making no secret of his desire to avoid him. Every time he spoke, the Ambassador turned away and Late couldn't work out whether he couldn't stomach his breath or whether the distaste was more fundamental. Earlier he had seen Ibrahim Masoud, in earnest conversation with the Ambassador, occasionally glance in his direction. He was also worried that Gomes-Little had suddenly become *persona non grata* in the eyes of the Tujanian authorities. His uncritical support for the little man was something else that looked like backfiring. Then he remembered how pleased the Foreign Secretary had been with whatever Gomes-Little had handed to him so perhaps things weren't entirely black.

In short, Late didn't know where the hell he stood. He remembered that he'd arranged a meeting of the Rep committee at the Marlborough at seven o'clock and regretted that he wouldn't be able to make it. The city was in such turmoil that there was no chance of anyone turning up.

Pity. He felt a desperate need to get out of the formal circuit that he'd been plugged into since early morning, a desire to relax with people who understood him. Still, civil war was civil war. He sighed deeply, fingered his boil, and helped himself to another gin and tonic.

II

Basil Earl had stayed for no such niceties. In spite of the Ambassador's warning that it would be unwise for anyone to leave the Embassy until the disturbances had died down, the Princess had no sooner stopped than Earl was hurtling the short distance to his house. Civil disorder held no terrors for him. It was the image of Maggie and Charles fucking that illuminated every cell in his brain.

He reached his house and burst in.

'MAGGIE!'

He careered through the building, flinging every door open before finding his house servant cowering at the bottom of the stairs.

'WHERE IS MRS EARL?'

The house servant began to tremble. 'Madam went out,' he stuttered, and the Aid Secretary let out a wail of complete hopelessness.

'She went out very early,' stammered the servant, desperate to say anything in an effort to calm his master.

Basil took a plate from an occasional table and hurled it against the wall. Then he sank to his knees, put his head in his hands and wailed, while his servant stood frozen to the spot.

III

'So that's your final word?'

Maggie nodded and put her finger to Charles's lips. 'It's not easy.'

'Would it make any difference if I decided not to go back?'

'No. I've told you, I couldn't live with Basil on my conscience.'

'Will you do me one last favour?'

'What?'

'Let me make love to you once more.'

She looked at her watch. 'I don't think . . .'

She was interrupted by the sound of people running, and an explosion shook the building. Charles and Maggie looked at each other and Charles rushed to the window. Men with guns were roaming the grounds, and fifty yards away a battle had begun for control of the power station.

Charles turned back. 'The place is full of soldiers. You'll have to stay after all.'

'I can't. Soldiers or no soldiers, I've got to go. Basil'll kill me if he finds I've been out. I've got to get back.' Charles showed no reaction. 'I'm serious. You saw how he was that evening at Late's. He's completely unpredictable at the moment.'

Charles rubbed his hand along his jawline. 'All right, as soon as the gunfire stops . . .'

'But that might be ages. I daren't wait till then. If you won't take me . . .' She moved towards the door.

Footsteps in the hall outside silenced them. There was a sharp rap on the door and after a few seconds Charles opened it. Three men with rifles stood there. They softened when they saw Charles and even in such extreme circumstances showed the Tujanian respect for the foreigner.

'Very sorry to disturb you,' the leader said in perfect English. 'Are you alone?'

Charles hesitated for a moment. 'Yes'.

The hesitation wasn't lost on the man. 'May I see?' He entered the room and saw Maggie standing by the bed.

'When I said alone, I meant just me and my . . . er . . . wife' said Charles.

The man gave a slight bow. 'Please excuse us, Madam. We are trying to start a revolution.'

Maggie managed a smile. 'Oh. Well, er, good luck.'

'Thank you, madam. I think we do not need luck.' He turned to Charles. 'It would be better if you and Madam did not leave this room for a time.'

He went out and Charles closed the door behind him. He turned to Maggie and shrugged.

'There you are. A revolution! What more do you need to convince you that we were meant to be together?'

Maggie frowned. Perhaps Basil would also be delayed at the Polytechnic. Her mind went back to the last time someone had entered the room unannounced.

'At least I was dressed this time,' she said.

'Mmm?'

'I said I was dressed this time.' But Charles didn't hear her. He turned to her, his eyes shining.

'Did you hear what he said? A revolution! They're trying to start a revolution! Perhaps there's hope for this country after all!'

IV

Stephen looked out of the storeroom window. There had been no shots for a while now and the compound outside the Department was deserted. He turned to Frank who seemed to have aged twenty years.

'Let's get upstairs while there's no one about.'

Frank shook his head emphatically. 'I'm staying here. No one will get us here.'

'Upstairs we may be able to phone.'

Frank shook his head again in a gesture that was becoming monotonous. 'They'll have cut the lines. That's the first thing they do in a situation like this. Cut the bloody lines.'

'Then we may be able to use Gomes-Little's radio. I know he keeps it in his office.'

'Probably locked up.' Frank was still looking furtively about him.

'At least we'll be able to see what's going on from up there.'

'And people will be able to see us.' Frank tried to inject some authority into his quavering voice. 'We must stay here.'

Renewed gunfire in the compound caused them to look round in alarm. 'They're probably not after us anyway,' Stephen said, with more conviction than he felt. 'At least upstairs we'll stand a better chance of seeing when the coast is clear.'

Bert at least was in agreement and as the two of them walked away he asked eagerly, 'How did the plan go?'

'Plan?' In the subsequent bedlam, Stephen had completely forgotten the plot against Gomes-Little. 'Oh, perfectly. Couldn't have gone better.'

'Wonderful!' Bert clasped Stephen's hand. 'Wonderful!'

As they opened the door, Frank joined them. 'I'm not staying here alone. But I still think this is a mistake.'

His fears seemed well-founded when, before they reached the top of the steps, a voice yelled out from the other side of the compound. The next minute students and men with rifles were running towards them and Frank trembled and cursed.

'I told you! Now we're as good as dead.'

'Relax.' Stephen tried to calm his companions. 'As I said, I'm sure they're not after us.'

Frank lapsed into a petrified silence. It was all very well for these other two bastards. They weren't under a sentence of death, didn't feel that every bullet was aimed deliberately at their hearts. They waited as students, still carrying placards and chanting slogans, gathered below, the men with guns forming a cordon round them. The leader began addressing the gathering through a portable megaphone. Stephen and Bert could understand little of what was said but Frank went pale.

Stephen turned to the trembling diplomat.

'What's he saying?'

'Death to all imperial lackeys and neo-colonialist bastards.'

'Is that all?'

'Isn't it enough?' Frank turned even paler. 'He's talking about us!'

Even Bert was now looking worried and Stephen again attempted to reassure them. 'That's just talk, just for public consumption.' He watched as the student with the megaphone and two of his colleagues broke away from the group and began mounting the stairs. 'Anyway, we'll soon find out.'

Frank looked round desperately for somewhere to hide and began scrabbling frantically at the back of the filing cabinet, trying to get into a space that wasn't there. The knock on the door surprised them. They hadn't expected such formality.

Stephen hesitated before opening it. The three students standing there saluted. Gunfire had begun again but it was sporadic and quickly subsided. Obviously the forces on the side of the students had beaten off what Stephen assumed was an attack by Government troops. He invited the students into the office and again they saluted as they confronted Bert and Frank who was pressed hard against the back wall.

The leader spoke. His English was good and his tone completely different from the stridency with which he had addressed the crowd.

'The Revolutionary Council of Tujan in association with its student allies and other progressive groups has overthrown the evil Government of Ali Al Hadi and has established an interim government as the basis for the foundation of true democracy in our beloved country.'

There seemed no obvious response to this and the three Englishmen waited. Artillery fire could be heard in different parts of the city.

'We have no quarrel with you. We shall not harm you if you stay here and keep your noses clean. We shall leave some people below to protect you.' He gestured towards the bookshelves. 'You can do your work.' He came smartly to attention and saluted. 'Long live the revolution!'

The Englishmen hesitantly echoed this sentiment and the students turned smartly on their heels. As they emerged, a great cheer went up from the crowd below. The leader gestured for silence and again addressed them, reverting to the tone he had used before. The three above listened and

Stephen again turned to Frank for enlightenment. Frank, relieved to find that a) he was still alive and b) no threat had been made against him personally, was recovering some of his dignity. And Frank on his dignity was not an endearing sight.

'He's saying they have captured three Englishmen and are holding them hostage against any resistance from the forces of reaction and imperialism.' He turned to the others. 'Holding us hostage! Who do these bastards think they are?'

'They're associates of the Revolutionary Council of Tujan,' Stephen said drily. 'They've just told us.'

Frank snorted. 'Revolutionary Council of Tujan! Bunch of bloody commies if you ask me.'

'Well at least they're not going to kill us,' Bert said brightly.

'They might,' Stephen said, 'when they realise we have no ransom value whatsoever!'

The three unlikely hostages spent a hot, restless afternoon. Frank had been right about the telephone wires being cut and Stephen searched the premises for Gomes-Little's two-way radio, finding it in a padlocked cupboard which he had forced open with a metal bar. He looked at the radio dubiously. 'Do either of you know how to work this?'

Bert nodded. 'We all have them. Now we should be able to contact somebody.'

He pressed a button on the radio. A red light came on and he began chanting: 'Tigger to Christopher Robin! Tigger to Christopher Robin! Can you hear me? Over.'

'Tigger to Christopher Robin! Who the hell is Christopher Robin?'

'The Ambo. He decided when we got these things we should all have code names out of *Winnie the Pooh* or *Wind in the Willows*.'

'And you're . . . ?'

'Alena and I are Tigger.'

'And Gomes-Little?'

'He's Owl.'

Frank had been listening to this with increasing impatience. 'The point is, can any of these bloody characters get us out of this mess?'

Bert tried again. 'Tigger to Pooh. Tigger to Pooh. Can you hear me? Over.'

'And Pooh is . . . ?'

'Pooh is Late.'

'But still no reply?'

'None at all. I'll keep trying.'

Stephen went to the window. He saw the two men who had been guarding the Department disappearing on the other side of the compound.

'Looks like our gaolers have gone,' he said. 'I told you it wouldn't be long before they realised we had no value.'

Frank and Bert went across to him. 'I don't like it,' Frank muttered. Some of his earlier fears had gone but he was still edgy. 'It looks like a trap.'

'What kind of trap?'

'Tempt us into trying to escape, then shoot us, you know the kind of thing.'

'But they said their quarrel isn't with us.'

'And you believe them? I tell you, if they see us trying to escape, they'll shoot us.'

'Well, we can't stay here forever. There's nothing to eat or drink, and it's getting dark. I think we should get out while we can. It all seems pretty quiet.'

Bert agreed and Frank reluctantly followed them down the steps. The silence in the compound was eerie.

'I don't have a car,' Frank said. 'I came with the Ambassador.'

'The Land Rover's here.' Stephen spoke with more confidence than he felt. 'We'll use that.'

'The gates will probably be locked,' said Frank for whom the assassination threat was again assuming significant proportions.

But the gates were not only unlocked but unguarded. Pickets and guards had disappeared. Explosions could still be heard in other parts of the city, but the area round the Polytechnic was quiet.

They climbed into the Land Rover and Stephen turned the key. The engine groaned like a hippopotamus in labour and he tried again. The engine turned over slowly, sparked once and died.

'We'll have to jump-start it.'

Stephen and Bert leapt out, followed less enthusiastically by Frank. The vehicle was heavy and the three men were tired. They pushed it out of the gates and, as it gained some momentum, Stephen jumped in and tried to start it on the clutch. There was no spark and he realised he'd forgotten to turn on the ignition.

Night was falling quickly on the city. The *haboob* had died and the afterglow of the sun still hung in the sky. But the road was dark as the three men took up positions around the Land Rover and tried again. Bert and Stephen were on either side and Frank was at the rear. Again the Land Rover gained momentum, again Stephen leapt into the driver's seat and attempted a clutch start. This time the engine roared into life and Frank fell as the vehicle spurted away from him.

Stephen braked, revving frantically to prevent the engine dying. Frank got to his feet and staggered towards it screaming.

'You all right?' Stephen called back to him.

'No, I'm not all right! I'm covered in bloody mud!'

Stephen and Bert turned back to look as Frank climbed into the back. The smell brought their stomachs to their mouths.

'That's not mud.' Bert said. 'That's . . .'

Frank looked down at himself in horror. The sewage that had been cleaned away for the Foreign Secretary's visit had returned with a vengeance and Frank had pitched headlong into it.

CHAPTER 21

I

Trying to ignore the stench coming from the back, Stephen put the Land Rover into gear and eased out the clutch. The engine coughed and spluttered, the wheels spun, and sewage flew in all directions.

'Don't let the bloody thing die,' screamed Frank. 'Not after I got into this state . . .'

Stephen suddenly remembered the vehicle had four wheel drive and this enabled them to move slowly forward. They phut-phutted through the sewage with the engine firing on what sounded like one cylinder and Frank becoming increasingly manic in the rear.

'Where the hell did this bloody heap come from?' he yelled, advancing towards the front seats.

'The Council,' muttered Stephen, holding his nose.

'Where?'

'The Council. Andrew Late.'

Frank snarled and sank back, grinding his teeth in frustration. That bloody fool Late again! Was there no end to that man's influence on his life?

The vehicle was now moving more assuredly; they had emerged from the sewage and were trundling towards River Parade. It was almost dark and Stephen tried the lights. The sudden demand for power caused the engine noise to dip alarmingly and he quickly turned them off. They were nosing forward in semi-darkness when Bert made out obstacles ahead.

'Looks like a road block.'

'What?' Frank's earlier fears, forgotten in the turmoil of the sewage and the faltering Land Rover, came flooding back. He hurled himself on to the floor of the vehicle, trying to cover himself with a piece of old cloth. Stephen glanced back.

'What are you doing?'

'Hiding.' Frank replied hoarsely. 'Don't want to be seen.'

'For God's sake. If anybody'd been after us, do you think they'd have let us escape so easily? We're not important enough.'

'You may not be,' said Frank darkly.

'Look, if they search us and they find you skulking in the back, then they *will* think we've got something to hide.'

The logic of this seeped through to the besplattered diplomat and he removed his cover. The Land Rover stuttered to a halt and the engine died. A soldier with raised arm and torch confronted them, peering into the vehicle and sniffing curiously.

Stephen apologised. 'I'm afraid my friend fell down in . . .'

He gestured towards the cowering diplomat. The soldier shone his torch into the back and said something to his companions who roared with laughter. All of them peered into the Land Rover, shining torches and holding their noses.

'Okay. You go.' The soldier, his mirth subsiding, waved them through. Stephen turned the starter, producing only the same fruitless whine.

'Could you, do you think . . . ?' Stephen made pushing motions.

Three or four of the soldiers began pushing the vehicle and the engine spluttered back to life. Waving his thanks, Stephen turned the vehicle into River Parade. The *haboob* had cleared and they could see the sky, lit up by the artillery and petrol bombs.

'So, an attempted coup,' Stephen said as they crawled along the tree-lined road.

'Perhaps it's more than an attempt,' said Bert, but Stephen shook his head. 'Those were government troops back there. They'd have been much more serious if there was any chance of the coup succeeding. Not that a change of government would do this place any harm.'

'Wouldn't do it any good either.' Anderson Frank, sitting in a back corner of the Land Rover, bounced around, the front of him covered in liquid shit, listening with half an ear to the conversation in the front. He could think of nothing short of total obliteration that *would* do Tujan any good. What he wanted was a long bath, a good meal, a couple of bottles of the best claret, and a flight out of this God-awful hole.

He sat up and looked out of the window. His knowledge of Omeldoum scarcely extended beyond the complex of Embassy houses and the Hilton. One place he did recognise, however, was the Marlborough Hotel and he saw its lights a little way ahead. A few more minutes even at this crippled snail's pace and they'd be at the Embassy where he could look forward to the things that made life worth living. Being held hostage by militant students, pushing obselete Land Rovers, falling headlong into sewage and being laughed at by little brown soldiers, while all the time labouring under the threat of imminent death – none of this featured high on Frank's agenda for an enjoyable life. He remembered what he had said to Late about experiencing the best and the worst that a place had to offer. Never had he expected the worst to be half as bad as this and he thought ruefully that the worst of Tujan was infinitely worse than the worst of anywhere else. Still, not too much longer . . .

Suddenly, with a noise like a man with acute diarrhoea, the engine exploded. Frank leapt forward. 'What's happened?'

'Looks like it's finally packed up.' Stephen tried the starter a few times.

'Don't do that!' Frank screamed. 'You'll flatten the battery.'

Stephen's patience with his strange companion was beginning to wear thin. He remembered his first impressions of Frank at the Hilton and felt they hadn't been so wide of the mark. His long-felt misgivings about the diplomatic corps were being justified to the full.

'So what do you suggest I do?'

'Try pushing it again.'

'I didn't think you'd want to.'

'Of course I want to. Why the hell you let it cut out in the first place beats me. Another half a mile and we'd have been safe.'

For the next few minutes, the three men pushed the Land Rover down Riverside Drive and attempted to start it on the clutch, but it seemed the engine had finally given up the ghost.

'One more try and we'll have to abandon it,' panted Stephen. 'Come on.'

A voice barking instructions startled them and the next instant a dozen soldiers emerged from the shadows. The assassination threat leapt back into Frank's mind as he explained in a tremulous voice that they were to leave the car and line up against the wall.

One of the soldiers pointed his gun at Frank, dropped into the crouch position and released the safety catch. The diplomat almost fainted.

'Don't shoot!' he screamed. 'I'll give you anything. DON'T KILL ME!'

The soldier sniffed at Frank and pulled a face. 'This man smells,' he said in Tujanian and the others laughed.

Stephen turned to the man who seemed to be in charge of the group.

'Could you ask that man to stop pointing his gun?' His calmness amazed him. A reaction to all this would surely set in soon.

The soldier barked another instruction and the man put his gun down. 'Don't mind him,' he said, in good English. 'He's mad!'

Another soldier came up. 'Give us cigarettes.'

Stephen looked round at his two companions. 'None of us smokes,' he said. The soldier shrugged. 'It doesn't matter. Just go home and you will not be harmed. We have no quarrel with you.'

Stephen relaxed a little. 'What's happened? Why all the fighting and the fires?'

The soldier's voice took on a warning note. 'Just go home and nothing will happen to you. You can leave your car here.'

The three men were left with little choice. It was, as Frank had said, not far to the Embassy, and they walked away with a feeling of relief as the soldiers went to examine their acquisition.

None of them noticed the other figures silhouetted momentarily on the bank of the river before taking cover behind the Land Rover. The next second the three men heard shots behind them and they turned, petrified. Little spurts of flame were coming from the abandoned vehicle. Four of the soldiers fell and the rest fled as half a dozen men emerged. Frank's fear spread to Stephen and Bert as this new terror confronted them. There, before their eyes, four men had actually been shot. The bodies were proof, dark shapes lying on the road, and the killers were advancing with rifles at the ready. It was the stuff of nightmares.

The leader of this new and terrifying pack of gunmen turned to his companions and spoke. He then smiled at the three men. It seemed again that, in spite of the bullets, the little spurts of fire, the bodies on the ground, as foreigners, they were in no danger. The leader spoke in Tujanian and again Frank interpreted.

'Their quarrel is not with us and we have nothing to fear.' The diplomat was an unwholesome sight, with dung caked all over his front and his face smeared where he had tried to wipe some of the excrement away. But his self-confidence was returning. This business in Omeldoum was a local quarrel. They were perfectly safe as long as they stayed out of it. Even the assassination threat receded. Perhaps he had got things a little out of proportion.

The man who had been addressing Frank turned and introduced two of his companions while the rest of the group watched for the return of the soldiers. Then they all shook hands. 'What a strange ritualised country this is!' Stephen thought. 'Here we are, shaking hands in a parody of civilised behaviour, with four men dead at our feet and parts of the city going up in smoke!'

Frank questioned the man about what was going on while Stephen and Bert waited helplessly, understanding only the odd word. Frank was looking intently, not at the leader but at the man by his side. Occasionally he nodded sagely, seemingly unaware of the spectacle he presented. There he was, trying to assume his best Foreign Office manner, coated from head to toe in human shit!

The leader eventually made a gesture and Stephen and Bert realised they were again free to go. The gunman by the leader's side stared hard at the departing figure of Frank. There was something familiar about him, something he should be remembering.

Stephen asked Frank what he had gathered and Frank, his dignity restored, responded imperiously. Who was he, this man who came regularly to this godforsaken hole yet couldn't understand the language? Stephen was informed haughtily that, yes, a coup was taking place. The men they had just spoken to were from the Communist Party of Free Tujan and they said they'd overthrown the Government.

'The Communist Party of Free Tujan? That's a different crowd from the ones we met at the Poly.'

'I know. Bloody ridiculous, isn't it?' But Frank's mind wasn't on the factions that made up the opposition to the Tujanian Government. Something was disturbing him, something that he couldn't quite put his finger on. It had to do with the man on the leader's right, a man he was sure he'd met before. He couldn't remember where but he was sure it had something to do with Late, the day the *haboob* started . . .

Behind, the man kept his eyes on the disappearing trio. Who was that man? Where *had* he seen him before? It was the day of the meeting in his father's house, the day when they had been interrupted by . . .

Suddenly he shouted and pointed towards the three men. 'That man, the one who was talking. He is the man who broke into my father's house and insulted his wives.'

The leader turned. 'You mean . . . ?'

'Yes. The man we have pledged to assassinate!'

And two hundred yards ahead, Late stopped in his tracks. 'The day at the dentist's! The son of that bloody communist!'

The next second a shot was fired into the air and Bert and Stephen looked round.

'What's going on?'

Frank's hunted look had returned. 'We mustn't stop,' he hissed. 'They'll kill us if we stop.'

'How do you know?'

'That's what they're shouting,' Frank lied. He suddenly realised beyond any doubt where the assassination threat had come from. And there, barely two hundred yards away, were a dozen men with rifles more than willing to carry it out.

'Then what can we do?' Stephen said. 'If we run, they'll catch us, if we stay here we're done for. Why have they changed their minds?'

'My boat!' Bert said suddenly.

'What boat?'

Stephen looked quickly at Bert. 'Of course. It's moored near here, isn't it?'

'Just ahead.'

'But what good will it do?' Frank screamed. 'Where the hell can we go in a bloody boat?'

'To the island. We can go to the island.'

Stephen looked at the men, who were still yelling and had begun to advance down the road. A surprise start was their only chance and he whispered to Bert to head for the boat.

'What about me?' cried Frank hoarsely.

'We'll stay here for a second and hope they don't notice Bert's missing.'

'But, why should . . . ?'

'Bert has to get the boat away from its moorings.' He looked at Bert. 'What about the motor?'

'I never leave it on the boat. We'll have to use the oars.'

'You mean we're going to escape in a boat without an engine?' Frank hissed incredulously.

'Don't worry. We'll be all right.' Bert sidled away and Frank reluctantly stayed with Stephen. The lights from the Marlborough flooding the road would make their escape very difficult. There were more shouts from the men as they continued their advance.

Stephen watched Bert steal along the riverside wall and disappear down the steps to the mooring pad. Suddenly, as if responding to Stephen's prayers, the lights from the hotel dimmed. Ahead, Bert jumped into the boat, releasing the mooring rope and holding on to the quayside. In the darkness, the shouts of the men became more urgent.

'Now!' Stephen whispered and raced off down the road.

'Wait for me!' screamed Frank already ten yards behind, his lungs bursting with the unaccustomed effort.

But Stephen was waiting for no one. Shots cracked again but this time they were not shots in the air. He remembered the four dead soldiers and his heart went cold.

He was just about to race down the steps when a figure appeared from the opposite direction and a small voice cried, 'Help me!'

'Dolores!' Stephen was astonished.

She gasped in relief. 'Stephen. Oh, thank God.'

Bert's voice came from below. 'The boat's ready.'

As Stephen led Dolores down the steps, Frank staggered along the road like a marathon runner on the edge of collapse. Reaching the top of the steps, he caught his foot on a protruding stone. His momentum carried him into space and, arms outstretched, he now looked like a diver competing several heights above his level of competence. His head cracked against the mast and some instinct told him to hold on. Now he was a fireman, called to duty after a drunken binge, sliding uncertainly down the pole. Finally, his semblance changed to a boxer having received the *coup de grâce*, clutching vainly at his opponent's legs before collapsing in a heap. Blood poured from a gash in his forehead.

So, in far less time than it took to describe, Frank had arrived in the boat and was ready for departure. Stephen and Dolores jumped in after him and Bert cast off. The moon had not yet risen and there was little light on the water. The island of Doum was about a hundred yards away.

They had drifted perhaps fifty yards in the shadow of the bank when Bert suggested they man the oars. The shouts of the men were close on the road above but it was soon clear that they had no idea where their quarries had gone. Belatedly, they looked towards the river, standing on the wall and firing blindly into the water. After a while, the shots stopped, the yells became fainter and Bert and Stephen began rowing. Frank lay unconscious in the bottom of the boat with Dolores ministering to him. They set course for the island as the first arc of a great orange moon appeared over the horizon.

II

The dark shape of Doum came closer and Bert steered towards the southern end where the island was unpopulated. Frank lay where he had landed, the gash on his forehead seeping blood. Dolores wiped it away and tried to manoeuvre him into a more comfortable position.

'How is he?' Stephen turned round, feeling that some enquiry about their passenger was in order.

'He'll live. I've just realised who he is. I've met him once before and he was unconscious then. Do you remember, at Andrew's film show?'

Stephen remembered vividly the evening of *Professional Foul* when he had first thought of his plan to get rid of Gomes-Little. It seemed a long time ago.

'That was when Andrew arranged tonight's meeting in the Marlborough. I had no idea things were so bad in the city. Those soldiers scared the shit out of me. Gang rape has never been an experience I've particularly craved.' She had been saved by the arrival of a senior officer. 'I hid in the shadows. When he'd gone they started looking for me. I'm sure it was only a matter of time before they found me.' Then, incredibly, she had heard Stephen's voice.

'It was providence that brought you there, Stephen. I don't know what would have happened if you hadn't come.' She planted a great wet kiss on his cheek, put her face against his chest and wept. Some response was obviously necessary although he didn't quite know what. He put a fraternal arm round her shoulder and managed a token 'There, there'.

Using the rudder and one oar, Bert steered the boat towards the beach. His eyes were sharp and his brain had recovered its old edge of enthusiasm as he began to see secondary benefits in their escape. A study of the nocturnal bird life of the island had always been on his agenda. He had a vague recollection of having spent nights on the island before but that was in another life, another dimension, almost, when birds had been the last thing of his mind. But now . . . he smiled to himself . . . things were different.

The moon had risen by the time they landed, a huge orange in the eastern sky. In an hour or so, it would be very bright. Dolores pulled her head away from Stephen's chest and looked at Frank stirring on the bottom of the boat.

'Do you think we should take those clothes off him? They're a bit . . . high.'

'There's a couple of blankets in the box you're sitting on,' said Bert as he steered the boat on to the beach while Stephen helped Dolores undress the hapless diplomat. Frank suddenly regained consciousness as Stephen was pulling off his trousers. He shrieked in terror. Was he being stripped as a prelude to some horrible torture?

'Relax, honey.' Dolores stroked his brow. 'You've had a bad time but you're OK now.' And Frank, soothed by her voice, relaxed. He let Stephen remove his clothes and looked up gratefully at the large woman smiling down at him. He was sure he'd seen her somewhere before, at a time when, as now, the emotions of fear and pleasure had been mixed. She stirred memories of mountain peaks, plunging valleys, vivid sunsets . . .

Dolores helped him out of the boat while Stephen and Bert pulled the vessel higher up the beach. The sand was bathed in the first glow of silver and the little group went as far as the vegetation line where Stephen watched Dolores in her Florence Nightingale role. Here was the kind of adventure he had longed for as a child, escaping to an island pursued by angry soldiers, an eccentric ornithologist securing their boat, having saved a rather large damsel in distress who was now nursing a wounded diplomat. But no childhood romance allowed for the horror of Tujan, the civil war, the mass destruction of an innocent people. And the illusion of innocence disappeared completely when the wounded diplomat fell asleep and the damsel came over to him.

'I can't tell you how grateful I am, Stephen.' Her face was alive with what he hoped was gratitude but feared was something else. 'It *was* providence, you know. I felt this bond between us that evening I saw you with the loo cleaner.'

Stephen coughed. Another wet kiss was planted on his cheek and Dolores took his hand, her fingers hot and podgy against his palm. 'We're safe here, aren't we?'

Stephen nodded. Safe from the turbulence of the city at any rate. On other scores, he felt substantially less safe and he shifted around in embarrassment. There was a limit to the number of 'There, theres' he could manage and he looked for Bert to act as chaperone. But Bert had disappeared.

Dolores snuggled in. She turned her face towards him, her eyes shining. Not a bad-looking face, thought Stephen. If only it hadn't been attached to such a vast body. 'I shall always think of you as the Harpic man,' she murmured and Stephen winced. At least her overtures conveyed the right image. 'Lavatory cleaner' was a phrase that sprang easily to mind when he thought of Dolores. Given her tendencies, he couldn't understand why she had objected to the attentions earlier in the evening. He was sure a whole platoon was well within her capabilities. Perhaps she only wants comforting, he reassured himself. She's had a nasty couple of hours. It's obvious she feels the need for a friendly cuddle, a sort of paternal presence.

A hand running up and down his thigh in a totally unambiguous gesture dispelled this illusion. 'There, there,' he said, hoping his avuncular tone would have the desired effect, 'There, there.' How was he to extricate himself from this? Having allowed him to escape from the fire of the city, Fate might have been kinder than to push him into this particular frying pan.

Suddenly inspiration came and he shot to his feet. Dolores gave a little whimper of disappointment. 'What are you doing?'

'I must try and let people know where we are.'

'But how . . . ?'

'Gomes–Little's radio. It's in my jacket in the boat.'

She struggled to her feet. 'I'll come with you.'

'I don't think that's wise.' He gestured towards Frank. 'I don't think we should leave . . . I'd hate anything to happen to him now we've all managed to survive this long.'

'But what can happen to him? You said we were safe here.'

'I know I did but we can't be too careful. These are very strange times,' he added with feeling.

'Bert can look after him.'

'Bert's gone bird-watching,' Stephen said, now grateful to Bert for his disappearance.

'Oh, all right. You can bring the radio back here.'

'Oh, I don't think . . .' Stephen blustered. 'It won't work very well . . . Interference from the water . . . I'll have to take it inland. Look after yourself, and . . . er . . . see you soon.' He suppressed an urge to say 'There, there,' and set off towards the boat.

CHAPTER 22

I

Stephen lay on his back and contemplated. The moon was a brilliant orb high in the sky and the grass around him was coated in silver. So many times he had been overcome by the melancholy beauty of this place, the strange, haunting peace that seemed to settle when the light had died and nothing remained but the afterglow of the sun, the patterns of the stars or the enchantment of a moonlit sky.

He had retrieved the radio and retired well away from the beach. Although he had used it as an excuse to escape the attentions of Dolores, the radio did provide the possibility of finding out what was happening and passing on the information that they were safe. But several calls of 'Tigger to Christopher Robin' had failed to arouse the Ambassador, who was obviously not one to lose any sleep over the city in turmoil and four members of the British community missing!

He had spent the next half an hour calling a variety of characters, a whisper of 'Tigger to Eeyore' producing a sudden sense of unreality, a realisation of the intense foolishness of it all. Swimming in the Club pool, conversing at dinner parties, teaching at the Polytechnic, and now, at the end of a sequence of calamities and embarrassments, lurking on Doum Island having escaped the attentions of homicidal gunmen and a sex-starved nympho and reciting a list of utterances that in any other circumstance would have led to questions about his sanity. And the over-riding feeling was no longer sadness or irritation, or anger, or fear, but foolishness. Sheer, unexpurgated, unadulterated foolishness.

He had almost given up on the radio when a final 'Tigger to Pooh' produced the sleepy voice of Late. Yes, there had been an attempted coup. Yes, it had been serious but the Government was back in control. The last pocket of resistance had been a group of communists near the Marlborough Hotel. But thank God they were safe. (Late had heard that Frank was safe with distinctly mixed feelings.) Oh, they had Dolores with them? Good, good. (Late hadn't known she was missing.) No, there was no need for them to move that night. (Late had a vision of the drive to the river – road blocks, security checks, gun-toting soldiers half-crazed by victory – and realising who would have to make that drive, he decided that, in the interests of safety – he didn't say *whose* safety – they should spend the night on the island.)

Stephen signed off and lay back. He looked at the sky and again felt the deceptive peace of the place. The conflict had died; no artillery fire, no gunshots, no angry splashes of sky, no movement apart from the occasional scuffle of a little creature on some nocturnal errand and he suddenly felt so satisfied that an unusual feeling of smugness came over him. The previous day, in spite of the coup attempt, had gone almost too well. There might well be some hitch, some final twist of fate that would render his game plan useless, but he could think of none. He had, in one go, discredited Gomes-Little and dealt as effectively as he could with the plight of the Westerners. And now that he had escaped the turmoil on the mainland, surely Fate could have no more tricks up its sleeve?

Anyway, it was finished, one way or the other. He'd brought all the strands together, all the events to a conclusion, and he felt as if, lying in bed, he'd passed the denouement in a whodunnit and could put out the light and turn over. The tension drained from him, his body relaxed for the first time in weeks, his eyes closed and he slept.

He didn't know how long he slept. Images churned in his mind, of Gomes-Little and Valentine, of blazing guns, of Charles and Maggie in the Green Grange. Nakedness and sex took over, primeval urges and recent images blurring before crystallising into a generalised lust.

He woke with a little cry, not realising for an instant where he was. But he recognised the feeling that was overpowering him.

Lust. An all-consuming need for sexual gratification that turned his thoughts towards the only immediate means of satisfying it. Dolores, the woman on the beach. Available, willing, even desperate. Not a prospect to set the pulse racing in times of plenty, hardly one to rate an entry in his list of conquests but this particular lust storm demanded that he enter any port. And Dolores wasn't so bad, he told himself. Quite pretty really. Quite a sensitive face when you thought about it. And a body that would engulf an army!

He had worked hard and successfully; now he was safe on Doum Island, secure from prying eyes, from gossip, from anybody finding out the depths to which lust proposed to take him. Yes, he decided, a quickie with Dolores. Let him indulge himself for once. He'd earned it.

He rose and made his way towards the beach. She would no doubt be pleased to see him, delighted by what he envisaged would be fairly perfunctory advances. He saw no need to prolong the foreplay. A quick indication of his intentions, then . . . wham, bam, thank you Sam. Stephen didn't rate himself the best lover in the world but he had little doubt that Dolores would find the next few minutes more than satisfactory.

He was pulled up sharp by sounds such as he had never heard before, similar to those that might have been heard by explorers discovering some outlandish forms of reptilian life. But these sounds were almost human. There were in fact two sounds, one a high pitched moan, the other a much lower grunt. The lower sound was possibly male, the higher . . . At the edge of the vegetation, his brain reached the inevitable conclusion seconds before his eyes confirmed it.

Lying on the sand, her great bulk white and luminous like some kind of albino walrus, was Dolores. She was emitting accelerating moans of pleasure that changed on the instant to little squeals while above her and on her, Frank had made a spectacular recovery. Looking like a Belsen victim enjoying his last request, he rode her with wild abandon, eyes wide, teeth bared, a kind of rhythmic mating call coming from his mouth.

Stephen watched for a few moments, fascinated by what looked like the frantic rites of two creatures threatened with extinction engaged in a desperate attempt to propagate their species. Then he turned and ran. His desires disgusted him. How could he have wanted to engage in such an absurd parody of love when occasionally he had experienced the real thing? He remembered his previous incursion into unwitting voyeurism – but that had been different. At the Green Grange he had felt an intruder on a scene of intense tenderness. What he had just witnessed was like stumbling on a pair of copulating elephants. And yet essentially the act was the same, nature's insurance that the human race would be perpetuated – God alone knew why!

He walked towards the southern tip of the island where the sand extended in a great bank and where, in daytime, many species of wading bird scavenged in the shallows. A shadowy figure, looking like a proponent of desert warfare, scurried across the sand and crawled to the top of a dune. The figure raised his head cautiously, turning round as he heard Stephen approach. Bert put his finger to his lips and with his other hand gestured over the dune. 'Tujanian nightjar, I think. Very rare species.'

Stephen whispered Late's news and walked on. He walked right to the end of the island and sat down, feeling again the melancholy of solitude. A long time ago he had strayed on to the same long strand of silver while the gaiety of a midnight barbecue had proceeded a few hundred yards away. It had been a night such as this and he had sat and pined for a love long since forgotten. He had moved on; life had moved on. He had grown older: perhaps even a little wiser, although he doubted it.

He lay down and dozed. Mosquitoes attacked him and he cursed and scratched before dozing again and then sinking into a deeper sleep. He opened his eyes as the first grey of dawn was appearing in the eastern sky and thought again of the scene on the beach. And his lust returned. Again he contemplated one last gratuitous act hidden by the remnants of night, again he rose and made his way to the spot where he had left his two companions. Reluctant though he was to follow Frank, he was now in the grip of an obsession. He needed a woman. He had to have Dolores.

As he approached the spot, he again heard noises. They were different from the previous ones in that he could make out only one voice. Again, as he emerged from the vegetation, the same two bodies confronted him. But this time Dolores was lying face down on the sand and Frank, astride her buttocks, was still riding her furiously.

Stephen was astonished. He couldn't believe that Frank, after being knocked unconscious by a mid-air collision with a hardwood mast, would be capable of anything more than a couple of tight-lipped kisses, let alone a night of the most frenzied sex. He found himself reluctantly revising his opinion of Foreign Office personnel, having to put grudging qualifications on his previous contempt. A sexual athleticism placed somewhere between the supernatural and the mythological was obviously the reason for their privileged positions in life. And although Frank, as he silently rode the screaming Dolores, looked as though he might die in the attempt, Stephen at that moment couldn't think of a more appropriate way to go.

II

It was almost dawn when Maggie returned home. The gunfire had subsided but Charles had insisted on accompanying her. Compared to the loss he was beginning to feel, the city held no terrors and they walked in a state of emotional numbness. Reaching the end of her street, she turned to him.

'I'll go alone from here.'

He nodded, not trusting himself to speak. He pulled her into the shadow of the trees and she responded to his final kiss with tightly closed lips, afraid that more intimate contact would shake her resolve.

'Change your mind.'

She shook her head. 'Basil needs me. I've told you.'

'I need you too.'

'You've got other things. Look how I've made you mess things up these last few weeks.'

'It doesn't matter.'

'Of course it matters. That's why you're going back.'

'I thought you'd come with me.'

She shook her head again. 'It wouldn't work. Building happiness on someone else's misery. It just . . . wouldn't work.'

He was silent, reluctantly accepting the truth of what she was saying. In years to come he would remember this scene in every detail, the last peck on the lips, the hopelessness in her eyes, her footsteps running along the street, the brown buildings silhouetted against the dawn. And Maggie Earl disappearing forever from his life.

She let herself into the house. The place looked as if a horde of vandals had passed through – crockery broken, curtains shredded, pictures smashed. She went quietly upstairs and looked into the bedroom. Basil was lying face downward on the bed, an empty gin bottle next to him. She sat beside him and as he stirred she stroked his head.

He looked up at her with wild eyes and as she carried on stroking he began blubbing like a baby.

'Hush' she said, hardly able to bear his cries. 'Hush. I'm home. And I'm staying home.'

His sobs subsided as she nursed him. She rocked gently to and fro, staring blankly at the wall, wondering whether it would be easier to live with loss than it would have been with guilt. At least she finally felt in control. And it meant nothing.

III

The sun was high by the time the party on Doum Island made their way to the boat. Frank was walking unsteadily, helped by Dolores who looked like the cat who'd finally got the cream. Wrapped round his head was a lace-edged bandage.

Stephen checked to see that nothing had been left behind. His feelings of the night before had passed and he was relieved that Frank had beaten him to the draw, as it were. But . . . He shook his head in disbelief. Whatever his other failings, the man's sexual prowess was nothing short of miraculous.

Before joining the others in the boat, he went into the bushes for a pee, glancing down as the yellow liquid gushed from him. And there he saw it, a familiar object half-hidden by undergrowth. It looked a little less proud, a little less distinguished, but it was still unmistakable and less than a stone's throw from the spot where Dolores and Frank had been copulating the previous night. He bent down and touched it. It was slightly sticky.

He looked up and smiled.

Dolores's screams and Frank's prowess were now explained. He walked to the boat, strangely content in the knowledge that the phallus from Old Joe's luggage had fulfilled its destiny. It was as though the last piece of the jigsaw had fallen into place.

Stephen and Bert rowed steadily. Frank stood pale and drawn, one hand on the mast, like the captain of a wrecked ship preparing to meet the natives with Dolores, the faithful handmaiden, sitting at his feet. On the bank, Late, Alena, and the Ambassador waved enthusiastically. It felt like the end of a long journey.

EPILOGUE

I

'So, Stephen, a strange visit.'

An unfamiliar face greeted Stephen from the other side of the desk, a face with puffy cheeks, full lips, and several small sores. Andrew Late had shaved his beard off and nothing in the recent catalogue of surprises had given Stephen a greater shock. Late ran his hand over his face in response to Stephen's raised eyebrows.

'Decided it was time for a change. That day at the Embassy, heard a few whispers – you know the kind of thing – Cypriot terrorist, Armenian bandit. The Ambassador even hinted that I looked a bit like Castro! So decided it was . . . time for a change. Didn't want to be mistaken for . . .' He giggled nervously, fingering his chin. 'How do you like it?' He smiled, a lewd, naked expression. The full lips were almost obscene.

'Well, it's different,' Stephen managed.

Late removed a breadcrumb from the side of his mouth and examined it quizzically. The boil on his neck had erupted again and an errant fly hovered close to it. 'Oh, people'll get used to it. Anyway, as I said, a strange visit.'

Stephen thought of the phallus, of Maggie and Charles, of Bert's anger, of Valentine's death and Derek's arrest. He thought of the Foreign Secretary's visit, the plot against Gomes-Little, the attempted coup, the antics on Doum Island. And now this. Andrew Late, beardless in Omeldoum.

'In some ways, yes.'

'You know, I never suspected Gomes-Little had those tendencies. I know we all sympathise with the West but I thought he would be the last person to use his position to try anything like that. Fancy presenting that document with a picture of himself on the cover!'

'Must have had a death wish,' Stephen murmured. 'He's protesting his innocence, isn't he?'

'Well, he was. Didn't seem much future in a confession at the time. But Fate moves in strange ways. The Foreign Secretary was very impressed.'

'Impressed with what?'

'Gomes-Little's courage.'

Stephen was puzzled. 'Courage?'

'Yes, and ingenuity. Presenting that list from the West the way he did.

That's the first bit of news. I understand a mention in the next Honours list is a possibility.'

'Honours?' Stephen's responses had been reduced to echoes.

Late nodded. 'Oh not a knighthood or anything like that. But an OBE was talked about.'

Stephen was now totally speechless and Late spread his hands in a sympathetic gesture. 'I know you didn't like Fairfax very much. But at least Derek's off the hook. I mean, just because a man runs a centre for refugees and has spent time in Western Province, to use this as an excuse to arrest him . . .'

Stephen swallowed hard, his relief at the news that Derek was out of gaol tempered by this latest episode in the Gomes-Little saga. 'Not much reason in this system,' he managed. 'What about Alena?'

Late stood up and came round the desk. He had forgotten his morning gargle and the rancidity, together with the boil, the full lips, the grey, fleshy cheeks, made him a most unwholesome experience.

'Well, normally she'd take over the project.'

'Normally?'

'Yes. If she was staying on.'

Stephen was puzzled. 'But I thought, now that Gomes-Little's discredited – in Tujan at any rate – her dismissal would be reviewed.'

Late smiled nervously. 'Don't worry, her good name is restored but she won't be doing anything on the strength of it in this place.'

'Why not?'

Late crossed to the telex machine and picked up a sheet of paper which he handed to Stephen. 'The second bit of news. Came through about half an hour ago.'

> British Government's decision on basis of Westerner's submission to Foreign Secretary. All developmental aid suspended pending political changes in Tujan.

'Seems Gomes-Little's taken you all with him. It was always on the cards. They've been looking for a reason to get out of this place for months. Gomes-Little gave it to them on a plate. So this is probably your last visit.'

'Unless there's a change of Government.'

'Judging how easily they sorted out the last little effort, I can't see that happening in a hurry, can you?'

Stephen shook his head. 'So I'm out of a job as well.'

'They'll find you something else, don't you think?'

'Perhaps.' Stephen felt no sense of loss or depression. That would no doubt come later. For the moment all he felt was relief. He thought back to the conversation in Late's garden at the start of his visit. Let the dying man pare his own fingernails for a change.

'The Earls have left. I hear on the grapevine that Basil's thinking of resigning. It all got a bit too much for him.'

'What about Frank?'

'It was all a bit too much for him as well,' said Late. 'A very strange man, Anderson Frank, don't you agree?'

An image of Frank riding Dolores as if she was an uncontrollable hippo flashed through Stephen's mind. He nodded.

'Anyway, he's been given six months convalescence to get over it. He's off to the South Pacific.'

'Six months . . .!' Stephen was speechless again. Frank in the South Pacific, Gomes-Little on the Honours list, the Tujanians without aid and Alena and himself without jobs! He looked at Late.

'What about you?'

'It looks as if I'm staying on for a while.' Late looked rueful. 'There was some talk of a transfer but I don't really mind another couple of years. I've just been planning a production of *Under Milk Wood* for October. Pity you won't be coming back. Should be excellent.'

'Will Dolores be in it?'

'Of course. What would a production in Omeldoum be without Dolores?'

'What indeed?' Stephen got up and shook Late's extended hand. *Under Milk Wood* produced by Late and starring Dolores! Perhaps it was just as well this *was* his last visit.

'Tujan's not such a bad place,' Late said without conviction as Stephen went to the door. 'I've got a new house servant, by the way.'

'Oh.'

'Yes. Got rid of the other chap. Once they start nicking lavatory cleaner there's no knowing where they'll stop.'

If Stephen was surprised at the original non-sequitor, he had the grace to blush at the follow up. There was something close to a twinkle in Late's eyes. How could he have underestimated the intelligence of this apparently bumbling man?

'Oh, and Stephen.'

Stephen half turned on his way out.

'Good film, *Professional Foul!*'

II

The departure lounge was, as ever, depressing: undermanned, under-equipped. Stephen bought the only drink available – a warm Pepsi – and went on to the balcony to drink it. The nights were now unbearably hot. He saw a convoy of military vehicles driving along the adjoining road, a platoon of troops double marching by the side of the runway. The liquid clung to the sides of his mouth.

Now, the thought that he might never return produced a wave of nostalgia mixed with a feeling of intense dissatisfaction at the way yet another plan he had regarded as foolproof had completely misfired. He hadn't fed one last factor into the equation, the factor of unpredictability, the endless capacity of people and events to behave and react in ways diametrically opposite to the ones he expected. The adroitness with which he had carried out his plan had led to three paradoxical results: the gnome was a hero, he himself was out of a job; and the Westerners were even more at the mercy of the Government. Fate had had more than one last card up its sleeve, more like a full hand of trumps!

A familiar figure waved to him from the other end of the balcony and Major Bakheet, back in uniform, came across.

'Mr Talbot.' They shook hands. 'So your Mr Gomes-Little was a bad man after all.'

Amazing, Stephen thought. The little shit had come close to destroying the project, treated his staff like dirt and yet was only officially classified as a 'bad man' when he unwittingly acted as the agent for people on the last edge of oppression.

'Misguided, perhaps.'

The major snorted. 'Why do you English always use euphemisms? Misguided! Bad! We all know what we mean.'

'I hear the British Government has suspended aid.'

Bakheet's eyes narrowed. 'A shortsighted decision. You see, Mr Talbot, we don't need your aid. We can manage very well without it.'

Stephen nodded. 'Is your leave over?'

'Yes. Back to the West. Back to do my little bit.'

Stephen nodded again. Back to kill a few more Westerners, to take a few more steps towards the grand design, to make sure that justice had no place on Tujan's agenda. He remembered that Bakheet had been charged with finding the submission and it occurred to him that being posted back to the

West was his punishment for having failed. If so, he was lucky to have got off so lightly.

He turned away, aware that for himself a form of justice had prevailed. He had used the submission of the dead and the dying for his own puny ends. He had tried to do what was possible and even in that he had failed. It was as if the world bridge championship had been decided by a swift and unsuccessful hand of Happy Families. The dying man now had no fingernails at all.

The picture of the President on the far wall caught his eye, baleful, accusing. As ever, he saw in it the face of Old Joe King. It was in this lounge that Joe had died. The view that Stephen was looking at had been Joe's last vision on earth. The face now had lost its humour; there was pain about the mouth, sadness in the sunken blue eyes.

He walked away as the loudspeaker system announced the departure of the British Airways flight to London.

POSTSCRIPT

Charles stood on the edge of the wasteland. The river had subsided further in the month he had been away and colonies of wading birds searched languidly near its shores.

The evening was drawing in as he walked along the bank above the river. The last light from the vanished sun hung in the sky like some theatrical effect. Pink changed to deep orange on the sight. And the blood of the sky reflected in the water like a metaphor.

A gust of wind scoured the landscape. Sand swirled into him and he covered his face. Then the wind died, night fell, and a deep melancholy settled over the wasteland.

'Now small fowls flew screaming over the yet yawning gulf; a sudden white surf beat against its steep sides; then all collapsed; and then the great shroud of the sea rolled on as it rolled five thousand years ago.'

(Herman Melville, *Moby Dick*)